Praise for Sui Lynn's

I0664619

The Pauper Prince

"By the end of this story I was hooked, not only by the variety of characters but also by the story line and I can't wait to see what is next for all involved."

—Literary Nymphs Reviews

"…a unique spin on the Vamp/Wolf relationship…"

—My Earnest Review

"I really liked the characters…"

—Night Owl Reviews

Goodreads M/M Romance Groups
2012 Member's Choice Awards
Nominee: Paranormal and Best World Created categories

Top Ten Finisher: Preditors and Editors Reader's 2012 poll

the
PAUPER PRINCE

SUI LYNN

Dreamspinner Press

Published by
Dreamspinner Press
5032 Capital Circle SW
Ste 2, PMB# 279
Tallahassee, FL 32305-7886
USA
http://www.dreamspinnerpress.com/

The Pauper Prince
Copyright © 2013 by Sui Lynn

Cover Art by L.C. Chase
http://www.lcchase.com

Cover content is being used for illustrative purposes only
and any person depicted on the cover is a model.

ISBN: 978-1-62380-866-2
Digital ISBN: 978-1-62380-867-9

Printed in the United States of America
Second Edition
July 2013

1st Edition published by Silver Publishing, 2012

To my support group, Angie and Sandy.
You believe in me and help me keep my eyes focused on the goal.

To Cori, who introduces me as "my friend the smut writer."
Gotta love ya!

PROLOGUE

"NINEoneone. What is your emergency?"

"There's blood everywhere. I'm trying to make it stop, but his throat's cut. How do I make it stop?"

"What is your address? I'll send an ambulance."

"2425 Pine Tree Way. You gotta hurry! Please, there's blood everywhere.It won't stop… I can't hold it together."

"Police are en route and I have an ambulance on the way…. Stay on the line with me, okay?"

"Please hurry! I don't think he's breathing anymore! The blood's everywhere…. How do I stop it? I can't hold the wound together…."

CHAPTER 1

I STOOD in the barn, my backpack filled with the items I'd found. Everything had a coating of dust, so I figured nobody would miss them; I'd return them when I was finished. I wasn't stealing—just borrowing.

A man walked into the barn, on the opposite side from where I stood. I froze—unable to even breathe—caught with my hands quite literally in the cookie jar… a big ceramic Pooh bear full of nails, which I'd been adding to my bag of spoils.

He was tall, at least six feet, clearly older than me by a year or two. My breath caught, and not because of what I was doing…. I'd never seen a man so ruggedly handsome. He was bare-chested and his jeans hung low on his hips. His body was lean and muscular. His skin was a deep golden brown that stretched across a muscular chest and ripped abs. He had spiked black hair and large sky-blue eyes. Surprise flashed across his face as he saw me, and in that instant—I ran. *Could have stared at him all day*, I mused as my sneakers pounded the dirt. He seemed exotically beautiful with those blue eyes and black hair. Another day—another lifetime—I could get lost in him. Today—no time—gotta run. With my spoils in my duffel over my shoulder, I made for the tree line at a dead sprint. He gave chase—on my heels, calling after me. I didn't turn around to see how far he'd follow. I just ran. The trees—the forest—they were my safety zone.

Where does he think he's going? I thought as I ran, my breath coming in controlled pants. He didn't stop at the trees. I could hear feet running after me. Crunch—crunch—pant—crunch—crunch— the rhythm of running and breathing,through the tree litterthat muffled our footfalls. I'm fast; you learn to be fast when your life depends on how quickly you can disappear. He steadily fell behind despite being taller than me. In no time, I couldn't hear him anymore. I kept going. It might've been the adrenaline from being seen, but the hair still stood up on the back of my neck as if I were being tracked or maybe hunted.

I put a couple miles between me and the ranch, following the animal trails I'd become familiar with. The Black Hills National Forest was thick and in this particular area, it was easy to lose your way if you couldn't recognize the signs of the forest. I'd lost him, but I continued to run anyway. I could feel the thrill of the chase, the high from evading a pursuer, a feeling of invincibility. So I ran on. Panting hard, I reveled in the heady feeling. A part of me never wanted to stop. I felt like I could outrun anything—anytime— anywhere.

"Ah!" I screamed. Pain stronger than anything I'd ever felt hit my stomach like a sledgehammer, knocking the wind clear out of my lungs, ripping my guts from my body until I was sure they were scattered across the forest floor. I fell, tumbling to my hands and knees—duffel bag sliding to the ground.

I curled into a pain-filled fetal ball, trying to hold myself together through the intense cramping. For the first time it hit me how alone and vulnerable it was to live like this, but only for a second as the pain came again in an overwhelming wave. My insides boiled and my skin crawled. I clawed at my arms, wanting to peel the skin from my body in chunks. I couldn't stand the scratchy, irritating touch of my clothes. I screamed in agony as I yanked on my shirt and pants, dragging them off, away from my oversensitive skin as quickly as I could. I struggled, trying to gasp for air, but I couldn't breathe because the air wouldn't go into my lungs.

I felt my bones turning to jelly and reshaping themselves. Joints were changing direction. My chest seemed to expand, getting larger and deeper. Fur. *Fur?* It seemed to force itself through my skin to cover my entire body. Claws and paws replaced fingers and hands, and I could see my nose... well, not *my* nose, but a large brown snout sticking out from my face. When the pain finally subsided and I could breathe again, I found myself standing on four legs and I had a tail. A thick chocolate-brown pelt covered my body, except for my stomach and feet, which were white. I walked in circles looking at my tail, in complete disbelief.

From all the parts I could see, I could only come up with one possible answer—I had gone completely nuts. *What the fuck!* WTF wasn't strong enough for this hallucination. I must be certifiably insane... bound for a rubber room... or a dog pound. People didn't just turn into animals. Somehow, I'd entered a Tim Allen movie and I'd become the Shaggy Dog.... No, something inside felt offended... not a dog—a wolf. Oh God, *American Werewolf in London*.... I was a monster. *Well, no surprise there.Now the outside and inside match. People will see a monster when they look at me, as they should.* Sometimes I hated my internal voice; I cringed and shivered at my own thoughts. After shoving the self-hatred back into a box in the corner of my mind and stomping on it hard, I shook my head, which became a whole body shake... fur twisting and flopping across my body all the way to the tip of my tail. It felt good.

I grabbed my clothes, what was left of them, with my mouth and buried them, along with my pack of treasures, under some bushes by a large tree. A part of me—there but separate—told me to hide everything. If I ever turned back into a person, I'd need to return and get my stuff. *If...* what the hell!

Well, at least I could think, so I was still me... sort of. I felt like me, but more, like something else lived in my head too. *Wonderful. Multiple-personality disorder... yes,Doctor, my other self is a wolf... wanna see?* I bet I couldn't find a psychiatrist who allowed pets in their office.

4

My new senses practically overwhelmed me with information. My sense of smell—I could smell everything. The forest was unbelievably filled with the aromas of animals and trees. If scents were cars, I was downtown New York on the busiest day of the year, caught in midtown traffic. But it wasn't my nose alerting me now, but my ears.Someone was still following me. My imagination hadn't been playing tricks on me. I quickly tried to cover up my trail and hid in the bushes. I wanted to see if the handsome man from the barn had trailed me here.

Damn, but he's hot! I couldn't help thinking when he broke through the trees. The wolf seemed to be in agreement. He was beautiful, just as I remembered, only now I could see his sexy sky-blue eyes, rimmed in thick long black lashes. He had the kind of eyes that would see clear into a person's soul. When he hit the end of my trail, to the point where my wolf paw tracks, which were huge, by the way, took over from the footprints of the person I used to be, he crouched down to look very closely at them. He looked around with a confused look on his face, and then he kind of smiled to himself. He stood up and began to circle around the area where the impressions changed over, as if he were looking for something. He went in ever-larger circles, widening his pattern, searching with a growing scowl on his face. It was obvious if I stayed, he'd find me in minutes. I had to leave. But before I could move, he walked past me and my new nose picked up his rich scent—thick musk, the deep woods, and the earth. He smelled heavenly. The wolf wanted to step right out of our hiding place and pant after him. He wanted to drop to the ground and show the man our white belly, with all four feet in the air, and give him our submission. He wanted to play and make the man chase after us through the woods. I told the wolf to just shut up and run. I darted off into the woods silently. I was hungry, thirsty, and I knew if I wanted, I could run like the wind. So I did, leaving the wonderful-smelling man behind.

I ran and ran and ran. The wind in my fur, the smell of the forest in my nostrils, pine needles and damp earth under my paws— it's impossible to explain how exhilarating and peaceful everything became. I had no worries about the future, no thoughts of the past, only my immediate need and its fulfillment. The wolf wanted to hunt and I let it; he seemed to know how to take care of his hunger. The wolf knew where the deer were without thinking about them, and I headed on silent feet toward the herd sleeping in the tall grass.

I moved in tune with all the life that pulsed all around me. I crept up silently, had the doe in my teeth, and snapped her neck before I realized what the wolf intended. The wolf had totally taken over, ripping through the hide and inhaling large amounts of steaming flesh, relishing in the coppery goodness and warmth sating his hunger. Somewhere in the back of my mind, my human self screamed, *Oh gross!*But the wolf gloried in his kill, and he felt exultant, content. When I finished as much of the venison as my engorged stomach could hold, I was sure I'd never be able to eat again. Completely stuffed, I lay down in the grass and rolled over. I didn't want to think about how much raw meat I'd just consumed. *I'll never be a vegan now.* I laughed to myself, the sound that escaped me sounding like a bark.

I was officially a killer. No surprise there.My dreams had been reminding me of my failings for quite a while now. I rubbed my muzzle on the grass, then licked my huge paws, cleaning them. I decided to head for the stream I could hear trickling nearby. I felt extremely at ease and comfortable in my new furry hide. I was at peace for the first time in what felt like years. The wolf was blissful, I was happy, and I had no idea why.

I couldn't get the vision of golden skin, black hair, and blue eyes out of my head. The memory of his scent and an unrealistic urge to have the man's hands running through my fur made me want to curl up and lick my own balls. Yes, I could reach them… no, I refused to give in to the urge to do so.

Night crept up on me, and darkness started to fill the forest. I wasn't sure when I decided to go looking for the young man, or maybe it was the wolf that decided. I found myself drifting back to where I'd stashed my stuff, the place where I'd last seen him. He was gone, of course, but his scent remained and it smelled so nice.

Sniffing around, I could tell he'd headed back toward the ranch. I wondered what he thought about wolf tracks picking up where the human trail he'd followed had disappeared. The wolf didn't care. He rolled in the hints of the man's wonderful scent. So very tired, my muscles and joints ached from running and hunting. The wolf wanted to sleep, so I stretched my new muscles, curled up among the roots of a tree, and fell asleep.

Cool fall morning light filtered through the trees. I was lucky it was still closer to summer than winter, no frost, but there was still a slight chill in the air. I awoke. Human. Naked. And I had company. A huge mound of gray and white mottled fur had curled up alongside me, keeping me warm.

"Shit!" I screamed in a voice that sounded like a little girl—at least it did to me. I made a leap for the other side of the tree. My scream awoke the owner of the fur, the largest wolf I'd ever seen. He—*yep, definitely a he*—stood up and peered at me curiously. He could've been a pony. His shoulders reached well above my waist, and he could practically look me straight in the eyes—He had sky-blue eyes. *Rare for a wolf to have blue eyes*, I thought, *but not unheard of.* I kept the tree between us as I watched him closely for any sign of aggression. He yawnedand stretched, cocked his head sideways at me, then looked down my previous trail back toward the ranch, growling softly.

Had I missed something, maybe someone coming up the trail? My senses were at a distinct disadvantage as a human. I made a run for the bushes and dug up my clothes, what was left of them, and my duffel bag of scavenged tools from beneath the hedge. I quickly pulled my jeans on, but my underwear was missing, forcing me to go commando. At least the pants were still intact.The shirt would need to be mended. The buttons were all missing, and there were rips along the seams. My jacket remained whole, and I quickly slipped it over my tattered shirt. I grabbed my bag and cut across my previous trail, heading for the stream.

The cool water felt good against my bare feet—I'd been unable to find my shoes. I headed upstream, roughly in the direction of myplace. It wasn't a home or even that great of a shelter, really, but it was my sanctuary. If I could get there, I'd be safe. Looking through the trees, I realized he was following me. The white-gray wolf ran along with me—not at my feet, like a dog would, but parallel to me. He kept watching me as we ran. I'd see him turn toward me, keeping me in sight. He didn't seem aggressive. I guess maybe my wolf self must've made a friend, although I didn't remember any other wolves. I didn't like the idea that I might've blacked out or lost time as a wolf. Not knowing what my wolf might have done was a horrible feeling. I needed to be in control of him. I might have become a monster, but it would be a cold day in hell before…. I didn't want to think about it. Emotionally, I couldn't even begin to process this new facet of my life. I prayed it wouldn't happen again.

The white-gray wolf didn't seem aggressive, so I decided not to complain. He'd take care of himself, and hopefully wouldn't decide at lunchtime that I belonged on the menu. He'd go away eventually. I took my time circling back around toward my sanctuary—my cottage—and felt sure no one would be able to trail me. I ran straight into the dilapidated structure. Immediately, I felt safe. The wolf followed, right through the nonexistent door, and stood there looking aroundalmost expectantly.

"What?" I looked at the wolf.

He shook himself, sat down, and looked at me, glancing out the doorway every now and then as if he expected someone. I ignored him. My sanctuary probably didn't look like much. It was a one-room mining cabin that had been abandoned sometime in the 1800s after the gold rush, and it'd seen better days. With four crumbling walls, no windows, an entrance with no door and a thatched roof that was in the process of falling in, the building had clearly been devoid of human occupation for a very long time. But to me it was perfect; it had a working fireplace and, as every Realtor will tell you, the thing that makes the sale—location, location, location.

I got busy digging into my small stash of clothing in the corner of the cabin. I found socks and a pair of sneakers I'd scavenged along a riverbank earlier in the season. Some swimmer had left them behind, but they fit me fairly well. I began going through my duffel bag. I smiled at what I'd been able to scavenge. I promised myself I'd return the things I'd borrowed and I'd leave money for the twine and the nails.

The wolf growled as I pulled things from the bag and laid them out on the floor.

"I know stealing is wrong." The wolf looked disgusted. "I'm going to return them. I just need to make a few improvements or I won't survive the winter." The wolf seemed to consider, looked up at the roof, shook his big head, and lay down with his head on his paws, watching me.

"I'm reasoning with a wolf.... I'm sooo headed for a rubber room," I mumbled to myself. I stood up, went to the side of the cabin for firewood, and started a fire in the fireplace.Looking around, I found a place for each of my new tools, keeping them separate from the things I owned.I didn't want to mix the two. I intended to return them to the barn when I was finished with them. The warmth from the fire took the chill out of the cottage, despite the lack of a door. I smiled and hummed to myself. I'd found a number of buckets and a couple pots during the summer, all abandoned by fishermen and campers vacationing in the national forest. I hung a bucket full of water over the fire to boil. I really wanted to wash up. I sang as I worked. I knew singing wasn't considered very manly, but I missed having real music. A radio was a luxury I didn't have. I'd discovered a couple of MP3 players, but they only held their charge for so long, then they became worthless except for the few bucks I could get at a pawn shop for them.

I took off my jacket and hung it on a nail. I replaced my tattered shirt with a clean one, and then I dug a sewing kit out of my backpack to repair the one I'd torn. I'd long ago learned how to sew, and I always kept the buttons from clothing that was no longer wearable.

As I waited for the water to boil, I looked around my sanctuary, trying to decide what needed to be repaired first. The hardest to fix would be the door. The water steamed and rolled. I carefully removed it from the fire and made a cup of tea from wild mint leaves. The wolf watched as I brewed the tea. I'd found the mint about three days ago in a patch that covered a large section of the forest floor. The tea warmed me from the inside out and I began to relax, the stress from the previous day finally fading. Even though the sun overhead declared it to be barely noon, I was exhausted. I decided on a nap.

I took off my jeans, pulled on a pair of shorts, and climbed into my sleeping bag. The wolf just continued to lie in front of the fireplace with his eyes closed; I guess he'd fallen asleep watching me. I stretched out and quickly joined him.

CHAPTER 2

"NO... NO...," I scream back at him as I try to run through the same blurry gray house filled with doors that only lead to more halls and more doors. I'm yanking them open and trying to run, but the carpet pulls at my feet and I stumble from room to room, trying desperately to get out.

"Come on, boy... time for your punishment." His laugh causes me to scream in terror, and I'm gasping because I feel like I can't breathe. I run, but it's in slow motion, and he's gaining on me. He's going to catch me and—

I must've cried out in my sleep. The wolf nuzzled my neck, whining softly, licking the skin under my ear. I woke just enough from the dream to know he was there. I sighed and sank my fingers into his thick pelt, so soft—so surreal, I didn't even notice in my half-asleep state—how completely unreal. A wild wolf woke me from a nightmare and lay beside me with his huge head across my stomach. How could this feel right and seem so natural? His presence made me feel safe again and the nightmare didn't return.

A new dream began: *We're running through the woods. I watch the wolf running with me. We dodge the trees and the low branches, leaping over downed trunks of long-fallen pines. As I watch, my huge white-gray wolf is running beside me.One minute, he dodges a trunk—then the young man with the spiked black hair is there, running. Then behind another tree and it's back to the wolf again. We run through the forest, playing and chasing each other.*

11

Sometimes I'm a brown wolf and sometimes I'm human. Not a word is spoken between us. We hunt together and eat side by side. I relaxed into the bliss of this good dream—strange, but good.

The late-morning sun woke me to bone-chilling cold. The upper elevations were cool until midday even during the height of summer, and now, with the onset of fall, temperatures in the forties and fifties until close to noon were the norm. I'd slept through the previous afternoon and the night as well. I shivered involuntarily in the cold, the fire having long since burned itself out.

My wolf was gone. His absence brought all my fears and confusion to the forefront, forcing me to deal with emotions I could no longer set aside. *What am I?* I'd actually turned into a wolf the day before. It hadn't been a dream. Surely I wasn't a werewolf! All the stories I'd ever heard, the movies I'd seen—the creature had been mercilessly tied to the cycles of the moon, silver bullets, and hunting people. They were mindless creatures, appearing halfhuman and halfwolf. They killed people for pleasure. My experience as the wolf had been nothing like that. The animal lived in me, was a part of me, my mind and thoughts—I was a part of the animal. *I can't be a werewolf. I just can't be... that creature,* I thought, *at least not in the traditional mythological sense.* I turned into a real wolf, not a half-and-half thing. Maybe the bloodlust—the evil—the hunting-people stuff—would come later? I tried to shake myself of the fear forming around my heart. *Maybe I'd have become a killing monster if I'd been closer to where people lived? Maybe because I was in the forest I became a whole wolf? Maybe being around people would make me a monster? Maybe I'd be a safe beast if I stayed in the woods?* I argued with myself, back and forth.I hadn't attacked the young man when he'd walked past me on the trail. I hadn't felt even the urge to harm him. In fact, my desires were of a decidedly more friendly nature. Maybe it wouldn't happen again.

I sat with my arms wrapped around my knees and rocked like a child as I struggled to deal with my increasingly overwhelming fear. Great shudders shook my body, and I began to concentrate on my breathing, trying to calm the terror that threatened to push me beyond my own endurance. I'd just about get a handle on myself when another wave would hit me, as I thought of some different facet or possibility of my new existence. Half the day passed with me rocking and holding my knees, unable to get a grip on my emotions as my mind ran in circles, out of control. I'd never felt so entirely alone, or hated myself and my circumstances more. I felt nauseous, as if I might throw up, but I couldn't. Fear had me rooted to the spot, swaying back and forth and trying to soothe myself.

By midafternoon, my distress had moved from incoherent occasional mumbling to being unable to breathe. I concentrated on taking slow even breaths, but I'd already begun to hyperventilate by the time I saw the wolf walk in the door. He came to me instantly, whining softly, and sat beside me as I tried to calm myself, feeling on the verge of passing out. I sank my fingers into his fur and held him to my chest; I began to feel a little better. I didn't feel quite so alone. I felt my racing heartbeat begin to slow and take up a more natural rhythm.

"What am I?" I asked the wolf softly between my gasps, panic coloring my voice.

The wolf whined softly. He shoved his nose between my hands, washed my face, and licked the sweat from my brow. I wrapped my arms around his neck, and he pushed his body up against mine. He rubbed his face against me and occasionally he would whimper, but he never complained as I attempted to work through my panic.

Slowly my grip on his fur began to ease and my breathing softened; I felt better. I felt more like myself. It wasn't that I knew any more now than I had before but I'd moved beyond the panic. I took a couple of steadying deep breaths and ran my hand from the wolf's head to his shoulder. I released a strangled laugh, managing to cough and choke at the same time.

"Sorry," I whispered into his coat as I wrapped my arms around him again in a reassuring hug. He might be an animal, but he'd helped me to regain my balance and my sanity. That thick fur I had my fingers sunk into assured me I wasn't alone.

13

"Thank you." I held him tight to my chest. He seemed to almost purr for a moment, his head snuggled close to mine, rubbing gently against my cheek. *Can wolves purr?* I didn't think so....

My brain and my survival instincts finally kicked in. The light had begun to wane as the afternoon progressed into evening. I was losing the day, and each was precious as winter was looming near. I got up from my sleeping bag and stretched sore muscles. Mother Nature was calling, and I walked out to the tree line to relieve myself before returning to the cabin. Damn, I missed plumbing. I washed my face in water from my bucket and brushed my teeth. Just the normalcy of those basic acts made me feel better, more like myself. I'd wasted enough time wallowing in self-pity. I couldn't afford to let myself be sidetracked. Nature wouldn't give me a pass because I had a mental breakdown over becoming a wolf. The seasons still passed, and if I seriously planned on being in the cabin for the winter, innumerable repairs needed to be done in order to keep out the cold. This would be survival of the fittest, and I obviously needed to be stronger to survive.

"I should've gone into town today. I need to get some supplies, and I need to stop at the library." The wolf watched me, a strange look on his face. He shook his head.

"What, you don't think I should go to town?" I spoke to the wolf as if he could know what I said. I laughed shakily, still not quite myself. *That rubber room's looking better all the time.* I stood up, stretched, and reached for my clothes. The wolf roused himself and went outside. I hurried, changed out of my shorts, and put on my jeans. Hunger had me grabbing an apple from my stash in the corner. I'd found a wild crabapple tree a couple days ago, and the apples were ready to eat. I'd amassed a substantial stash of them; they made a good breakfast in a pinch.

I grabbed the burlap sack I'd scavenged earlier in the season and headed for the door. I'd pick up cans along the roadside and turn them in at the recycling station for a couple extra bucks, and then I'd go to the landfill and see if I could find some plastic sheeting to line the inside of the windows to keep out the winter wind. A door would be nice too. I walked outside, apple in hand, to find the wolf sitting in the afternoon sun as if he were waiting for me.

"You can't come into town with me, you know." He didn't look at me. He just stared out into the forest. His fur glistened in the sun. I didn't say anymore, I just ate my apple.I tipped my face up to the sun and relaxed. The wolf turned and began to watch me almost expectantly. I was about to tell him I didn't have anything to give him as I didn't think he'd really want my apple core. In that moment, the pain reached up and clawed its way through my stomach.

"Shit!" I screamed, doubling over. My skin crawled. I moved faster this time, ditching my clothes, knowing where this was going, but the change seemed to be happening faster too. I got my shoes, jeans, and T-shirt off before the wolf exploded out from my body. When I finally opened my eyes, panting hard, I stood trembling on four legs, and I had a tail... again. I shook out my fur and took a deep breath.

The wolf in me wanted to celebrate his freedom. I could feel his joy. He wanted to run and hunt. He saw the other wolf, standing a little ways off, and my beast immediately became territorial. He didn't know this wolf. *No!* I silently screamed at him. *This is my friend.* He ignored me and growled a warning at the trespasser. I tried to take control away from him and force him to lie down, but the wolf was stronger and he had to defend us and our sanctuary. The strange wolf had come into our territory, and my wolf wouldn't allow it. The white-gray wolf's head dropped low and he snarled back at me, teeth snapping and hackles raised. I couldn't believe it; he'd never so much as growled before. The fur on my back rose, and I lowered my head menacingly. The white-gray wolf approached me slowly, his own head down, andsnarled a warning. We came together in front of the little cottage, both of us aggressive and circling each other, our fur on end, sniffing at one another.

The other wolf smelled familiar to my wolf. *Of course he does, I spent most of yesterday and this afternoon with him.* My wolf didn't agree; he knew this scent, but not the wolf who wore it. The white-gray wolf had an inch or two on me in height and was a few pounds heavier, as well. My wolf knew we couldn't take him in a fight—he was Alpha and we were barely out of puppyhood—but this was our territory. My sanctuary belonged to us, and it was ours to defend. He growled but didn't attack, sniffing me from one end to the other, and I carefully sniffed him in the same suspicious way. A whine escaped the throat of my wolf; I found myself on my back with my feet in the air, pawing playfully at him. He snarled, but it sounded like approval to my wolf's ears. He clenched his jaw around my jugular in seconds. He was dominant, and my wolf told me we'd follow him anywhere and he'd take care of us.

Just like that, we were accepted. The white-gray wolf liked us. The two of us took off running. The snarls, yips, and nips were light and playful. We ran together through the woods, leaped over downed logs, and splashed through the stream. We hunted together and brought down an elk, taking pride in our joint venture. We both ate our fill of the kill 'til our bellies were distended with the meat. My dream from the other night played out in reality as we ran, played, and slept in the sun while the afternoon turned to evening. We curled up together as the last rays of the warm sun stroked our fur, my chocolate brown mingling with his white and gray as we snuggled. He rested his head on my paws and I rested my head over his shoulder—perfect contentment.

We watched as the sun set, turning the sky vivid red and purple as dusk swallowed the last of the evening light. My wolf was happy; we had a pack and our Alpha was glorious. I lifted my head to look at him. He did the same, looking deeply into my eyes. He rubbed his face against mine, snuffling as he did. I rubbed back; I liked the affection and my wolf couldn't get enough touching. Together, as if we had one mind, we both stood and shook our coats.

The silvery tip of the moon just beginning to rise above the horizon now ruled our play. I could feel… something… expected… something, but had no idea what. My Alpha opened his muzzle and his tongue fell out in a wolfish grin. I cocked my head to the side. He took off running, barking back at me. I took off after him, running, chasing him. He led me to an open meadow. We watched the moon rise over the horizon. Suddenly he threw back his head and set to howling, a deep, throaty song. The sound pulled at my soul and figuratively curled my toes, beckoning me to join in, and before I even realized I'd done it, a second voice joined his. I'd thrown back my head and begun baying in perfect harmony.

Nearby arose an answering howl, and not just one—a chorus rent the night. The sound shocked me. I dropped to my belly in fear. Too close! Way too close! My wolf trembled in fear. We looked to our Alpha, but he seemed happy with the answering call and immediately bayed again. He glanced down at me cowering at his feet.

The sound of his voice on the wind clawed at me and drove me to my feet. I had to answer his call. It ripped from my throat before I could stifle the sound.

I knew we were in trouble, my wolf knew we were in trouble, but our Alpha—he moved closer to me and draped his head over my shoulders in a protective and soothing manner. My wolf calmed immediately; our Alpha would protect us. We wandered through the moonlight, heading slowly back toward the cottage. The more I thought about it, the more the wolf in me didn't like the proximity of the other wolves. They were too close. We shouldn't—couldn't—stay at the cottage. We'd have to leave; the two of us couldn't defend our territory from a pack. We'd have to convince the Alpha to follow us.

THE fact I woke up as the early morning sun peeked over the horizon further attested to my nervousness. I woke human and in my sleeping bag, alone. The white-gray wolf had left again, probably returning to his pack. I got up and stretched. I looked around. A profound sadness welled up in my chest. I couldn't stay here. The other wolves were too close. I'd encroached on their territory and the white-gray male had to belong to their pack. I needed to move on.

Damn... just damn. I sighed from my heart, a sound full of regret and disappointment, as I began to pack all my things in my bags. I pulled out my large frame backpack and began fastening the various bags, pans and totes to the frame, then secured my bedroll to the bottom. I pretty much lived from that backpack, so it didn't take long to get it together. First I needed to return the borrowed tools to the ranch. I wasn't about to leave with that on my conscience. I decided to leave the big pack at the tree line above the barn, taking the duffel with the tools back, and then retrieving it on my way out. South seemed like a good direction since, adding in travel time, it wasn't likely I'd have a warm place to keep me out of the winter weather. I had some money. I'd try to hitchhike first. Maybe head for the forests of the southern Rockies in New Mexico; that would be a good place to head for the winter. There would still be snow, but nothing like the winter I'd have to face here in the north if I stayed.

I twitched in my fear. I wasn't used to being on the road and traveling on my own, but the wolf in me felt confident. I was glad one of us did. I'd discovered I could hear my wolf all the time, and if he had an opinion, he wasn't afraid to share. We wondered where the white-gray wolf had disappeared to. Would he miss us? Would he follow our trail away from the cottage? I caught myself already thinking of myself in the plural and that unsettled me further. I sighed, grabbed the duffel with the tools, my backpack of belongings, and headed out at an easy jog.

I arrived at the tree line above the barn in much less time than I'd expected. On the good side, it seemed I could run effortlessly over large distances and my wolf said,*See? This isn't so horrible after all*. On the bad side, well, it hurt like hell to shift, but that seemed to be the only drawback. Maybe the change would get easier with time.

I looked down at the ranch from my vantage point. I wasn't even winded. I let my pack slide off my back to the groundand hid it in the bushes at the base of a large tree just inside the tree line, well off the main trail. It would be safe there for the short time I'd need to return the items I'd borrowed.

I sprinted to the barn. I didn't see anybody around, so I moved quickly, putting the tools back where I'd found them. I had the strangest sense of déjà vu when I realized I was being watched. I turned suddenly. The young man leaned against the far door, his arms crossed, smiling at me.

"Again?" he asked. His voice was deep and it sent an involuntary shiver up my spine. *Yep, again,* I thought. I closed my eyes briefly and took a deep breath. Again, I noted how utterly beyond handsome he looked. And againI sprinted for the tree line. Again, he followed, right on my heels this time, but I still had a bit of a head start and I put on a burst of speed. I was faster, even though he was taller and his legs were longer. I poured on the speed when I hit the trees. I leaped over downed logs and let the wolf tell me where to go. He had me running like the wind. At the stream, Iran down along its length and then across. Mr. Drop-Dead Gorgeous seemed unusually persistent but was falling farther and farther behind with every step. When the wolf felt certain we'd lost him, I circled back around toward the barn. I needed to pick up my stuff. Then I could be out of here.

Back at the tree line, I'd just pulled the straps over my shoulders and secured the belt around my waist, holding the pack in place, when he appeared, walking around from the far side of a tree.

"Thanks for bringing back the tools," he said with a smile, his hands raised in surrender. I watched him carefully as I continued to make sure I had everything. I couldn't afford to leave anything behind. I didn't say anything and I didn't intend to.

"My name is Andrew. Who are you?" He leaned against the tree with his arms crossed, smiling at me like he was my best friend. Wow! His smile dazzled; he'd stop traffic effortlessly. 'Course, you had to notice it first—his sky-blue eyes had me at "Thanks."

I blinked and gave myself an internal shake. There was nothing to say, so I just looked at him, narrowing my eyes with suspicion. I didn't trust him, so the next best thing was to try and ignore him.

Turning abruptly, I started walking back into the woods. Of course he wasn't giving up that easily, the man couldn't take a hint. He followed me… again.

Gonna try and keep up again. I took off at my newfound wolf jog. I didn't run to get away from him this time, I just pretended he wasn't there. He didn't say a word, just ran along with me. I kept going, heading due southwest. Eventually I'd run out of the Black Hills and then I'd have to find the highway. A good hour into my run—him keeping pace without a single complaint—I shook my head and sighed. I thought he'd eventually get tired, stop, and go back to his ranch. I couldn't figure out why he insisted on following me. I'd returned his property. He had no reason to keep going. I stopped and he stopped with me. He looked at me expectantly.

"What do you want? I returned your stuff, now leave me alone."

"You haven't told me your name yet." He smiled at me with that devastating grin. I swear my heart paused for a second to admire that glow. He didn't seem to be any more winded than I was.

"I'm not going to tell you my name. You don't need to know. I don't plan on staying here, so what does it matter?" I looked around, trying in vain to keep from being pulled into those eyes. I'd unconsciously made my way back toward the cottage. I knew where the river flowed, and I needed a drink.

"Why're you leaving?" His smile had disappeared, replaced with a frown. He looked confused, almost sad, like a little boy whose best friend was going away, leaving him behind.

"Because I don't belong here. Time to hit the road before I wear out my welcome." I drank deeply of the little stream, wanting to hold the memory of it inside of me. The water tasted good and cold. I missed my wolf friend already, although in a way I didn't mind delaying my journey in order to talk with the handsome Andrew. Maybe the wolf would make an appearance before I left his territory. I closed my eyes and sighed. Enough procrastinating. If I intended to get south before the snow, I really needed to leave. I didn't want to have to turn myself in just to stay alive.

"Look, just go on home. It was nice to meet you, Andrew, and thanks for the tools." I headed southwest again, still at my jogging pace. He didn't follow me this time. I sighed with relief. Looking into his eyes had completely unsettled me. I felt like I could see into his soul. I couldn't understand the feelings behind those unguarded eyes. I'd never met an adult who didn't hide their emotions. Andrew's every emotion shone for all the world to see, right there in his sky-blue eyes. What a dangerous and painful way to live. If people saw too much of you, they'd know how to hurt you.

I kept running through the woods. I couldn't exactly say how I knew which way to go, but I knew, without looking for moss on trees or checking out the sun in the sky. I felt like I could never get lost again. The cottage quickly fell behind. Soon it would be just a pleasant memory. Nature would take the ramshackle structure back, and my few improvements would soon mean nothing. I felt kind of sad, as though the cottage had become a friend and I'd failed to save it, instead abandoning it to its fate. *Damn, I'm getting sentimental.*

The afternoon continued as I jogged on through the forest, the unhurried miles passing beneath my feet. Eventually I emerged from the woods.The highway stretched out before me, a black line dividing the past and a possible future. Dusk settled over the hills as the sun disappeared behind the trees.

Preferring the woods to people, I decided to stay in the forest one more night, then head for civilization in the morning. I really hated the idea of going into town. This remote nature reserve had come close to feeling like a home, closer than I'd ever come before.

Maybe my white-gray wolf would find me here at the edge of what I hoped was still his territory. I moved back into the forest and made a camp. I'd stretched out my sleeping bag under the trees and was considering starting a campfire when it began.

In all the nights I'd stayed in the national forest, I'd never heard the howling sound so dismal. Goose bumps prickled my skin, chilling me. The wolf in me wanted to cry back, but I made him remain silent, determined to stay human. The sad song continued. I struggled to hold myself together, wrapping my arms around my knees. The wolf had had enough; the pain in my stomach told me the change was starting. I began to shed my clothes. The mournful howling continued. It called to my wolf as the transformation took over. This could be a serious problem. If I couldn't control when these shifts happened—granted, they were getting easier and less painful, this time better than the others—there would be no way I could live in a city. I could be at a grocery store and get a whiff of the deli case and go all wolf! That would be bad—very bad. Ihad no desire to become a lab experiment.

I'd no sooner donned my fur coat than the wolf in me set to baying at the top of his lungs. The answering song, though quite a ways off, sounded joyful and ended with a yip, and my wolf wiggled like a puppy from nose to tail. *He's coming.* Our white-gray wolf would be here soon. *What am I supposed to do with a wild wolf in town?* I thought. My wolf didn't care; he ran forward, intent on meeting our Alpha.

It didn't take long. My wolf was right. He seemed thrilled to see us. He leaped into the air and tackled me, rolling both of us across the ground. We ran and played all night, hunting together in the early morning.A small deer fed the two of us quite well. Snuggled into each other's fur, we lay together completely at ease, just enjoying being together, before the sunrise and reality could disrupt my happiness. Our Alpha was warm, affectionate, and wonderful. I began to lose my apprehension. My wolf couldn't be happier; he wanted to stay. The white-gray wolf wouldn't let anything happen to us. Trust our Alpha. He seemed to be convinced we couldn't go wrong. I'd been trying to leave this contentment, and I seemed to be losing out to the wolf. *I'm the person here*, I told my wolf, *I make the decisions*. My life, my choice, not his. I was ignored, and we fell into the dreamless sleep of the wolf.

I woke up as dawn peeked over the treetops. I turned and realized Andrew sat against the tree, looking down at me, stroking my fur. He smiled down at me, a guilty grin on his face.

"I wondered when you'd wake up, my*àluinn*," he teased gently. Andrew wore only a pair of jean cut-off shorts—completely bare-chested and barefoot. He didn't seem the least bit concerned about the large chocolate-brown wolf curled beside him, whom he was petting like a Labrador retriever. But, damn, my wolf wanted to rub all over him and lick that beautiful bare chest—*Yummy!*—in a good way, not as lunch.

The wolf in me knew Andrew and the white-gray wolf were the same immediately. My wolf nose couldn't be fooled. My wolf stood up and began rubbing against Andrew, and a happy thrumming sound came from my chest. I guess wolves could purr, because I did. Almost as quickly as the wolf became overjoyed, I became appalled. Andrew and the wolf I'd spent so much time with in the cottage were the same. He'd seen me at my weakest… my nightmares… my demons… and witnessed my theft, although he did see me return what I'd borrowed. I'd cried like a baby into Andrew's fur, but the wolf in me couldn't have been more pleased to see him.

"You know you should really just come home with me. The others would be more than happy to meet you. There really is no danger. I'd protect you, my *àluinn*."

I shook my fur. Both of us, the wolf and I, were in agreement. We couldn't take that chance. He kept saying that word, *àluinn,* like it meant something special. I had no idea what it meant, could be "bastard" for all I knew. The wolf and I had an understanding; we might not want to go anywhere near the other pack, but we wanted to be closer to him. I couldn't explain my instant attachment. Yes, the man was beyond hot and I wanted to lick every inch of his yummy dark tan skin, but something more tickled at the edge of my mind that I couldn't readily name.

I'd never wanted to be around anyone before. The wolf thought the danger of approaching other wolves simply too big of a risk, and so did I. I didn't trust people, even wolf people. But Andrew—I wanted him to stay. I shook my head and my fur and lay back down beside him. I put my head in his lap, pushed my head against his chest, and sighed, a frustrated whine escaping.

"I don't understand your reluctance." He sighed, putting his hand on my head and petting me soothingly. "No one would hurt

23

you. My mother and father would be thrilled to meet you. We've a fairly small pack. There are my two younger brothers and my baby sister. I have uncles and their wives, and my cousins, but they're spread out across the Black Hills and don't come around much. I wish I knew where you'd come from. We don't see too many of our kind passing through. There're very few of us, you know. When I saw you in the barn that first day, I didn't know you were like us, not 'til I found you in the woods, where you'd transformed."

I listened to him intently. I was trying to absorb every word like manna from heaven, but I continued to growl softly so he'd know going back to the ranch wasn't an option. The lush silky tones of his deep voice soothed my soul. I nuzzled against his chest. He chuckled softly, stroking my fur.

"I went looking for your people. I felt sure they'd be close by. We don't usually travel by ourselves. The wolf is a pack animal and being alone is uncomfortable, you know. But I couldn't find anyone. I had to return to the ranch, to tell my family you were here. Later, when I came back, you'd transformed back to your human form, but you were so cold. I shifted and stayed with you, kept you warm. I figured your family had to show up eventually to take care of you, but they didn't, so I stayed.

"You were nervous at first when you awoke, but you didn't seem to mind me. I didn't realize you didn't know what you were until I came back to the cabin the next day and found you in the middle of a panic attack. I was afraid to transform then, because I didn't want to make it worse. You were so freaked out and seemed to have no idea what you were, and I finally realized you were completely alone. I tried to comfort you as best I could. I didn't know what to do. We usually grow up knowing what we are. Our families are so tightly bound together it's inconceivable to me how you could be lost and have no one looking for you. I grew up watching my family transform before my eyes, pulling the tails and ears of the adults, and waiting for pubertywith anticipation, when the first change occurs. I tried to imagine what it would feel like to transform, to not be ready for it and not know what the pain is, to just have it happen and completely rock your world. I have to say, I've only the vaguest clue how you feel. You must be so confused and scared, not understanding the instincts and what the wolf is telling you. I couldn't leave you, you'd have no idea what to expect. So I stayed close, waiting for the wolf to emerge again. I thought I should go and get my folks, but you were too scared, and then you started talking about going to town and I knew you'd never make it before the wolf showed up again."

He ran his fingers through my fur and I inched closer, liking the feeling of his body next to mine. I'd never liked it when people touched me, but having Andrew's hands on me—gently, softly stroking my head and shoulders the entire time he spoke—had to be the next best thing to heaven.

"We're shape-shifters, sometimes called skinwalkers or weres. Some names are preferred in certain parts of the world. Some shifters with purer bloodlines can take more than one shape, but most just take one. In this part of the country, we seem to be predominantly wolves, although I have an uncle who's a bear and a cousin who's an eagle." I lifted my head to look at him, startled, and he chuckled.

"For some of us it's a choice, for others... not so much. We're a very old, long-lived race, second only to the immortals—the vampires. Our lives can extend for hundreds of years. The oldest of us is two hundred and twelve years old." Andrew's hand paused in my fur and seemed to tremble a bit. "He's ancient but he remains vital and strong. He has very little human blood in his bloodline. It's said he's learned to transform into numerous animals over the centuries. He says each form brings its own understanding and its own wisdom. He appears to be middle-aged, maybe forty or so. There's no sign of actual physical age on his body." Andrew rambled while I listened with fascination as he explained shape-shifters and bloodlines. I could tell he was trying very hard to explain everything and not freak me out any further. I whined a bit and looked off toward the south, contemplating making a run for it. Everything he said seemed so strange, yet I could hardly deny it, seeing as I was a wolf lying beside him. I didn't know what to think. It dawned on me that I couldn't run from myself. From everything Andrew had been explaining, the animal was part of me and I could no sooner deny the wolf than I could deny my arm or leg.

"Please don't leave. Whatever the problem is, we can fix it. I'll help you. You don't have to be afraid. You don't have to be alone."

Andrew's hand never left my shoulder. I put my head back down into his lap and pressed against his stomach, closed my eyes, and sighed. I never thought I'd be the one to think this, but I liked not being alone. I really wanted to trust him, but I didn't easily trust anyone. I didn't know how to begin to trust. The very idea of giving someone the power to hurt me went against everything I'd learned growing up. But the wolf wanted to lean on him badly. The wolf tried to convince me that Andrew wasn't like the others, and I saw that he had a point. Andrew was a shape-shifter, like me. Maybe I could trust him. But trusting others had never ended well before. Besides, I'd always be able to tell what he was thinking. He couldn't hide anything in those sky-blue eyes.

Andrew had fallen silent, but my mind kept working. I couldn't understand why, but he made the wolf feel extremely safe. I loved lying here with our head in his lap, listening to his silky, deep voice. Still, part of me trembled, afraid to believe in him. I'd never had a home. I didn't know what a real home should feel like, but these woods made me feel like I'd finally found one. I'd never felt wanted before, or even just comfortable anywhere, except for right at this moment, with my head in his lap. Andrew made me feel desired and welcomed both, but he shouldn't. He continued to stroke my head and shoulders, quietly... waiting. I felt the stress leaving my body, relaxing as he kept stroking my fur. I could feel the change coming on, knew that I'd be back to a person soon, and for some reason I felt he knew it too.

"We'd better go and find your clothes." He smiled down at me. "Unless you want to walk around the woods naked? Can't say I'd mind the scenery, but I think you might get cold," he teased. I growled menacingly, but he only laughed.

26

I didn't want to end up naked in the woods. The man was too gorgeous and I'd be walking around sporting wood with no pants to even begin to cover it up. I needed my clothes. I got up and shook out my coat. I headed back toward the road at a brisk jog. We weren't far from my campsite. He kept up in human form, able to run almost as fast as he could in wolf form. We were by the highway in a couple of minutes, back at my campsite; my clothes were scattered about haphazardly. Andrew moved to stand at the edge of the woods, looking down at the highway. I stayed in my campsite. I could feel the change coming on. When I came out of the woods, he stood leaning against a tree with my backpack at his feet.

When he saw me, his eyes softened and he smiled.

"Hello,*àluinn.*"

I brushed off my jeans and my dusty T-shirt. I tried to pick the leaves from the rat's nest my hair had become.

"What's that mean…*à-àluinn*?" I asked, staring at the ground at his feet.

"Beautiful."

"Beautiful… hardly." But I smiled back at him, shaking my head in bewilderment. Seeing him standing there, it struck me just how different we were. He towered over me. I'd always been short.The bane of every guy in high school, to be shorter than average. My five foot five inches—with shoes on—height was a constant point of contention. I barely came up to his shoulder. His chest was broad and muscular, not too much muscle, but what I saw I wanted to run my fingers over and rub myself across. I just stopped the needy whine my wolf wanted to make, begging to be allowed back out to play. Having spent so much time living the life of a scavenger, my body was much leaner. I was skinny, probably too skinny. The muscles I had were tight and wiry. Andrew probably weighed around two hundred pounds of beautiful tall golden-skinned Adonis. I, on the other hand,would weigh closer to one twenty five in the rain. The man could blow me over if he sneezed.

"So, do I get to know your name now?" He smiled smugly, a little condescending, even, as he teased me. His eyes glittered.

"Lance. Lance Fitz…. Nice to finally meet you, Andrew." I sat down in front of the tree, drew out a comb from my backpack, and attempted to pull it through my hair. He chuckled and sat down behind me. He took the comb from me and began to work it through my now shoulder-length brown hair. I normally never let it grow like this, but since I'd gone out on my own, I hadn't had time to have someone cut it for me.

"So you followed me as a wolf. Where'd you get the shorts?" I couldn't help but ask. If my clothes would disappear and reappear when I shifted, that would be way cooler than having to worry about destroying my meager wardrobe.

Andrew held up his wrist, where a wristband was wrapped a couple of times, secured with Velcro. "I wrap the shorts as small as I can make them with this cord and hang it around my neck before I shift. Once I start shifting, I step through one of the cords so it ends up like a cord harness around my back and chest with the jeans hanging under my belly. Shorts are small and my fur tends to hide anything I carry."

"That's cool." It was a bit disappointing that my clothes wouldn't shift with me but, well, that only happened in books and movies.

"Some things will shift with you, but it has to be small and natural fibers like wool or cotton, but your clothes are just too much of a foreign fiber to transform with you. This cord is nylon, so it won't transform when I shift."

"So shifting and taking your clothes with you is out." I rolled my eyes and shook my head.

"So where are your people?"

"I've no idea. I've always been alone. I've been in the foster system for as long as I can remember. I've never had a family. I've never had a permanent home. I don't even know my parents' names. I've been shuffled from state to state. I couldn't even tell you where

28

I started out at, for sure, without checking the records. I don't trust people... easily," I warned him, seriously. His hands paused in my hair and he seemed sort of stunned, but quickly recovered and continued working.

"You're free. In a way, even as bad as growing up among humans probably was, freedom is something I'll never have." Andrew spoke so softly, I wasn't sure if he spoke to himself or me, but I had no idea what he meant and it wasn't the response I'd expected. I'd been prepared for pity and apologies, not sadness, or maybe... envy?

"What do you mean? You aren't free?" I stammered, confused.

"Our people are born into servitude, until we're freed by our benefactor, our master, except we never are.Our stories tell us about some who are free, but I've never met anyone who's been freed or had anyone in my family freed." Andrew's fingers lingered on my neck, caressing it so lightly that my breath caught and I stifled a small groan.

"You can stay, but I can't leave. I'm tied to these hills, to my family, and my master. I can go no farther than up to the highway. I can't cross it or follow it for more than a couple miles along this side."

"What would your master do if he found me?" A chill ran up my spine.

"Maybe nothing. Your presence means nothing to him, really. He probably wouldn't even realize you were any different from the rest of us. He's pretty ancient and doesn't notice change. He lives in his own world for the most part and is preoccupied with the social life of his kind.He doesn't come around much. If he calls, we go to him."

Andrew pulled me back against him, inhaling the scent from my hair. He cradled me against his broad muscular chest and wrapped his arms gently around my shoulders. I could feel his apprehension in the slight stiffening of his body behind me, as if he feared I might sprint to the other side of the road and be forever beyond his reach. I couldn't understand his feelings.Maybe it was a wolf thing; he was possessive because we saw him as our Alpha. He wanted me to stay. I tried not to be nervous; being held by Andrew like this felt so intimate, but I didn't want him to let go of me either. My wolf loved being held by him and wanted me to just relax and let him care for me. I couldn't remember the last time I enjoyed having someone touch me. My head fell back against his shoulder. Never in my life had I voluntarily allowed anyone to be this close.

"If you won't come back to the ranch, then at least please stay at the cottage. I'll help you fix the place up and get it ready for winter. We could make it our place, if you'll let me share it with you. I can come and stay with you sometimes, if you let me, and you can get to know my family slowly. I'll teach you about our people, and then in the spring you can decide what you want to do. No pressure...just me." Andrew was pleading now. "Please, Lance.Please stay."

A shock went through my body when he said my name. I couldn't stop the shiver that ran up my spine and thanked the heavens I sat with my back to his chest so he couldn't see my face. I couldn't suppress how happy just hearing him say my name made me. My wolf danced at the sound. I couldn't deny him his joy. The wolf in me howled that we had to stay. He demanded we not leave Andrew. I turned around to look into those cerulean eyes, and I shyly reached up to touch his face, feeling the scratch of whiskers, before I pulled back. I couldn't even explain why I decided to agree to his proposal; everything about this went against my better judgment. Connections were a bad idea, and trusting others never turned out well. We'd regret this, I tried to tell the wolf. He ignored me.

"Okay, I'll stay at the cottage... for now. But no promises. If you want to help me prepare for winter, I'll take all the help I can get. You're welcome to come and see me whenever you want. We'll decide what to do from there." I could hear myself saying the words, but I couldn't believe I'd actually agreed to trust him. "You can't tell anyone I'm here. Nobody in your family can tell anyone. I can't get caught here. I don't want to get anybody in trouble."

"Are you old enough to be on your own?" Andrew asked nervously, holding my gaze.

"Yes, I turned eighteen a couple weeks ago. But I wasn't of age when I ran, and I don't know if anyone's after me." I had no intention of telling him why I ran. There wasn't enough trust in the world to get me to spill those beans."How old are you?"

Andrew chuckled, a touch of mischief in his eyes. "How old do you think I am?"

"Couple years older than me, I guess."

"You're a cub compared to me. I've degrees in mathematics and physics that are older than you. I've been published," Andrew teased.

"Okay, so more than a couple years… you can't be thirty."

"Once a shape-shifter changes into his animal for the first time, we age very slowly. Until we change, we're the same as everyone else, essentially human. I changed for the first time when I was seventeen… you think I appear a couple years older than you and your eighteen years."

"Quit fooling around already." I gave his chest a playful shove.

"My twin brothers appear to be in their early teens, but are thirty-six.They both shifted very early, at fifteen, and will probably continue to look like teenagers for decades. I will be seventy-seven years old in November." Andrew's hold around me tightened, as if he feared his age would scare me off.

"No fucking way!" I turned in his arms to stare into his youthful face. There wasn't a wrinkle, not a gray hair, not a line to give any hint at his true age.

"We turn into wolves, and my age is something you have a hard time with." Andrew rolled his eyes.

"Yeah, but… seventy-seven!"

"You're gonna give me a complex. My parents are much older. Mom is ninety-three and Dad will be ninety-eight this year. They both appear in their thirties. Lance, we aren't human. Our lives are much longer." The color had begun to drain from Andrew's face, nerves setting back in as I struggled to grasp this added bit of strangeness.

"Damn." I let my head fall back on his shoulder with an exaggerated sigh. I mean, really, if I was going to accept it, there was no point in getting stuck on something like age. I just... wouldn't think about it. "Okay, old man, let's go home."

A brilliant smile lit up his face, and my breath whooshed from my lungs like I'd been punchedin the gut. Happiness shone from his eyes, and I'd never seen anything so fucking beautiful in my life. He hugged me close. His joy overtook everything, and my soul sang because I had made him feel that way. I couldn't understand why my being here was so important to him. I liked him and I hadn't given myself permission to like him yet or even begin to trust him, but seeing as how I was doing both, it was too late to second-guess my decision.

I sighed and ran a hand through my hair, amazed to find he'd gotten all the snarls and leaves brushed out. He handed me the comb; I shoved it into my backpack and he pulled me to my feet. We broke camp and returned to the cottage.

CHAPTER 3

REPAIRS to my sanctuary progressed much more quickly with two of us working on them. We spent our afternoons together, enjoying each other's company. Andrew told me about his family. His mother had homeschooled him and his brothers when they were young.She was currently teaching his little sister, and sometimes his cousins. His father worked on a construction crew in town; he brought in money for the family. Andrew, as the eldest son, ran the ranch. Mainly his responsibilities were to take care of the animals, the fields, and keep his brothers out of trouble. Andrew had explained that since his brothers had transformed at such a young age, their wolves were truly still impulsive adolescents and often got the twins into trouble if not kept busy. The animals kept him and the twins busy in the morning, but hespent therest of his day with me. I spent my days making plaster and sealing cracks in the mortar of the stone walls, usually humming or singing as I worked.

About a week into working on the cottage, Andrew brought me a battery-operated radio. It was the best present ever, even though he said he did it so he wouldn't have to listen to me sing anymore. Somehow I knew better. I loved music, and the radio kept me company when he went home in the evenings.

Fall was a time of radical temperature changes in the Black Hills. By noon the temps were in the upper eighties, though they drastically cooled to the forties after sunset. I didn't mind seeing Andrew hanging from the rafters wearing just his jeans and no shirt as he worked on the roof. Sometimes I'd catch him grinning down at me and I'd always smile in return, trying not to blush.

I balked one afternoon when he arrived with a heavy new door in his arms.

"What the hell is that?" I frowned at him as he carried it toward the cottage.

"What do you think… it's a door, of course." Andrew smirked.

His upturned lips and crinkled eyes always intoxicated me, and for a moment I was stunned as he leaned the door against the outer wall. "You can't bring that here; I've got no money to pay for it." I stroked the cool, smooth heavy oak. It was beautiful and solid. This door would keep out most everything Mother Nature could throw at it.

"I'm not asking you to pay for it. I paid for it, so don't worry about it." Andrew reached over and ran his hand down my arm. I trembled slightly. I couldn't get over how he always seemed to have his hands on me. Always calming me, but also distracting me from my argument.

"I will worry about it. Look, you can't just be buying stuff for me."

"What stuff?It's a door. You've got to have a door."

"What if I end up leaving?You'll have spent money to fix up a place you'll never need."

Andrew growled. He pushed me back against the wall, his body covering mine, his hands curled around my biceps,keeping me from running. "Quit talking about leaving. You already promised to stay through the season." He leaned forward and rubbed his cheek against mine, but stepped back when I put a hand on his chest.

"Andrew?"

"If you leave after that, the cottage will be a nice place for my family to use as a hunting cabin, or I can use it to get away from the family. God knows my brothers make me crazy enough to need a place to get away." He let go of my arms, turned away, walked over to the door,and leaned against the wall.

"Fine, I guess. Thank you." I rolled my eyes and watched while he hung the door. I couldn't say no; every time I said yes, he'd get so happy, and I liked seeing his eyes shine. He went back to the ranch after that, but returned later, carrying a small table. Making a second trip, he went back for the chairs. All I could do was say thank you. I had nothing to pay him with other than my gratitude. I'd never been exposed to someone who gave because they wanted to and asked for nothing in return. Yet Andrew seemed to find joy in the giving.

BY THE end of the second week, we began bringing slate rocks from the river canyons and laying a new foundation for an additional room.

"But we'll never get it finished," I argued.

"Of course we will. If things start to look like we aren't going to make it, I'll get my brothers up here and they can do the heavy lifting." Andrew laughed.

"Nobody else comes here, Andrew. You told me it'd be me and you." I growled, not liking the idea of anyone coming to our cottage—our sanctuary.

"You're right, it'd only be as a last resort, and I don't see that happening. We'll have the place done with plenty of time to spare."

I couldn't do it. I wanted to do it, but I couldn't. I couldn't say no. I just shook my head and gave in. "Fine. It's your place, after all; I'm just a freeloader. Let's go get the damn slate."

His face lit up like Christmas, and he picked me up and swung me around like I was a feather. "Knock that shit off!" I practically snarled, but it didn't stop him from keeping my hand in his and pulling me off in the direction of the river.

"Come on, Slate Canyon is just upstream, and we should be able to find some nice pieces to build the foundation. Will you make the mortar, like you did for the walls?"

"Sure, no problem." I ran after him, holding his hand and trying not to think anything of it. *Wolves are touchy-feely creatures*, I kept reminding myself. He didn't mean anything by it.

"We need to get enough for a bedroom, a bathroom, and a nice-size closet for storage." He planned as we ran. "If we hurry, we'll have it completed before the first serious frost."

"Bathroom? Andrew, hello? Have you noticed that we don't have running water?"

"We will have, Lance. The water table's fairly high here, and it won't take much to bring a four-wheeler up here. I can bring up some equipment and have a well dug in a day or two. We can lay some pipe and have water in before the ground freezes. We can even put in a small septic system and…."

I stopped, pulling my hand out of his. "Andrew. Seriously, I think you're getting way carried away here. I'm content with a roof and a door."

"But I'm not." He stopped and came back to me, his smile crinkling the skin around his eyes. "A bathroom and running water are necessities in the winter. The creek will be frozen over, and sometimes we don't get a lot of snowfall until spring. You'd have to chip away at the river and try to bring chunks of it to the cabin to thaw. Having a reliable water source is a necessity. Let me do this for us."

I tipped my head back and stared at the sky above me, shaking my head in frustration. Why couldn't I tell him no? "Fine," I grumbled. He howled with glee and grabbed my hand and towed me after him… again.

"Besides, I'm so not going to miss peeing on trees and burying my shit in the woods, even if it does mark this area as our territory." I just shook my head and laughed.

Andrew was as good as his word—it all happened. We laid the foundation, he brought up equipment to dig the well, and we put in the pipes, burying them a couple feet below the frost line. I had to laugh, stumbling, barely keeping my feet, the day I walked out of the cabin and found him in his wolf shape digging toward the well, but it was much faster than anything we could've done with a shovel. Still, seeing his wolf pawing at the ground, dirt flying out behind him between his back legs, tail waving above as he furiously worked at the trench for piping, was hilarious. Especially when he lifted his head and looked at me with dirt covering his face and muzzle, tongue hanging out. He looked like a puppy burying a bone or digging up a flower garden.

"You look ridiculous!" I guffawed. Andrew growled and shook so the dirt and grass flew from his coat. "I know, hurry up and get my ass to work, but you really look like a bad puppy. I should be punishing you for digging up the yard." I hooted with laughter as Andrew charged me, knocked me to the ground, licked my face, and covered me in wolf spit while I was pinned beneath him. His feet, coated with mud and dirt, soon had me as filthy as he was and he sat back on my stomach and yipped. Even as a wolf, I could tell he was rather satisfied with himself, before I shoved him off me so I could get to work.

His generosity seemed to have no limits; I didn't know what to say. I'd never known anyone who wanted to give me anything and he continued to come day after day, trying to give me the world, or at least a house. Secretly I ached for a bathroom, and hot water would be so wonderful. My last real shower had been at a campground facility; since then I'd washed from buckets of water brought from the river and a camping shower kit hung in a tree. I felt guilty for accepting his gifts, but whenever I tried to hold him back, he'd get this lost-puppy look on his face and all I wanted was to see him smile. I couldn't figure out what the hell was wrong with me. Toward the end of the third week of renovations, he asked me if he could bring his father up to see the improvements.

"I need his advice. I'm not sure how to join the old roof and the new one. The angles are going in opposite directions. I don't want the roof to leak where the two join."

"So, what… you're going to have him come up here and look at them?" I frowned and tried not to tremble at the thought of his father, his Alpha, coming to the cottage.

37

"He won't be here long. Just long enough to check that I've got the right idea on how to put it together. Then he'll leave. You don't even have to be here if you don't want to. You can hide in the tree line at the edge of the meadow, if you want. He won't hurt you." Andrew tried to reassure me.

"Fine, but I'm not going to hide in the damn trees. I'm not that big of a wuss." I grumbled unhappily. Part of me thought, *He just wants to introduce me to someone from his family.* I couldn't stop shaking. I'd seen Andrew's family from a distance both in wolf form and in human. His dad was a big man and he terrified me.

I had nightmares that night for the first time since Andrew had talked me into staying. I dreamed of the man who chased me—his evil laughter, him catching me, and the beatings—before Andrew woke me. I'd been screaming; I woke to find myself in his arms.

"Wake up, beautiful. Shh... nobody's going to hurt you. I promise." Andrew rocked me back and forth in his arms. He held me against his chest, his arms wrapped around me, holding my flailing arms so that I couldn't hurt either of us. "Easy, baby, I've got you," he whispered. He didn't ask about the dream and I didn't offer anything. He just held me and stroked my hair. Once the trembling stopped and I relaxed, I fell asleep with Andrew keeping a watchful vigil nearby.

I COULDN'T believe how nervous I felt. I washed my hair and combed it out, then fussed over what to wear, finally giving up and putting on a pair of clean jeans and a T-shirt. It wasn't like I had a lot to choose from. I stood in the doorway of the cottage to watch for their approach, feeling like I wanted to freak out. My wolf wanted to run and hide. I seriously considered doing just that as Andrew and his father emerged from the tree line. I struggled to stay human, fighting the wolf's urge to run, because Andrew had told me running would trigger his father's alpha wolf to chase me. I didn't want to be chased anymore. My wolf whined, and a whimper actually escaped my lips as Andrew's dad came out of the trees. There was no doubt the man approaching was the Alpha of the pack. I had to stand my ground and meet him, even though he terrified me. I could do this; Andrew wanted this. I won the battle. The wolf listened to me, albeit reluctantly. We stood our ground.

Andrew watched me carefully. I know they both saw my hands twitch, giving away my nervousness. He smiled encouragingly to me as they slowly approached. Pointing at the roof, they talked to each other about the lay of the thatching. One step at a time, letting me get more comfortable with him being here, they drew nearer. Andrew smiled at me again and waved me over to join them.

The two men watched me approach, slowly. Andrew's father was a large man who really did appear to be in his midthirties. Although Andrew was a couple inches taller, his father was broader, more barrel-chested. He wore jeans and a short-sleeved, snap-front plaid shirt and cowboy boots. Around his neck hung a necklace with a carved-bone wolf head howling at the moon, with three carved-bone wolf claws dangling below it. One claw appeared to be pure white while the other two were golden, and a spot remained where you could see something could be added to the necklace in the future. His father smiled warmly, like his son; he seemed to be friendly. He had long straight black hair but his eyes were gray as steel, hard and suspicious, but curious; he watched me closely. He appeared to be trying very hard not to spook me.

Andrew put an encouraging arm around my shoulders, gently but firmly, holding me in place. "Dad, this is Lance Fitz. Lance, this is my father, Maxwell Reed."

I took a deep breath and raised my chin, met his gaze, and extended my hand, praying that it wouldn't tremble.

"Nice to meet you, Mr. Reed." I put on the best meeting-the-newest-foster-parents smile I possessed and tried not to make my shoulders too stiff. When he frowned slightly, I knew he could see right through my bravado to the fear underneath.

"Max, please." He shook my hand and clapped his son on the shoulder. He must have been okay with what he saw, because he relaxed and smiled at his son. "Now, let's see what we can do about this roof." Together the three of us moved toward the cottage. Andrew took my hand firmly, and I stayed at his side while they talked about angles, the best way to place the rafters, and how to join the new roof to the old. Andrew's touch relaxed me, as always. He was so warm my body trembled, and I knew he felt it. I stared at the ground, grateful his father didn't seem to notice me blushing. He didn't even seem to realize or care about Andrew holding my hand. It was hard to envision a society so open to touching one another, where a father wouldn't have a problem with his son touching another man possessively. I had to admit, though I might've been embarrassed, the reassurance felt nice.

I paid no attention to what they said. I just followed along like a puppy on a leash, trying to keep from hyperventilating. In the end, Andrew and his dad came to some agreement. All I understood was Andrew came away knowing how to fix the roof.

"See you later, son, and nice to meet you, Lance."

Max Reed trotted off to the north, back toward the ranch.

He'd left and I was okay. Adrenaline and panic washed through me, and I began to shudder. I concentrated on breathing but I didn't know if I could stop shaking. My knees buckled and I leaned into Andrew heavily, almost collapsing where I stood. I grasped for the doorframe of the cottage to keep from falling. Andrew wrapped an arm around my waist as I swayed. "You really were afraid," he said in complete disbelief as he held me upright.

"Yes. I don't like people. I don't trust people." I struggled to find the words to make him understand. He pulled me into a chair at the table. "Andrew, you're the first person I've let near me since I ran away from my last foster family. I don't allow anyone to physically touch me, ever. But I trust you more than I've trusted anyone in my life. Yet, every day I wake up and think 'Okay, is it going to be today? Will today be the day he hurts me?'" I whispered, confessing my fear, even though I knew I was giving him one more way in which to hurt me. I could feel his pain as I admitted how little confidence I had in him. Even after everything he'd done for me. I sighed sadly. I wanted to tell him the rest, but how to explain it without revealing too much? It wasn't that I didn't want to believe… to trust. My heart just couldn't survive if he were to ever…. No point in even thinking about it; it wasn't a possibility if I didn't have a heart to give.

He never asked me about my past. He never pushed, but I could feel his curiosity. I needed to explain at least some of it so maybe he'd begin to understand a little. *He is far better than I deserve, and I don't know how to deal with better.* Sighing, I rose and sat down on my sleeping bag. I held out a hand for him to join me, which he did without hesitation, and I turned to look at him. Andrew draped an arm around my shoulders, pulled me snug against his body, then settled me across his lap. I leaned my shoulder against his chest; I needed to be able to read his expressions, to make sure he understood what I had to tell him. His eyes still reflected hurt, as if I'd kicked him in the stomach with my confession. I felt bad, but I wasn't sure if my explanation would make the pain any better.

I took a deep breath, "Okay, here's the thing. I'm damaged goods. Part of me is broken, and I don't think there's any way to fix it." I watched carefully for his reaction. He pulled me tighter against his chest. He didn't say anything; he just listened intently, waiting for me to continue. Unbidden, I let the memories of childhood— loneliness, fear, pain—and the horrors of my life flicker briefly through my mind's eyes, knowing he'd be able to read some of the agony and fear reflected there. He flinched slightly, but he didn't look away.

"People had never been kind to me before you. I went from being in children's homes to foster care, to juvenile detention, and back to foster care. I've gone from school to school, never fitting in anywhere. I've been in more than twenty-five homes in the past sixteen years, and I've never stayed in one place very long." I turned to stare at my hands, clenching them on my thighs. "My name has been changed so often even I'm not really sure what my original last name was. I'm considered a trouble case—the homes don't get better once they label you. You end up in homes where you're just a paycheck, and those are the better ones. One family would lock us kids up after school so they didn't have to deal with us. There were seven of us there. One day one of the kids went to school with bruises, got sick, and was sent to the infirmary. The nurse sent for social services to check out the home. That was the end of that. From there I went back to juvenile hall, because no one wanted to take a child involved in a court case dealing with abuse. I ended up being sent across state lines to yet another foster family."

I shook my head at the dark memories; I'd barely scratched the surface. I knew there'd be nightmares tonight. I picked nervously at my jeans. Andrew's arms were rigid and he held me still tighter against his chest. I glanced quickly up to see his eyes, afraid I'd see pity reflected there. He stared at the ceiling. His eyes were hard and angry, but thankfully they held no pity. I could deal with anger, especially as it wasn't directed at me. "The last family, the one I ran from, the husband kept leering at me like I belonged to him. She wasn't able to keep him off me, and I'm not really certain she wanted to. She cowered away from him like a beaten and broken animal. There were others, young girls in the home who he'd already broken. They would whimper when he entered the room and cringe in fear. I couldn't stay. I ran—I'm a coward." I lied about this last one just a bit, refusing to look him in the eye. He didn't need to know what really happened, but I got the feeling he knew part of the story was missing.

"Noone will *ever* hurt you again. I won't let them." Andrew snarled. His wolf barely under control, his fangs had dropped and his hot breath panted at my ear as he struggled to stay human. "Never again! You're with me and I'll protect you. Just stay with me. I swear you're safe. You're not broken, just healing," he insisted. A deep red flush covered my cheeks. His words were so adamant, I almost believed him. I wanted to believe him; I prayed he'd keep me safe forever. I couldn't believe how much like a child he made me feel, as I rested my head against his chest, struggling to keep my tears from flowing. I hadn't cried about this crap in…. I couldn't remember ever crying over this. He reached for my chin and tipped my face up to look into his eyes. "I *will* keep you safe. I won't let anyone ever hurt you again as long as I live." His declaration felt more like a vow or a confession. He saw the disbelief in my eyes; I couldn't hold it back. I knew it hurt him. "I'll prove it. You *can* trust me."

"I want to, Andrew. Please believe me, I do. But that's part of being broken. I don't think I'm capable of trusting anyone anymore. Not totally," I said, looking into those sad blue eyes. "It has nothing to do with you. *I'm* broken. *I* can't be fixed. *I* can't fully trust anyone." I tried to make it perfectly clear. My damage wasn't his issue. I rested my head back against his chest: begging, pleading with, praying to whatever gods were listening to find a way to help me trust him.

He held me for a long time, 'til my trembling stopped. I'd occasionally feel his face rub against my hair and his hands stroke my arms as he petted me. I had barely touched the surface of what I'd been through before meeting him. There was so much I didn't want to tell him. Nothing he could do about it, anyway. I tried to convince myself it didn't matter, the things I'd been through. Maybe Andrew would let me stay close by—maybe as his friend. We could still be our own pack. Perhaps what I'd told him would be enough for him to understand. He didn't seem to mind. He still held me even though I was damaged goods. I just hoped he understood I didn't do it on purpose. We sat in an easy silence, neither of us talking, just comforting each other.

"Come on. Let's go run." He smiled my favorite smile, trying to push the sadness away, but I could still see the pain and anger just under the surface. I would have the worry gone before we came home tonight. His eyes should never have to hold my pain. He'd been nothing but kind and generous to me, and I'd hurt him. I needed him to forget, for the smile to return to his beautiful sparkling sky-blue eyes.

"Okay." I smiled too, both of us trying way too hard. He saw my pain regardless. The man was far too observant sometimes. He stood up and pulled me up with him, yanking off his shirt before he got to the door. I undressed and shifted in the cottage; he shifted outside. For some reason this had become our evening ritual.

His beautiful white-gray wolf waited for me when I emerged from the cottage as the chocolate-brown wolf. My shifts were becoming easier and faster, practically pain-free. The wolf came when I called for him and left when I wanted to be human. We'd had no more surprise changes from one form to the other. Andrew had explained uncontrolled shifts usually only occurred in the beginning or during times of great stress. My shifts would be completely under my control as I became accustomed to the wolf. The change felt like a shimmering from the base of my spine up to my head and all my bones would be like jelly, remolding to their new shape almost instantaneously.

My wolf danced around Andrew, prancing in front of him. I dropped down in front of him, my ass in the air, wagging my tail, as if I were a pup asking to play. Andrew's wolf growled, clearly not in a good mood, and my wolf blamed me. My wolf knew how to get Andrew going. He stood and began rubbing himself along Andrew's body, first down one side and then back up the other. He dragged his tail under Andrew's nose. Andrew shook his head and nipped me hard in the neck behind my ears, a gentle pinch to remind me of his dominance. I dropped instantly down in front of him, looking up, licking the bottom of his jaw, growling playfully but in complete submission to him. He nosed me gently, rumbling his satisfaction, and took off running. I sprinted after him. He shook his head and his sour spirits were left behind as we played and hunted long into the night.

The moon glowed golden in the autumn sky before we returned to the cottage and curled up on my sleeping bag in our usual dog pile of limbs. I probably should've warned Andrew before we fell asleep or made sure he'd gone back to the ranch. I woke to the sound of my own screaming, still seeing the nightmare. I felt Andrew rocking me as he gently clutched me to his chest. A soothing stream of whispered reassurances and kisses to my forehead calmed the terror, bringing me out of the dream and into a sense of safety I'd never felt before. He had me cradled in his arms like a child. "Shh...*àluinn*, it's okay. I have you now." Andrew rubbed my back. "Wake up, Lance. You're safe. I've got you. I won't let anything hurt you."

Finally awake enough to realize the horror was over, and that Andrew held me, not the evil man of my nightmare, I opened my eyes and stared into Andrew's. He felt the change in my body first as I relaxed. Tears flowed silently down my cheeks, tears I didn't know I'd shed until he wiped them away. He continued to calm my nerves, humming softly in my ear, cooing as if to a small child. He stayed with me all night long, fighting my demons for me as they came, over and over. Andrew didn't let me down. He wasmy guardian angel, my Alpha. In the morning, he returned to the ranch reluctantly to do his chores. I could see the worry etched into his face. Part of me feared he wouldn't return. I'd shown him some of my haunted soul, and perhaps he couldn't handle it. I laughed and joked around before he left, acting as if this morning was no different from any other, although we both knew better. He clearly hadn't realized how much talking about the past, having to explain and relive the horror, would cost me. Andrew returned my laughter and jokes, a beautiful smile on his face. He seemed determined that if I could act like nothing was wrong then so could he. I knew he was worried—he knew I was scared. We both said nothing. We let sleeping dogs lie, and no one knew when to do that better than a wolf.

MY MORNING routine included getting water from the stream that flowed close by the cottage. As always, I kept a lookout for things I could scavenge. During one of these morning forays, I came across a pile of elk bones. Dried and bleached, they looked like they had been lying in the sun for years. Andrew didn't wear any jewelry, but his dad wore a stunning necklace. There was one way I could repay Andrew for some of his generosity. I really liked the style of the necklace Max wore. I liked the bones and the way each piece seemed to have meaning. It'd be time-consuming, but something similar, made of a natural material, with each carved bead having its own meaning, would be perfect for Andrew. I didn't know if he'd like it, but I wanted to make him an armband, and maybe a necklace, depending on how well the bones withstood carving. I'd also have to be sneaky. I wanted to surprise him with the completed band. It was the first time I really wanted to give a gift to someone else, just because I wanted to. It needed to be special. I smiled as I began to plan the pattern I'd weave to string the bones to make the armband. I gathered together the pieces I could use and began designing it in my head.

BY THE end of September, things at the cottage were progressing smoothly. During the day we worked on the repairs, and at night we ran and played as wolves. When the wolves got tired, we'd return, snuggle up together—usually as wolves—and sleep.

Andrew surprised me one night, after our hunt. His human self and not his wolf snuggled up against me. He sighed, sank his fingers into my fur, and inhaled deeply of my scent, as if he was trying to memorize it. "I have to go away for a couple days, maybe longer… I don't know. My master's called and I've delayed him as long as I can. I must go and see what he wants. I'm not sure how long I'll be away. I'm hoping that whatever he wants I can take care of it and come right back. I'll try to get word to you if I can." Andrew growled and fisted my pelt in frustration.

"I hate leaving like this. I promised to keep you safe always, and now I have to go. There's no reasoning with Stephon. He's my master and I can't refuse. Please, Lance. Please wait for me here. My family will protect you, and no one else knows you're here. I know you don't like other people up here, but with winter pushing at us, we don't have time to wait until I get back. My little brothers'll be coming in the morning to put up the rafters, and then again the next day to complete the thatching on the roof. They won't bother you. They'll just work on the cottage. They'll let you know if they get word from me. If you don't want to be around when they're here,

46

you don't have to. Stay in the woods nearby until they're gone. They won't be offended if they don't see you here when they're working. Just don't leave. Please," Andrew practically begged.

I pushed my head into his chest but I didn't change to human. I couldn't reassure him. I couldn't make him empty promises. I'd try to stay. The wolf wanted to stay and that'd help. I hoped the wolf could keep me here for Andrew's sake.

"Please, Lance. I can't follow you if you leave. I can't come and find you. No matter how much I'd want to, and I *would* want to desperately, I cannot leave here without my master's permission. Please don't leave," he pleaded. I could feel the passion he felt and his fear that he might return and find me gone. His eyes were so dark, and so fearful, they tore at my soul and I couldn't stand to look at them. It became obvious that Andrew had feelings for me. Feelings I'd been trying to deny, writing them off as just the protectiveness of an alpha wolf or the touchy-feely ways of shape-shifters, but clearly he cared about me, enough to beg and plead for me to stay.

I phased to human. I needed to try to ease his fear, his pain. Andrew shouldn't ever hurt like this. He should be joyous. I still wouldn't be able to tell him—to promise him anything—but I could reassure him that I wanted to be here for him. I just couldn't promise to stay.

I reached up with a hand and caressed his face. I slowly lifted myself to kiss him. His mouth came down to crush against mine, filled with want, need and desire. He stroked my naked skin, pressing me against him. We slid into the sleeping bag. I could feel his erection pressing against my thigh, but he didn't reach for anything other than to rub my back and clutch me tighter against him. His kisses—first powerful and need-filled—became tender and soft, wonder-filled and maddening. Every touch felt like liquid fire on my skin, yet so sweet, as if he feared I'd break. Our breathing became ragged. We held each other tight and kissed, drowning in each other's caress.

"I love you," he whispered into my ear. I heard the words but pretended I didn't. I couldn't bring myself to say the words back, because the ache in my heart screamed at the impossibility. I locked my mouth over his, preventing him from speaking again. He'd be gone by morning. The pain that thought brought made me lock my arms around him, press myself against him. Showing him what I couldn't say. I trembled, fearing he might take our kisses further, feeling icy panic begin to seep in and take over the heat of our lust, but he didn't.

"I love you. Shh… it's all right, I just want to hold you, and I wanted you to know how I feel." Andrew's voice tickled the little hairs at the back of my neck. I knew the control he was exerting. I knew he wanted me but that was another part of me that was broken. As always, Andrew was as good as his word. He didn't pressure me or try to force anything. We held each other long into the dark hours of the night, gently kissing and touching each other. Eventually we both gave in to the night and slept in each other's arms, a sweet dreamless sleep. Andrew stayed with me, keeping the nightmares at bay.

In the morning, unlike I'd feared, he still held me when my eyes opened. He'd stayed the whole night. We held each other and tried to prevent the dawn. I stroked his face and tried to memorize every nuance, his scent and the feel of his skin. The way his hands moved through my hair and along my back, touching and kissing, prolonging the inevitable.

I saw it happen. If I hadn't been looking into his eyes, I'd have missed the moment of intense agony before he whipped his head around to the north and then turned slowly back to me.

"My love, I must go. My master calls. He knows I'm stalling, keeping him waiting, and he won't wait any longer. Please, please stay here, and I'll return as soon as I can." His eyes were filled with sadness and fear. He fought his connection with his master, a link that forced him into servitude.

"I'll stay." I said the words I wouldn't have been able to say if I hadn't seen the sting in his eyes. Andrew was literally fighting physical pain to stay with me just a few more moments. He smiled radiantly at my words, squeezed me tight once more, and kissed me deeply. He stood and transformed, his body becoming liquid silver in one moment and then the white-gray wolf the next and gave me a long look as if to burn my image into his mind.

Before he could leave, I grabbed the armband I'd been working on for him from where I'd hidden it inside my backpack. I'd finished it the day before, but hadn't gotten the chance to give it to him. I didn't want him to leave without my gift. He'd have a piece of me to remind him of me in case I couldn't stay.

I'd strung the cream beadlike bones I'd carved on a small thin braid of my hair, locking each delicate bone in place in a weave pattern. I'd whittled a howling wolf head out of a bone that had discolored to a shiny reddish-brown. I'd hung it between the three bands of the woven bone beads, then secured it in place with a cord of my hair. He whined, and I threw my arms around his neck, hugging him close to me. I grabbed his front left paw and securely tied the armband above the knee, cinching it tight so the band couldn't slip as he ran. Andrew trembled as I secured the armband, then rubbed his face into my chest, whining. I let go of him and ran with him to the edge of the woods. He looked back once, howled mournfully, and disappeared into the trees. I wanted to chase after him and never let him out of my sight, but I'd promised and I'd keep my promise. I would stay.

I slowly walked back to the cottage with my arms tightly wrapped around my chest, trying to hold myself together, shaking slightly but not from the chill in the morning air. What was wrong with me? I'd been alone most of my life, so why was this so hard to bear?

I needed to get dressed. Andrew's brothers would be here soon to work on the roof. I knew he'd be gone a minimum of two days, because his brothers would be around for at least that long. I'd do everything I could to make them feel welcome. I'd make myself be warm and friendly. I could be what Andrew needed me to become. I'd find a way to truly trust him. He loved me, and I knew I loved him too. And wasn't that just the shit, to admit your feelings for someone after they were gone.

49

It hurt knowing he wouldn't be back today. It took everything I had to keep from changing into my wolf and chasing him down. My wolf knew I could catch him if I tried. We were faster than Andrew, after all. I wanted to cry, but I refused to allow myself to be weak. I'd be strong for Andrew. He'd asked me to stay and I'd told him I would. I'd keep my word for him. I loved him with all my heart and I had from the very beginning. Now I had to prove I wouldn't be the one running away. I'd be here when he came back. I had to be.

CHAPTER 4

I HAD tea brewing in the fireplace and the radio blaring music loudly when Andrew's brothers arrived. They were identical twins. The two were similar and yet distinct in appearance compared to my Andrew. They had the same dark rugged complexion and the same straight black hair, but theirs grew long and had been braided. Both brothers had blue eyes, but not the sky blue of Andrew's. Their eyes were a darker, smoky gray blue, like slate. Both of his brothers were markedly shorter than Andrew, more like their dad, but still had a few inches on me. It became almost immediately obvious that they looked nowhere near thirty-six years old. They truly looked years younger than Andrew and me both, maybe fifteen or sixteen.

They had the wooden trusses hung over their shoulders as they walked hesitantly into the clearing from the tree line around the cottage. Determined to be a good host, for Andrew, I put on my friendliest smile and stepped out of the doorway of the cottage toward the approaching pair.

The only thing giving away my nervousness was the fact I couldn't seem to unwrap my arms from round my chest. I felt like my heart would fall out if I let go. They stopped cold in their tracks. Obviously, Andrew had told them I probably wouldn't be there. I smiled and waved. They looked like kids. I could handle a couple of teenagers. Even if they really weren't teens, in wolf years they clearly looked sixteen, or maybe seventeen at the most. They looked at each other, then waved back, picking up their pace. They appeared to be good-natured and friendly. I could do this.

"Hi, guys," I called as they got near.

"Hey, Lance," they greeted me cheerfully, as if we were old friends.

The first brother stopped in front of me, while his twin stood a bit farther back because of the struts they carried.

"I'm Jack and that's Joe."

"Like I'm going to be able to tell you guys apart," I teased. They smiled widely. Of course, the wolf in me catalogued instantly which was which, because of the difference in their scents. Jack smelled like running water and fresh-cut grass, while Joe smelled like running water and crushed pine needles. It would be impossible to mix them up—their scents would always give them away.

"We'll get right to work." Jack walked toward the cottage.

"We'll have a roof over your head in no time." Joe laughed, and then they were on top of the cottage walls before I could even offer them a cup of tea. They worked steadily, teasing back and forth between them. They occasionally sent a joke my way at their missing brother's expense, but kept at it throughout the day with an expertise that belied their apparent years.

I'd decided to keep busy, and since I knew nothing about roofing and would be more of a hindrance than a help, I decided to indulge myself in an old love. Since they were building me a proper cottage, I'd make myself some pottery dishes and bowls. Yes, I guess you'd call me artistic. I'd always enjoyed working with my hands and I was fairly good at it. I loved making things: jewelry, carvings, pottery, needlework, painting, knitting. I knew most people didn't consider these manly activities, but I found them relaxing. I'd never be able to make a living at my crafts but they worked to occupy my mind and hands when I needed to lose myself.

I'd found a rich thick layer of clay near the stream when I'd been making mortar for the walls. It had been perfect for the job, heavy and thick. I'd also discovered a vein of scoria on a canyon wall downstream. I powdered the scoria and added it to the clay, making the clay a beautiful red color. Kneading it with water, I removed all the larger rocks until I had a thick smooth earthen medium. I worked the clay and sipped my tea, sitting in the sun, listening to the radio.

Pottery throwing was a craft I'd learned several families back from a very creative woman who'd taken me in as a foster. She taught me to carve as part of the process of decorating the clay. But she said I "cramped her mojo" when she realized I had talent. When my amateur bowls and carvings sold in her shop more readily than her own wares, I found myself in need of a new foster home. These wouldn't be quite as good, because I didn't have a pottery wheel and the clay wasn't exactly commercial grade, but I could still work the clay and form the bowls and plates. They wouldn't be perfect, but they would be unique. I hoped Andrew would like them as much as I'd enjoy making them.

The twins wrestled and played while they worked, accomplishing more than I'd thought possible. Before I realized it, the day had passed and they were climbing down, the trusses in place. I had several bowls and plates setting out in the evening sun to dry.

"Hey, guys, is there a place nearby that does pottery craft? Maybe a crafting supply store that offers firing and glazing, anything like that?"

"I think there's a shop in Rapid City called Pottery Place or Hut. They might do stuff like that." Joe eyed the drying pottery. "Those are really beautiful, Lance."

"Thanks. Do you think you could check for me? When my pottery is finished drying, it will need to be fired and glazed before I can really use it."

"Sure, we'll call around and let you know." Jack rubbed his shoulder against mine, admiring the pieces I'd completed.

"I can pay you for it."

"No problem, really."

"You wouldn't mind taking the pieces into town and bringing them back for me later?" I'd etched depictions of Andrew's wolf into the cups and the plates. Some were running, some were sleeping, some howling at the moon. I'd even made a large serving bowl where I'd carved the wolves into the edge. The piece had a decidedly delicate look even though I knew it was sturdy and heavy.

"Sure, we'll take them in for you. Hey, Mom's birthday is coming up." Joe grinned at Jack, then asked, "You think you can make an extra piece for us to give her for her birthday—say, maybe a nice vase? We could pay you for it." Jack nodded, agreeing with Joe.

"I'd be happy to make her a piece or two. Since you're taking the pottery to town, I'll pay for the firing and glazing." The twins grinned like they'd won the lottery. "What do you want it decorated with, or do you want me to stick with the wolves?" I asked.

"The wolves," they both said together.

"She'll absolutely love it." Joe laughed. "They're perfect!"

"Okay, no problem."

"See ya tomorrow morning, Lance." They laughed and ran from the clearing, waving as they went. I had to smile in spite of myself. I'd had a good day. Andrew's brothers were playful, open, honest, and warm. They acted much closer to their apparent years than their actual age. They made me feel like Andrew was close, even though he was gone. How could I not like them? I went back into my cottage and brewed some tea.

LATERthat day, I started working on a necklace to go with the armband for Andrew. I'd already chosen the bones. I'd taken some of them and put them among the coals in the fireplace. Some I toasted black, others to a golden sheen. This piece would be more intricate than the armband, but I had a clear picture in my mind of what I wanted to create. I'd need a ring, maybe in white gold or platinum because silver just seemed wrong. The ring would be at the center with the other pieces around it. The ring would be the only part of the necklace I couldn't make myself. I hoped the twins could find what I needed.

My wolf wanted out, but I didn't trust him not to chase after Andrew. I decided to keep my wolf locked in and instead tried to dream of running with Andrew's white-gray wolf through the meadows. The wolf song began about midnight, waking me from my usual nightmares. Andrew hadn't starred in my dreams like I'd hoped. I recognized the howling immediately: Andrew's family singing of their successful kill. I almost lost my hold on my wolf. He wanted to answer them, but I stayed quiet, hoping to hear Andrew's answering call. None came. I didn't realize how much it hurt to not hear his voice in the night. As I drifted back asleep, the nightmares picked up right where they'd left off.

THE next morning the twins arrived early. They rode in on four-wheelers loaded with thatching for the new section of roof. The day flowed much like the previous one, which melted into the next… and the next… and the next.

When it was ready, the twins carefully took a load of my pottery back with them. They'd checked around, and the Pottery Hut did offer firing and glazing for a fee. I'd made them a tall vase and carved wolves into the clay. I'd also put stretching wolves with their heads pointed to the sky, their backs arched, one on each side, forming handles. The twins loved it.

We settled into a pattern; the twins would work and play, and I'd work on my pottery, or on Andrew's necklace. Sometimes I'd just wander about the woods, lost in my growing misery. As time passed, I let my wolf out to hunt, always careful to make sure he didn't try to go after Andrew. My heart grew increasingly restless each day he was gone. I wanted him to return soon, and hoped he hadn't forgotten me or decided he no longer wanted me.

The nights were the worst. If I let the wolf out at night, he'd howl mournfully up at the sky, his sadness unbearable. If they were hunting, the family would call back as if to console his bleeding, lonely heart; but more often than not, they'd just let him cry. It was as if they knew nothing they did could ease my pain except Andrew's return.

The nightmares continued unceasingly, but with a slightly different script. They started now with me searching for Andrew, trying to find him. The evil laughter, as always, continued to form the soundtrack, haunting me from previous nightmares. I now saw the man as Andrew's master. Black-cloaked figures chased me as I searched for Andrew; I had to find him before the man could get to him. The black-cloaked figures were getting closer. No matter how fast I ran, they gained on me. I'd hear Andrew's tortured howl as I'd last heard him when he left me, and I'd run toward the sound as fast as I could. His cry would be cut short by a gurgling sound. It spurred me on to run faster, only to enter a clearing and find Andrew's wolf lying in the center of it on a bed of flowers, all stained red with his blood, beaten until his pelt had been peeled back in strips along his back and sides. The evil laughter filled the air around me as I saw Andrew's throat cut from one ear to the other. He lay dead in my arms, my hands covered with his blood. I'd wake up screaming, shivering in the night... alone.

So much for another night's sleep. I'd get up, make tea, and try to find something to do until dawn, every shadow in the dark resembling the man who chased me.

We were into week two when Laura, Andrew's mom, came to visit. Okay, ten days, twelve hours and fifteen minutes, to be exact... not that I was counting. The twins had just finished the roof when I saw her. I'd been refereeing their latest wrestling match—okay, I was pulling them apart, like usual, and sending them each to their neutral corners.It was the only way I could find out what they were squabbling about this time—when she appeared on the edge of the trees. I froze, completely unable to move. Jack and Joe felt me

56

freeze and followed my line of sight. She just stood at the tree line and waited for me to acknowledge her.

"Hi, Mom," Joe called and waved. He watched me very carefully.

"It's okay, Lance, I bet she has mail for you or something." Jack smiled at me encouragingly.

"Bet it's something from Andrew," Joe teased.

I took a deep breath. I put my smile back on and waved at her, trying not to panic. She smiled, waved back, and walked slowly into the meadow around the cottage. I sent the twins to opposite sides of the cottage and told them to stay put 'til they were done fighting. They went to their respective corners, but the fight had definitely ended. They were both watching me intently. I just shook my head and walked forward to meet Laura. I could do this. For Andrew, I'd smile and be friendly to his mom.

"Hi, I'm Lance." I extended my hand and tried to smile.

She was a beautiful woman, petite to the point of being almost tiny, maybe five feet tall, max. She had a light complexion and had long curly blonde hair that flowed in waves down her back. She wore a pair of blue jeans and a lovely yellow eyelet blouse. She had Andrew's sky-blue eyes, and it took my breath away to see them shining out of this tiny woman's face. I clutched at my chest with one arm, trying to hold myself together.

"Hi, Lance, I'm Laura Reed. I'm sorry to intrude, but I know Andrew would want me to bring this to you." Instead of shaking my extended hand, she handed me an envelope. I gingerly took the envelope, like I feared it would bite me. My name had been written on it in a beautiful script. It hadn't been opened. I hadn't expected a letter, but Andrew had promised to contact me, and it wasn't like he could text me or call me. I didn't have a phone, and probably couldn't have gotten a signal if I did.

"Thank you so much. He said he'd try to get word to me if he was going to be a while. He had hoped to be back quickly." I stared at the envelope, struggling to keep my emotions under control.

"Lance, do you mind if I ask you some personal questions? I know how much my son's in love with you, and if I can help him to smooth the road so you can stay, I'd really like to help," Laura said softly.

"I don't mind. I—I'll try to answer whatever I can." I led her back toward the cottage. The twins had come out of their corners to the front of the cottage and started to wrestle again within sight of the door. I think they wanted me to know I'd be okay, my dynamic duo of moral support. I just shook my head and went into the cottage with Laura, clutching my envelope like a life preserver.

The afternoon light filtered into the cottage through the open door.

"Won't you have a seat? Would you like a cup of tea?" I asked politely.

She smiled and just shook her head. "No, thank you."

She'd said her son loved me and didn't seem upset. I wondered again if this was due to an overall acceptance of homosexuality within shifter society or a demonstration of the fabled unconditional love some parents had for their children. I tended to believe they loved him so much it didn't matter, which left me wondering about the rest of our kind beyond Andrew's family.

"What can you tell me about yourself?" Laura asked, sitting across from me.

"Well, my name's changed a couple of times over the years. My full name originally may have been Lance Fitz, but I'm not exactly sure. I've no idea who my birth parents were. I have no memory of them or any idea what happened to them. My last foster family lived in Custer.Before that, I lived in Hot Springs, then Lincoln, Nebraska; then Omaha, Nebraska; then Kansas City, Kansas; Wichita, Kansas; Oklahoma City, Oklahoma. I don't remember what came before Oklahoma. I would've been about six or seven then."

"I think we've a good place to begin. The twins are experts with computers. If the information is out there to find, they'll hunt it down. I'll start by having them look for any records dealing with your life and parents—a birth record—hospital records where you were born, maybe? We'll see how far they can get us." She reached over and patted my hand, but stopped when I winced at the physical contact. "With luck, we'll be able to find some information about your family. Then we'll know which bloodlines you come from and be able to get approval from Stephon for the two of you to be together. Assuming you'd like to stay. If nothing else, we may be able to get you in touch with your real family and find out what happened."

"Thank you," I mumbled softly, not sure what to think about getting in touch with a family who'd never tried to find me. "Okay, please ask the twins not to read the files on my foster homes. A lot of them are... ugly... and some are inaccurate. I witnessed and was a part of things that should never be part of anyone's bedtime reading." I didn't want the twins to change their opinion of me because of what they saw in those records.

"Oh, dear, don't worry. We don't put much stock in anything the humans have to say about us. I'm sure you were treated horribly. You see, they instinctively dislike us. They can sense we're different, even if they don't know why. The twins won't believe most of what they read. They won't judge you for anything they run across. They're just going to be tracking your movements, looking mainly for your birth records," She smiled. She seemed really nice. I could see where Andrew got his soothing nature. Laura's eyes made me feel like a part of Andrew sat with me, telling me not to worry.

"Just so you know, I'm doing this against his wishes. He doesn't want us to push you. He's terrified you'll leave if any of us get too close, but the twins kept saying you're okay with them, so I thought I'd try. I've never seen Andrew get so passionate and protective about another person in his life. It's good to see."

"If there's anything else you want to know, I'll try to answer." I smiled shyly. I had no intention of telling her how I felt about her son, when I hadn't even been able to tell him. She rose from her chair and I followed her out the door.

"Oh, and if you need anything… clothes, food… just ask. Try not to worry. Andrew will be back soon and everything will be fine. If you ever get to feeling lonely here by yourself, please know you're always welcome down at the ranch." Laura put her hand on my shoulder and smiled up at me warmly.

"Thank you. I'm fine," I lied. I barely kept from flinching from her touch. I missed Andrew so much, I felt my heart would burst into a million pieces, but even her sky-blue eyes, so much like his, couldn't induce me to go down to the ranch.

"Jack, Joe, let's get going. Your dad will have chores waiting for you to finish before nightfall if you intend to go hunting tonight." Her sons came running, and the three of them trotted toward the tree line. Jack and Joe turned to wave to me before disappearing into the trees.

I still clutched the letter in my hands, pressed to my chest like a drowning man clutches a lifeline. I carefully opened it and pulled out the letter, penned in Andrew's beautiful script.

Lance, My Love How I miss you. The pain is unbearable. Thank you so much for the armband, it's beautiful and so intricate. It's what's holding me together here. I love it.

Stephon has a rather time-consuming issue he wants me to address. I'll tell you all about it when I come home to you. Please, don't leave. The only thing getting me through each day is believing you're waiting for me.

I'm hoping my bratty brothers aren't making a nuisance of themselves and they're actually working at getting the cottage finished. I'm hoping that although it's only been two days for me, by the time you read this letter you'll have a complete roof on the cottage, and the twins will start putting in the plumbing.

I love you with all my heart and soul, and I've left them at the cottage with you. Please, take good care of them for me. I miss you and I dream each night of you. See you soon in my dreams.

All my love, Always, Andrew

My hands trembled as I read and reread the letter.

How could he manage to write such sappy things? It was definitely the mushiest, most cavity-inducing thing I'd ever read. I couldn't believe how my heart soared at those sweet love-filled words. He hadn't told me anything about what he was doing, but I really didn't care. I just wanted him to come back. My heart ached; the letter filled me with love both sweet and sorrowful.

As Andrew had predicted, the twins arrived in the morning with pipe to begin working on plumbing for the bathroom and kitchen. Oh, the joy of indoor plumbing! God bless the Romans for inventing indoor plumbing. Miraculously, my shack was being turned into a beautiful retreat, and I began to cherish Andrew's brothers as if they were my own.

Week two gone and still no Andrew. I didn't let my wolf out much anymore.He couldn't seem to do anything but howl sadly. The nightmares continued unabated. No rest for the weary, and damn, was I tired.

WEEK three had me becoming more withdrawn, and still the twins came. The sun was about to set and they'd finished, but seemed to be hanging about a bit more than usual, like they had something unpleasant to say but didn't know how. They'd been pretty quiet most of the day. Their attitude was curious, and because of it, I'd had a hard time concentrating. I couldn't even work on Andrew's necklace; just touching the bones hurt. Finally, I decided I'd get it over withand ask.

"Guys…." They came running, as they always did when I called. "What's up with you two today? Why so deep in thought? If you have something to ask or say, just say it." They paused as if they didn't know how to begin.

"Lance, we found your birth record. We know who your parents are and recognized one of the names—your mother's. If the name on the records is who we think it is, there will be lots of questions you probably won't have answers for. We know where you were born, and we're going to give the information to Mom and

Dad tonight. We figure they'll want to talk to you in the morning." Joe frowned thoughtfully.

"We didn't go into too many of the other records. We tried to stay out of them as much as possible, but when we hacked into the police records, we saw some of what you dealt with, man. That stuff.... Humans can be such ugly creatures. We had no idea they'd messed you up that badly." Jack stared at the ground and shook his head, as if trying to get a bad taste out of his mouth. "Mom and Dad will probably want to take you in to see Dr. Carlson for blood tests after they see the names on the records. The name we recognize is that of a well-known family, but history tells us they were all killed. So the only way to be sure will be through genetic testing. Dr. Carlson's the best." Joe punched his brother in the arm, scowling at him.

I didn't like the twins knowing what I'd run from, regardless of how much they did or didn't believe the human records they'd read. It was bad enough that they even suspected the kind of shit I grew up with. It was ugly and embarrassing. I feared they would never look at me the same again. "I told your mom to tell you not to read those records. You heard me tell her." I tried not to yell, to keep my shame from turning into anger. "The foster system can be an ugly place to grow up. I'm actually much better now than I've been in years, and a lot of that's due to Andrew, you two brats, and your family." I smiled, trying to lift the gloom on their faces.

"Okay." Joe seemed to get a grip, shaking his head as if to dissipate what he saw in his head and get down to business. "Your full name as it appears on your birth record is Marcus Lance Fenrir Fitz. Your mother's name is Sasha Lorelei Gail Fenrir. Your father's name only gives the surname of Fitz. You were born in Denver, Colorado."

"Wow." I didn't know what it meant. I had no idea my first name wasn't Lance, but I preferred Lance to Marcus. "What does it mean?"

"Well, let's not worry about it 'til the folks get you to Dr. Carlson for testing. It may mean absolutely nothing. We just wanted you to know and warn you that they'll probably both be here in the morning. Also, to let you know we aren't going to tell them anything about what we found in the police records. In fact, we're going to forget all about them as soon as we leave." Jack laughed and rested his arm on my shoulders for an awkward hug. Joe had come around the other side of me and wrapped his arms around my waist. I'd become a twin sandwich, and for the first time, other than Andrew, I didn't mind being touched.

"Thanks, guys. I appreciate it." I hugged them both. Of all the kids I'd known as a foster moving from family to family, these boys were the first I'd ever felt like I could have as brothers. I cherished them.

"Oh, one more thing. We picked these up today." Jack trotted over to the four-wheeler and brought back a big box—my pottery, all fire-glazed and shiny. They'd come out fabulously, some of my best work. "Gwen at the pottery shop said if you ever want to sell some of your work, to give her a couple pieces and she'd fire and glaze them, then put them in her window. Mom loves her vase, and the wolf heads you cut into the rim and the handles are stunning."

"I'm so glad. Thanks." I couldn't help the grin of pride knowing they liked my work. "Maybe I'll make a couple more pieces for Gwen. Who knows, maybe she'll be able to sell them." I'd never considered selling my pottery. If there was a market for it, I might be able to make some money. It'd be much better than gathering cans from the highways, and might be more lucrative too.

"See you later, Lance!" The twins waved and climbed onto the four-wheelers, then headed across the meadow for the tree line.

The twins were becoming a lifeline for me. Of course, more than once, I'd found them brawling on the grass, wrestling over something one or the other had said. Once I'd had to send them home for new clothes, because the argument went from brawling boys to thrashing young wolves. Even as wolves, they appeared identical. They were both smaller than Andrew and me as wolves, clearly younger. They were all legs and they hadn't grown into their chests yet, just adolescent wolves. They both had sandy-brown coats with white blazes down their muzzles and between their eyes. Unthinking, once I'd grabbed them by the scruff of the neck, one in each hand, and pulled them apart and sent them home with their tails between their legs, embarrassed. They could've ripped me apart, but I never even considered the possibility of them hurting me when I separated them. I was less experienced as a wolf, and yet I knew I was stronger than either of them… and so did their wolves.

The next morning they were at the tree line, cutting down trees and pulling up tree stumps, then bringing the split wood to the side of the cottage to be used during the winter. Around midmorning, I saw Max and Laura at the tree line, as the twins had predicted. They hadn't been there long, because the twins saw them at the same time I did. The twins' warning had helped to prepare me to deal with them emotionally, but my wolf whined uncomfortably. I waved and told myself I could do this. I forced myself to stay still, although everything told me to run and run now as they slowly made their way toward the cottage, smiling warmly, hand in hand. Obviously, this was where Andrew got his sense of love from, because there was no doubt that Laura and Max were very much in love.

"Hi!" I called to them as they approached and waited for them to join me, because if I moved my feet, I was afraid they'd take me away.

"Hi, Lance," Laura said as she eyed me critically, then she took my hand and pulled me into her arms for a quick hug. I couldn't help my shock, but I hugged her back stiffly, trembling. I eyed Max nervously. She kept an arm around my shoulders and handed me an envelope. My name seemed to flow across the paper, written in Andrew's beautiful script. A wave of joy and loss washed over me as I took the envelope from her, my hand shaking, my emotions threatening to overwhelm me.

"We need to talk to you about what the boys found in your records," Laura said softly.

"They told me last night you'd want to take me to see a doctor in town for genetic testing," I whispered, my voice cracking because of the emotions generated by the envelope I clutched in my hands.

"Well, those two didn't tell us that they'd talked to you about anything. I'm going to have to have a word with them," Max said, looking toward a now empty tree line, a deep growl coming from him.

A wave of fear for the twins caught me. I chuckled, shaking my head, trying to lighten Max's mood. "They didn't tell me why the names are significant. Just prepared me for your visit." I caught Laura's eye. "I'm glad they did.I don't do well with surprises."

"It's going to be okay, Lance," Laura soothed, rubbing my arm, exactly as Andrew had done. I trembled at the force of the memory.

I wish she'd stop touching me, I thought. I knew she was only trying to comfort me, but it was making me even more twitchy. Dealing with my emotions and her constant contact was pushing the limits of my control.

Max waved a hand and shook his head, as if he were trying to erase my fear for his sons. "We do need to have your DNA verified. The name we recognize is your mother's, Sasha Fenrir. She's a well-known name in our history, and Dr. Carlson knew her personally." Max sighed and looked at Laura, who nodded."We need to warn you about Dr. Carlson, though, because we don't want you to be frightened or surprised. Dr. Carlson is a vampire… a drone. We can't exactly go to a human doctor, now can we? Our physiology is different from humans after our first shift. Muscle tissue and bone that change their shapes take on a different appearance from normal human bones and tissues, so regular doctors are out of the question. Dr. Carlson has been our family's doctor for about 150 years, so no worries. Okay?" Max tried to make his words soft. I could tell he feared I'd run.

I struggled to keep my place and willed my body to relax, concentrating on my name on the envelope. Laura's grip on my hand tightened momentarily, telling me she wouldn't let go, so I couldn't run.

I tried to take a deep breath. "I figured eventually I'd have to meet a vampire, I just never figured he'd be a doctor." I put on a brave face and told myself I'd be fine. "When are we going to do this?" I didn't like doctors in the first place, and a vampire doctor didn't make matters any better.

"How about now, before you can think about it too much and get scared?" Laura smiled at me sheepishly.

"Oh... um... okay. I guess that's actually a good idea." I couldn't tell her she was already too late to prevent my fear.

Max took my hand on the other side, and we started walking toward the tree line. Soon we broke into a quick jog, Laura and Max pulling me along with them. When we caught up to where the twins were cutting down trees, Max stopped and smacked each one gruffly on the back of the head, mumbling grumpily. He didn't hurt them. It was more of a loving cuff than any form of discipline I'd ever known. He quickly caught back up, took my hand again, and we were soon at the ranch.

They really must have been nervous about getting me to the doctor, because they had the car waiting for us at the tree line. I saw the car and stopped dead in my tracks. Max ran ahead and held the door for Laura, who coaxed me forward. She had to pull a bit to get me into the car, an older model Ford of some sort, but the engine roared with power that the exterior of the vehicle hid. She climbed into the backseat with me and wrapped her slender arms around me, trying to comfort me. It was stifling, and she made me feel even more nervous than if she'd let me be, but I didn't want to hurt her feelings.

I clutched my letter and prayed this would be over quickly, before I panicked and freaked out. *Please let it be over quickly.* I struggled to keep the wolf from sprinting away the minute the car door opened.

Max pulled out onto the highway and headed for Sturgis. We didn't have far to go before we hit the city limits and pulled into the parking lot of a small private practice clinic. *Dr. Tim Carlson, MD. Family Practice* the sign out front read. It probably should've read *DVM* too.

We went in. Laura and I took a chair while Max went to talk to the receptionist. He came back and sat on the other side of me with his arm draped across my shoulders. "She said Dr. Carlson will be with us in just a bit," he reassured us. I fidgeted nervously and stared at my hands, still holding Andrew's letter—my lifeline. Somehow the letter kept me calm. I stroked the envelope, reminding myself to breathe.

"Mr. Reed, the doctor will see you now," the receptionist called from a little doorway. All three of us stood, but only Max and I followed her through the door, down a hallway, and into an examination room. The room looked exactly like every other doctor's examination room I'd ever been in, which reassured me a little. I was glad Max had come with me. He took the chair while I sat on the exam table. We waited in silence, me staring at my envelope, 'til the doctor opened the door.

He appeared to be a young man, in his midtwenties, blond and very pale with black eyes. He looked like every other person to me. Perhaps a bit too pale, except for those eyes—they sent shivers down my spine. "Well, Max, who do we have here?" he said with a smile that showed no hint of fangs. Believe me, I looked for them. He took Max's hand in a warm handshake, the two obviously on friendly terms with each other.

"Hi, Doc, this is Lance. Lance, this is our friend, Dr. Tim Carlson."

"Hi Dr. Carlson," I said, my voice barely above a whisper. "It's nice to meet you." It took all I had to meet those black eyes and keep on smiling.

"How can I help you two today?" Dr. Carlson asked. He smiled softly, but he looked at me intently.

"Well, Doc, Lance is a bit of a mystery. He's been in the foster care system all his life. He has no memory of his family. He transformed for the first time eight weeks ago, just outside our ranch, into a brown wolf. He and Andrew are interested in each other, and with what we found on his birth record, we thought some genetic tests were in order," Max answered truthfully, hiding nothing from the doctor.

"Okay, well, what did the paperwork show?" Dr. Carlson asked, his gaze never leaving my face. His staring sent uncomfortable shivers down my spine. My wolf wanted to pace like a caged animal; he was growling deep inside. I knew fear had to be radiating off me in waves; I could barely control myself.

"Easy, Lance." Max stood and rubbed the back of my neck, as if he could take my wolf by the scruff of his neck and help me control him. In that moment he was 100 percent Alpha and my wolf claimed we could take him, but I didn't want to. I didn't want to hurt Andrew's father. I submitted to the controlling hand on the back of my neck. "His mother's listed as Sasha Fenrir, and his father's surname,Fitz, is all that's shown. Does that make any kind of sense to you?"

"You were right to bring him to me. Those names definitely mean testing is in order. It's not out of the question—they very well could be his parents. I was there when Sasha went animal. Her protector...." Dr. Carlson looked at my confused frown. "Think of him as a kind of bodyguard. He would've pledged his life to protect her if her mate weren't able to do so.At the time, he was a shape-shifter named Henry Fitz. He went animal with her. It'd be rare, but definitely within the realm of possibility that he could be their son. I'll get some supplies, take some blood, and run some tests. You do know I have to send the results to your benefactor. Is Stephon aware of him?" Dr. Carlson asked.

"Andrew's with Stephon now. I don't know if he's told him or not. Is there any way you can hold off telling Stephon about this until Andrew returns? I can't see him being gone much longer." I shivered involuntarily as Max talked about Andrew.

"Well, I don't see any reason why not. I'll call you when the results come in. It'll take a couple of days to get them and I may send the samples to a couple of different labs just to be certain there are no mistakes." Dr. Carlson smiled and left the room. He returned almost immediately with a blood-draw kit in his hand. When he approached me this time, he paused and took my chin in hand. His touch was very cool, but firm and gentle. He studied me carefully. He seemed to be studying the structure of my face, turning me first to the left then the right. "Well, isn't that interesting," he mumbled to himself. I trembled self-consciously at his touch.

"Oh, I'm sorry, Lance. I don't mean to be so rude." Dr. Carlson apologized, shaking his head, as if he was disgusted with himself.

"What is it, Doc?" Max looked confused, watching the vampire closely.

"I was very young in those days, Max, barely more than a newborn drone by vampire standards. But I was there when my Lord Nathaniel brought her home. I'd been created by Lord Nathaniel's father, Lord Basil. I was uneducated and a savage by most standards at the time, but I remember her very well, you see, because I still fought the bloodlust. When she was human, she appeared very tempting. Sasha's bloodlines were impeccable. Looking at young Lance here, his facial structure and eyes are very like my lord's lady, and his scent is almost identical to what I remember. The hair color is all wrong, and his skin tone is different. Physically, he's taller and more muscular, but the resemblance is uncanny. It struck me the minute I walked in the door.

"Still, we won't know anything for certain 'til the results come in. I'll call when I have them." He adeptly took the blood. "Give me a couple days and we'll be able to confirm who you are," he said with a smile, as if he already knew but needed the data for confirmation.

"Thank you so much Dr. Carlson. Talk to you soon," Max said, getting up from his chair. He slid his hand behind my back, guiding me before him out the door after the doctor.

"Thank you, Dr. Carlson," I said softly, following him out, not meeting those black eyes. I had no idea how he did it. How did a vampire handle blood without freaking out? Oh well, I'd ask Andrew someday. I also wanted to know what they meant by "going animal," but right now I just wanted out before I lost the internal battle with my wolf.

Max gave an encouraging squeeze before letting me go, but left his hand at the small of my back. He whispered, "Home stretch now, almost done."

Laura waited for us, anxiously wringing her hands, in the waiting room. When we came out, she took one look at me and went to open the front door for us. I still clutched my lifeline, my letter from Andrew. My breath came in pants, betraying my internal struggle with the wolf. My thoughts were circling, trying to find the meaning in their cryptic words. Nobody seemed to want to talk about "it" until "it" was confirmed. They totally confused me, but I didn't really care. I couldn't wait to be alone to read my letter. I didn't want to think about their "it," I just wanted Andrew to come back, to come home.

Max got us in the car and Laura wrapped her arms around me once again, trying to help me keep myself together. She didn't realize how confined her restraining arms were making me feel. As soon as we were at the ranch, Max let Laura and me out, then went to park the car. Laura and I stood at the tree line. I trembled with the desire to leave her in the dust and make a run for my sanctuary.

"I know you must want to return to the cottage, unless you'd like to stay and have dinner with us? You're more than welcome, you know." Laura smiled, giving me a little hug, then finally releasing me.

"No, thank you. I'd like to get back. Another time, maybe." I tried to be polite and I surprised myself that I could speak at all. When I looked toward the tree line, toward my cottage, I was amazed by what I saw—a wide swath of trees had been cleared. You couldn't see the cottage, but a chunk of the forest was missing. I didn't know what they'd planned, but I knew whatever they did it was by Andrew's design and I'd find out before too long. The day seemed to be slipping away. I needed to hurry so I could get back to my cottage and read my letter.

I smiled at Lauraand then headed up the clearing at my normal wolf trot, but took off at a full-out sprint as soon as the ranch disappeared from view. I arrived quickly at the clearing, gasping as the adrenaline produced by the stress of the trip began to leave my body. Dealing with people had been harder than I'd expected. I especially hated doctors, although as doctors went, Dr. Carlson seemed to be one of the better ones, even though his eyes were disturbing.

The twins were nowhere in sight as I approached the cottage. Relief washed over me as I went in the door and sat down at the table, clutching my letter to my chest. I struggled to hold myself together. I felt like I held a piece of Andrew in my hands.

My Leannan,

Lance, I'm so sorry I'm stuck away from you. I miss you so very much, sometimes it's hard to even breathe past the ache in my heart. So much time has passed. By now I hope the twins have completed most of the renovations to your cottage. I hope to be able to return very soon. I hope you don't mind my purchases. I've ordered a few things for the cottage. They should be arriving soon, and the twins will bring them up.

You've given me so much joy in the little time we've been together, and I can't bear the thought of you making do with anything less when Ican make you much more comfortable. Please don't be concerned. I'm not making any demands, and I don't have any expectations. I just love you so much, I want you to know it and feel it even though I'm not there to tell you in person. Please, let me make things as comfortable as I can for you. I want you to be happy.

I find myself staring at your gift every day. I'll never take it off. It's so intricate and I am

*thrilled you used your hair. I feel like I have part
of you with me even though we're apart. My heart
aches. I pray you're still there and waiting for me.
Please stay.*

You hold my heart in your hands, Leannan.

I love you always, more than life.

Andrew

I reread the letter over and over. He loved me. He said he loved me. God, how could he write such sweet things? His words were a balm for all my aches, even though I knew I'd never be able to respond in kind. The wolf rejoiced at his words. Part of me panicked, and part of me just wanted him to come back. I had no intention of leaving now. I clutched the letter to my cracked heart and glanced down at my hands; I was almost surprised that blood wasn't flowing from my chest. The pain was so intense I felt positive an actual wound had to be there. I wanted his arms, craved to feel them wrapped around me. I needed to kiss him, to be with him, always. I picked up the necklace with a renewed spirit and began to work, putting my heart and soul into the intricate carving.

As the afternoon wore on, I began to hear a steady growling sound. As the sound drew nearer, I decided to see what was going on. Max was slowly driving a large plow through the ground toward the cottage. The twins followed, bringing a grader and a truck with a load of gravel; they were building a road. They drove up to the side of the cottage, waving as they turned around, and then repeated the process back toward the ranch. I returned to the cottage to reread my new letter and wallow in self-pity. I looked around as I walked in. Jack and Joe had been working hard and it showed. The rebuild was almost complete.

I'd finished several extra pieces of pottery to take to the Pottery Hut in Rapid City, where the twins had said the owner, Gwen, was interested in selling them on consignment. I'd made two large vases and a large bowl, as well as a set of four stoneware plates, cups, and saucers. They all needed to be fired and glazed. I'd changed up the motif on these. I'd stuck with wolves, but I'd done a couple with eagles and buffalo as well. I decided the next trip the twins took into town, I'd ask to tag along. I wanted to give Gwen the pieces, hoping they would sell and I could purchase the ring I needed for Andrew's necklace.

The nightmares came that night, gruesome as always: my inability to find Andrew, the insanely cackling laughter, the endless search for him, the dark forms chasing after me as I tried to find him. The difference this time was that when I saw the man, he had black eyes and pale skin, and everything he touched appeared to freeze. Then the sad howling, Andrew's howling, cut short by the gurgling sound. When I found him, his throat had been slit from ear to ear, and I held the blade. I woke up screaming, as usual. I sat in the dark, striving to hold myself together, fighting off the fear and panic.

IT FELT good to be going into town. As much as I loved my cottage, I was beginning to go stir-crazy waiting for Andrew to return. Every little noise practically had me running for the door to see if he was back. Jack and Joe were ready to go, and they'd carefully packaged up my pieces and placed them behind the bench seat of the old red Dodge Ram truck and headed down the highway toward Rapid City.

The closer we got, the more I realized that I didn't miss the people or the traffic of living in the city. Jack and Joe dropped me off at the Pottery Hut with my carefully handled stoneware. They had said they needed to run errands for their mom, and something about the hardware store for electrical wire, breakers and junctions, which I didn't understand. I understood they would pick me up at the bookstore afterward.

A bell tinkled merrily as I opened the door.

"Hi, welcome to the Pottery Hut." A woman in her midthirties stood behind a counter.She wore an apron with clay splattered across the front.

"Gwen?"

"Yes, and you are?"

"Lance Fitz. Jack and Joe told me you might be interested in selling a few of my pieces?" I was nervous, now that I was there, that maybe she'd turn me down.

"Oh! You're the artist that made the pieces with the wolves. Yes. I'd love to be able to sell your work!" Gwen grinned and stepped out from behind the counter to shake my hand but took the box of pottery from my arms instead. "I assume this is a few more pieces?"

"Yes. Just a few."

"May I?" she asked and waited for my nod before diving into the box. She oohed and aahed as she pulled each bowl and vase from the box.

"Excellent. I'll get these fired and glazed and put in the front window. They'll have people pouring into the shop. Anytime you want to bring more, feel free." We haggled on pricing. I agreed to give her a percentage for the firing and glazing. I left feeling really proud and good about myself. It was a new feeling and I liked it. I even found myself liking Gwen, which was a new experience for me.

I went to the corner to catch the bus. The used bookstore was downtown, on Main Street. The drone of the engine as it motored along the route, stopping and starting to pick up passengers had me completely zoning out. I lost myself in the repetition of the sounds and motions around me as I waited for my stop. As we pulled up to the next stop, two girls waited to get on. They looked familiar. It took a moment for me to place them. They used to live in the same foster home I did—the last one, the one I ran from. I panicked instantly. The horrors of my last foster home slapped me in the face. I'd been forced to watch as these girls had been abused. I got up and headed for the door at the rear of the bus. Maybe they wouldn't see me, and I could catch the next bus…. Too late.

"Lance!" one of the girls called out. I shoved people out of my way as the two girls tried to catch up with me, pushing through the crowded bus.

I made it out the door and headed down the street at a quick pace, trying not to look too obvious. I hoped the girls would stay on the bus, but no such luck. I couldn't understand their reaction. I thought they would've wanted to leave me alone. Instead, they were running after me, trying to catch up with me. I took off at a sprint, trying to find a way to duck out of sight and lose the girls.

As I ran down the sidewalk, past all the storefronts, I saw my worst nightmare come true before my very eyes—a police car. I had no place to go, nowhere to hide. I was a fugitive on the run, a murderer.

The girls were flagging down the cop car, and I tried to run faster. The car had pulled over and its lights were flashing. I ran around the nearest corner and headed down the block as quickly as my feet would take me. There were no businesses here to duck into, no place to hide. I'd turned into a residential area. I ran on. I could hear the police car now. The siren blaring, it was gaining on me. I couldn't be caught—I couldn't go back to juvenile hall or worse yet, jail. They could try me as an adult now, since I'd turned eighteen. My sentence would end in prison or maybe the death penalty.

The wolf struggled inside me. The more I panicked, the more he wanted to be free, but I couldn't let him out in town. The police car seemed to be stuck at the end of the block. I made another turn and tried to get out of sight. More houses.No place to hide. I hadn't been paying attention to where I was running, but ducked down an alley that opened into the back parking lot of a grocery store. I cut around the side of the building and saw Jack and Joe, and the pickup truck. The police car was gaining on me now. I could hear it, but I couldn't see it. The twins were loading groceries into the back of the truck.

The side door had been left open. I dove in. Changing instantly, before my hands touched the vinyl seat, I had paws. I'd kicked off my shoes but the rest of the clothes would be destroyed. I pawed my clothes under the seat, praying I made it before the police car pulled into the parking lot, and that I wasn't seen changing.

"What the—" Jack yelled as he saw me change on the front seat of the truck.

Joe smacked him hard as the police car came rolling up alongside, slowly, the lights on, the siren blaring. The officer turned off the siren.

I jumped onto the front seat and tried to play "dog." I let my tongue hang out of my mouth, panting and wagging my tail. I held my tail curled up over my back as much as possible instead of down. The wolf in me felt stupid. *Think dog....think dog...* became my mantra.

The officer stopped the car. The girls were in the backseat, looking around like they desperately wanted to find me. I trembled in fear. I guessed in their eyes a murderer must be worse than the rapist monster who'd hurt them. I'd never considered how they'd feel or what they'd think of me.

The officer came over to Jack and Joe, the side door of the truck still open so he could look in and see that no one sat in the truck, except for a dog.

"Hi guys, did you see a young man come by here? I could've sworn I saw him jump into your truck." The officer stared into the cab.

"Beau's the only one in the truck, officer. I'm sure you aren't looking for him," said Joe, smiling. He'd shortened Andrew's nickname for me into a name for the wolf. I didn't know he called me *àluinn* around his family.... How embarrassing.

"No. Sorry, boys." The officer waved, then drove around the parking lot before going into the grocery store.

Jack and Joe finished putting everything in the truck, then casually got in and drove out of the lot.

"Oh man, Lance... you okay?" Jack draped an arm over my wolf's shoulders. A whine escaped from me. My panic started to fade once we were headed away from town and back toward the ranch. My wolf wanted to run, but I felt safe seated between Jack and Joe. I continued to whimper occasionally, but Jack's arm never moved. He just gently stroked my fur, telling me everything would be okay.

We were back at the ranch in about half the time it took to get to town. Joe sped the whole way. He seemed to know I was freaked out, and only the cottage could calm me.He didn't even pause at the ranch but drove me straight home. I got out of the truck, and the familiar comforting scents of my sanctuary settled in. Safe and home once more, I went into the cottage, transformed, and got dressed.

My clothing options were starting to become a bit limited. I might be forced to ask Laura for a few things. I went back out to see the twins nervously pacing in front of the cottage, waiting for me.

"Hi, guys."

"Oh, Lance!" They both hugged me at the same time. I'd become a twin sandwich—again.

"Are you okay? What happened?" Joe asked, not letting go of me, holding my hand, pulling me down to sit with him and Jack in the grass as Jack took my other hand. I knew I needed to get used to this touchy-feely life. Shape-shifters appeared to be very tactile and were always touching each other, especially during times of stress.

"I came out of the pottery shop, and I got on the bus and then my past jumped me. Two girls I knew in one of the foster homes I used to live in spotted me. I ran and they chased after me. They flagged down the cops.I ducked into the truck and transformed. I don't want to get your parents in trouble." I didn't know if they'd found the file naming me as the primary suspect in a murder. I hoped not.

"When I saw the truck door open, I hoped the cop wouldn't see me leap into the truck and change. I figured I couldn't be recognized as the wolf." I also didn't want them to know I'd almost completely lost control and transformed in panic.

"Well, you're safe here, and the cop doesn't suspect anything. We'll have to tell Mom and Dad, in case the police want to talk to us again. They won't turn you in. They don't want you to leave either, you know. None of us do, and Andrew should be back soon." Jack rubbed my arm gently. The adrenaline rush was fading fast. All I wanted to do was curl up and sleep.

"We got you something." Joe smiled. He went to the truck and pulled out a small bag from among all the other grocery bags and handed it to me.

I opened the bag to find a box of Earl Grey tea, my favorite. I grinned at the two of them. "Thank you. I'd run out a couple days ago."

"We know, you've been brewing that horrid generic crap lately. That stuff stinks... literally," Jack teased.

"We probably won't be back for a couple days. Dad has some big projects around the ranch he wants done. I know we don't usually say much, but after today, we didn't want you to think we weren't coming back because of the cops. We have to do some fence work on one of the northern pastures. Andrew planned on working on it, but he didn't get the chance before Stephon called him. We have to get it repaired before we can move the herd in for the winter." Joe leaned into me, bumping shoulders.

"We also gotta talk to Dad about the electrical. We got the stuff he said we needed and the wiring indoors is ready to go. Just a few things to take care of and you'll be able to join the rest of civilization." Jack smacked his brother on the shoulder.

"Thank you for telling me. I would've worried." I hugged them both. They got back into the truck and headed back to the ranch with a wave.

They didn't come back for two days, but when they did, two large trucks arrived, filled with stuff. My mouth hung open as I watched them pull up the road and park beside the cottage.

"What is all this?" I asked, completely taken aback as I saw furniture piled into the open beds of the trucks, tied securely in place.

"Andrew ordered you a few things. He said as soon as it arrived we were to deliver it." Jack smiled at the stunned look on my face.

"No. Guys, this is too much!"

"Hey, we're just on delivery. Look, Lance, don't worry about it. Andrew's an old dude who's been living with his parents for years while getting paid the big bucks. Sure, he works the farm now, but he didn't always." Jack laughed as I frowned.

"Old dude? I didn't even call him that." I just stood back, getting out of the way. Andrew and I would be having a talk about all this when he came back.

"Kris Kringle himself never had such a haul to deliver." Joe laughed at my astonishment. They moved my old table out of the cottage and set it outside as a picnic table, then began to unload the trucks, running into the cottage with armloads of things. I offered to help, but they laughed and had me sit down at the table instead, refusing to let me assist them in any way.

I watched as they first filled the cottage with bathroom things: sink, glass shower walls, a huge whirlpool bathtub that would fit three or four people easily, commode, and vanity. Then bedroom things: a large oak bed, an overstuffed mattress, a dresser, two tall armoires, and thick evergreen rugs. Then there were things for the kitchen: a huge oversized sink, a refrigerator, a range and other appliances, an oak table and chairs. Finally, there were a few things for the living room: an evergreen-print love seat depicting wolves in a forest, an overstuffed evergreen-colored armchair, with an ottoman, and a moss green rug. As the twins carried the last of the items into the cottage, I got up and followed them in. The cottage had been transformed from an open empty space to one filled with warmth and extraordinary beauty. I saw Andrew reflected in each carefully chosen piece.

"It's beautiful!" I managed to say around the lump in my throat.

"We're almost through here; give us about an hour and we should have one last surprise for you." Joe grabbed his brother, and the trucks soon growled off down the road. It didn't take long before they were back, fussing outside at the edge of the cottage. I wandered out to see what they were up to.

"This is your breaker box. We're tying the cottage into the ranch's electrical system. We just strung the wire, and tomorrow

79

we'll bury it so nothing messes with it." Jack attached the last of the connections and secured the breakers in place. Leaving the switch off, he nodded at Joe.

Joe grabbed his two-way radio and pressed the button.

"Okay, Dad, we're ready, turn them on at your end."

"Okay, they have power." Max's voice came over the radio.

Jack threw the master switch and light filled the cottage. "We have light. We're good on this end. Thanks, Dad."

"When you're done, get on home. Your mom's waiting dinner on you two."

"We'll be there soon." Joe turned off the radio as he watched Jack close and secure the breaker box.

"This should do for tonight, then we'll finish the job up tomorrow and have Dad come by and make sure we did it properly and up to code." Jack grinned as I stared at the cottage, trying to keep the tears from my eyes.

"I don't know what to say. You've performed a miracle here." I stammered, my throat tightening as I led the guys back into the cottage.

"We're glad you like it," Jack said bashfully, turning red with embarrassment as I moved around the kitchen and living room, running my fingers across the furniture in disbelief. I could hardly believe my eyes. Andrew's generosity overwhelmed me.

"Thank you so much, Jack. I don't know what to say."

"Geez, Lance," Joe said teasingly, walking through the door. "We're just the work crew. You'll have to thank Andrew when he comes home." He carried a box of what looked like groceries from the truck into the cottage.

"Have you heard anything from the pottery shop?"

"Not yet. Are you waiting for something?" Jack began to unpack the groceries, putting them in the cabinets and refrigerator. Joe went back outside only to return with another armful of grocery bags.

"Yes, once Gwen has sold some of the pottery, I need to purchase a solid platinum ring about an inch in diameter. I need it for a gift I'm making for Andrew. It can't compare to this, of course, but I'd really like to surprise him with it. If you could pick one up for me, once the pottery sells, I'd really appreciate it. I'm in no hurry to return to town anytime soon."

"Sure, Lance. No problem," Jack said with a smile as he shoved the last of something in a bag into the freezer.

I ignored their protests and hugged them both to me anyway. They turned red, patted my back and hugged me, and then excused themselves, telling me to go snoop and see what I could find. Closing the door behind them, I stared at my now quaintly furnished cottage. The lights were on in all the rooms, and as I'd said thank you to the twins, twilight had fallen. It had taken them all day to install and unload everything.

The rooms were exquisite. I wandered around, seeing where the twins had put everything. The longing for Andrew felt fuzzy and warm while being cold and desolate at the same time. I could feel his presence everywhere.

Among everything, I found Andrew's personal things. His clothes were in one of the armoires. His combs and razor were in the bathroom. I was happy to find his belongings among his gifts. We hadn't talked about him moving in, but I ached so much to have him here that when he returned, I intended to never let him leave. I clutched his sweater to my face again and inhaled deeply. Traces of his scent clung to the weave. Smiling, I put the sweater back where it belonged.

My chest hurt, where my cracked heart beat out the minutes of his absence. I was sure having someone use a spoon to rip my heart from my chest would have been less painful. The cottage was finished, and all I wanted... all I needed... was him. I walked back out to the kitchen and found my two letters lying on top of my sleeping bag in front of the fireplace. I stroked the paper and gazed longingly at the beautiful handwriting. If his generosity showed his love, then he loved me with overwhelming passion. I put the letters

81

on the table, folded up my sleeping bag, and put it in the corner. It looked as lonely and pathetic as I felt surrounded by such beauty, and just as out of place.

I thought about what I should do first, but I couldn't focus enough to think. I sat down at the table with my letters. I didn't get far in my thinking because the family began to howl, interrupting everything and sending chills running down my back. At first I thought they were hunting, but this call had a joyful and excited tone, unlike anything I'd heard since Andrew had left. I couldn't put my finger on exactly what—I dropped the letters and ran to the cottage door—

He stood rock still at the tree line, peering toward the cottage as if he were afraid to move. My white-gray wolf... Andrew... was standing as if he were afraid to come any closer.

"Andrew!" I ran straight for him, breaking whatever held him frozen in place. He came barreling out of the woods with an excited yip and sprinted toward me. We came together in the center of the clearing. I fell to my knees and wrapped my arms around him. He pushed me back into the grass, his wolf tongue licking me; then Andrew's arms went around me, his kisses sending little ribbons of fire all over my face. I had my arms around him, kissing him back as ardently and completely as I could. I felt light-headedas I clutched him to me, tightening my arms, refusing to release him for fear he'd disappear if I blinked my eyes.

"You stayed! Oh, you stayed!" he gasped between kisses, inhaling my scent and clutching me to his chest.

"I told you I'd stay. I'm here. Only you could've made me stay." I gasped when he let me speak, raking his shoulders with my fingernails, and I trembled when his erection pressed against the hard bulge behind the zipper of my jeans, our desire and excitement impossible to hide.

"God, Lance, my*leannan*." His arms crushed me, he held me so tight.It felt unbelievably good, and I felt safe, cherished.

"Andrew, I'm here." I pushed him back a bit so I could look in his eyes.

"I saw the lights of the cottage and I almost couldn't believe I'd come to the right place." His voice cracked with emotion. He picked me up in his arms and ran, carrying me, into the cottage. He looked around at the interior as we fell into the huge armchair, me on his lap. He traced the lines on my face, then stroked my hair. He kissed my eyes, my lips, my neck, and my hands. He held me close to his heart and sighed deeply, apparently content for the moment, despite his erection, just to have me in his arms. He looked like he'd been running for a long time. He was exhausted, dirty, and appeared to have lost weight. There were dark circles under his eyes, but no sign of pain, so I didn't care so much about the rest. I held Andrew in my arms—the rest of the world could wait.

"I missed you so much," I said into his chest as he stroked my hair. I wanted him to know everything. I looked up into his eyes and put my hand over his heart.

"I didn't realize before you left how much you'd touched my heart and how much I'd begun to heal." I took a deep breath. "I can't stand being separated from you. You've made yourself my whole world. Without you—there's nothing." I had to look away. I was on emotion overload. The floor held my attention, and my hair fell forward to cover my face... hiding me as I confessed how much I loved him.

He brushed my hair back from my face, then drew my chin up to look into his eyes. "I've missed seeing you. You're so beautiful, my love. Never hide from me." He gently kissed each eye and then my nose. "You're my whole life, my world too. Nothing else matters... I only need you. My *leannan*."

"What does that mean?" I gazed into the blue of his eyes, serenity and joy coming from him in waves.

"*Leannan*—it's a Gaelic term of endearment, kind of like 'lover' or 'beloved'. Our bloodline originally came from Scotland, and my mother can speak fluent Gaelic, although I only know a word here and there." He traced my jaw with a fingertip.

83

"Tell me what you did. Where'd you go? I want to know everything. I want to feel like we were together," I told him. Chagrin, embarrassment, and irony seemed to flash briefly in his eyes. He didn't want to talk about his time away. I really didn't care as long as he continued to hold me and talk to me. Instead of letting him answer me, I reached up and kissed him. I let my tongue trace his lower lip, feeling the texture of it and memorizing the taste of him. I felt him shudder under my hands. I smiled at his reaction and heard him growl softly. I answered him with a small growl of my own, which made him chuckle. His tongue came to taste my lips in return. The kiss was sensual and heady. I wanted to melt into him and never leave his embrace.

We parted, gasping for breath. "The twins finished the cottage today. I can't thank you enough. Everything is so…. It's so much more than I ever dreamed. You've made my small broken sanctuary a home. I've never had a home before." I stroked his face. "You look exhausted. Can I make you something to eat or run you a bath?" The dark rings under his eyes and skin stretched across his cheekbones, as if he'd not slept well in a long time, proof that the time apart had been as hard on him as me.

"There's no way you're leaving my arms. I may never let you go ever again," he said, his voice husky and filled with need, despite the fact he'd be asleep in minutes if left alone.

"Come, then," I said and pulled him to his feet. "Let's get cleaned up so you can sleep." I wrapped his arms around me; his chest lay heavily across my back as I pulled him with me to the bathroom. We were both too dirty to sleep in the new clean bed; me, from sleeping on the ground in my sleeping bag and bathing in the river for longer than I cared to think about; he, because of the miles he'd run from wherever he'd been with his master. Grabbing towels, soap, shampoo, and sponges, we moved toward the shower. He helped me to remove my T-shirt and jeans, and I heard his breath catch. I grasped his arms and wrapped them around me. He pulled me back to his chest.

"Better hope your brothers didn't get the hot and cold mixed up," I teased breathlessly as I turned on the water. I leaned my head back against his shoulder. It sent shivers down my spine and he trembled in response, our bodies speaking to one another without words. I stepped into the shower, then pulled him in behind me. The glass box filled with warm rushing water. *God bless the twins*, I thought. He caressed my shoulders and then sank his hands into my hair. Andrew took the shampoo from me and massaged my scalp and hair into a cleansing lather.

The stress of the past several weeks, of being without him, melted away with his touch, rinsing clean away.

I turned around, took the large sponge and body wash, and began massaging the muscles of his chest. I spun him around. He went down to his knees, and I leaned over his shoulder, kissing him on the side of his mouth. He groaned softly, and I pulled him back against me. His head rested against my heart as he sighed, the stress leaving his body. I shampooed his jet-black hair. I worked the muscles of his back and shoulders, kneading the tension out of them.

His armband remained securely tied, just as I had left it. I could tell from the knots and braid that he hadn't taken the band off. I felt a bit ridiculous, but it made me happy to think he'd kept it on the whole time he was away. I washed every inch of his body 'til he began swaying with my every movement. He was almost asleep in the shower. I pulled him up to his feet. His eyes were half closed; exhaustion was trying to claim him, pulling him toward sleep.

I turned off the water. My breath caught as I looked at him. He was so beautiful, his body wet and glistening, the water creating little rivers over the muscles of his chest and stomach. I began to dry him off. He smiled down at me and shook his head, sending water spraying everywhere. We both laughed. He toweled my hair and body as I dried his. It was so intimate, to wash and dry another person, but I couldn't have stopped touching him if I'd tried.

I led him to our bedroom and our bed. He climbed into the bed and I joined him between the white sheets. We kissed deeply, and I ran my hands over his body. He trembled violently under my hands.

Clutchingme to him, he snuggled his head to my chest. I held him there, my hands buried in his thick hair. The feeling of his fingers moving in strange patterns across the skin of my back and down my thighs ignited a fire in my soul. I couldn't have hidden my rock-hard erection if I'd tried, and even in his exhaustion, his hard cock pressed against my thigh.

I began to hum softly, a melody I vaguely remembered from my very first foster family, "St. Judy's Comet." I ran my fingers through his hair and stroked the side of his face. His fingers slowly ceased their movements and his breathing became steady. He slept in my arms. I'd never been so happy to have someone to hold, to be able to touch someone and be touched in return. I laced my fingers in his hair. I held Andrew safe—no one was taking him from me.

CHAPTER 5

I SLEPT dreamlessly. How could I not? With Andrew at my side, the creatures of nightmares were powerless. I was safe. I awoke with the dawn sun streaming through the window over the bed, kissing his face. Curtains were going to be a must-have purchase, at least for the bedroom. His head still rested on my chest and his arms clutched around my body. I didn't think we moved all night.

I smiled and fingered the armband. It seemed such a simple thing, but I couldn't explain how much pride I felt knowing he'd worn it the entire time he was gone. The braid remained in excellent shape and the hair showed no sign of fraying, as I'd feared it might. I sighed gently, completely content.

Even unconscious, he held me locked in his arms. Between the time when I'd first seen him standing in the doorway of the barn while I borrowed his tools until this very moment, I'd unconsciously decided happy endings could come true. I seemed to be living one right now. I lazily played with his hair and watched him sleep, careful not to disturb him. A heavy black scruff of whiskers covered his jaw, shading partway down his throat. I resisted the urge to run my fingers over the rough, coarse whiskers. He fascinated me—his beauty and the flawless innocence of his face. I trusted him unquestioningly, which scared the hell out of me. I could no longer deny him anything. He had me completely. A betrayal now would mean my death, but I had no fear of him ever doing that. This man might own my heart, but I claimed his as well.

"I love you," I whispered into his hair. "My Andrew." I stroked his hair. Even though I knew he slept soundly, he seemed to relax and sink deeper into sleep, as if he heard me and knew how I felt. He sighed deeply and moved for the first time in his sleep, inching his way up along my body 'til his face was out of the direct sun from the window. He came to rest with his head partially on my shoulder and partially on the pillow, lying on his stomach, but his left arm still clutched my body, around the waist. The sun's light now glistened along his broad, muscular back.

I'd never noticed before, but his back was covered with a crosshatch of scars. I recognized them immediately for what they were. He wore scars from a whip, and they were much more extensive than the ones I carried. Someone long ago had beaten my Andrew, repeatedly and harshly. The marks of the scars had overlapped and healed, one on top of the other. My wolf snarled and wanted to kill whoever had done this horrible thing to so kind a man. Furious didn't define the anger I felt. It took everything I had to keep from waking him.

I consoled my wolf—the scars were old. I couldn't do anything about them now but hold him close and swear in my heart never to allow it to happen again. He kept telling me he'd always protect me, but obviously I needed to protect him as well. The feelings of protectiveness and possessiveness I felt washing through me for this man astounded me, but left no doubt I'd kill for him. *And why not? I'd killed for much less, why wouldn't I kill for the one I love?* That thought didn't upset me nearly as much as I thought it should.

"I love you," I whispered softly, fiercely kissing his hair. The confession made me feel like a weight had lifted from my heart, allowing me to feel things I'd denied myself for so long.

Being human, well, almost human, wasn't always convenient. I wanted to stay curled up with Andrew around me, but nature had other ideas. Sure that Andrew slept deeply, I slipped out from under his arm, kissed his forehead, and crawled out of bed. I paused for a moment to grab some clean clothes from the new dresser and armoire—jeans and a T-shirt, of course—and went into the bathroom. The convenience of the bathroom was a pleasure after living off the land for so long. I got dressed, brushed my teeth, washed my face, and forced a comb through my hair. When I returned to the bedroom, I found Andrew sitting up in bed, staring anxiously at the bathroom like an abandoned puppy.

"I'm so sorry," I said softly. "I didn't want to wake you, and I thought I'd be back long before you woke up." I moved to sit at the edge of the mattress, only to find myself pulled across his lap. He kissed me soundly, his face softening a bit, but the fear was still there. I draped my arms around his shoulders.

"I missed you. I couldn't hear your heartbeat. I thought you'd finally left, or I might wake up any moment because you were just a dream." His voice shook on the last word.

I gently took his face in my hands and looked deeply into his troubled sky-blue eyes. "Where would I go? I only want to be with you, Andrew. I love you. I never want to leave your side," I said with all the sincerity and honesty in my heart. I held nothing back. I wanted him to see the love and know everything I felt for him.

He looked stunned for a moment, but only a moment. Then his eyes lit with joy and fire. I saw his love shining straight from his very soul. He howled at the top of his lungs, a sound that shook the windows. He laughed and clutched me to him. The joy and happiness jubilantly bubbled from his heart and soul. Nothing could contain his emotions. He howled again, giddy with love.

"My*leannan*, I love you too!" he saidsoftly, and then his feelings ripped from his throat again in a full howl. I laughed at his exuberance and excitement. My soul sang to see him so happy. Whatever happened now, it was worth it to see him so full of joy. "You really do love me?" he asked shyly.

I smiled into his eyes. "I love you more than my own life."

He howled again. I laughed and joined in his outrageous howl, which made him bust up laughing even more. He leaned in and began to kiss me,then ran his hands down my back and cupped my ass. I froze in place and began to shake uncontrollably.

"Lance?" Andrew stopped instantly and clutched me against his chest, moving his hands to my back.

"I can't—Andrew. I-I'm sorry. I—" I stuttered, trying to push back away from him. Images of the man's hands touching my body, rutting against me, flashed through my mind, turning me instantly cold. I could practically smell him. Memories overwhelmed my mind, my body, my senses, as if I were with him and not Andrew. Even though I knew—*knew*—he wasn't there, I could still smell the scent of stale sweat, blood, wet leather, and vomit that had permeated the room, and hear the vile laughter. I began to hyperventilate.

"No no no no…. Shh, baby. I'm sorry. Sooo sorry. I shouldn't have pushed you like that." Andrew began rocking me gently. He ran his fingers through my hair as he held my head pressed against his shoulder. His lips grazed the top of my head. He apologized over and over, swaying back and forth, consoling me like a frightened child. "It's okay,*leannan*. I love you… love you." I sat with my eyes squeezed shut and struggled to get a hold of my breathing. He hadn't meant anything by it, and I hadn't really explained too much of this in depth, but he seemed to know.

"I'm okay… I'm okay," I mumbled over and over in response to Andrew's consoling touch. I could tell from the way he was holding me that the desire that had risen between us was gone in light of his fear. I pushed the memory away from me, burying it, away from Andrew. He would not be sullied. I wouldn't let that man dirty the love I held in my heart for Andrew. "I'm sorry, Andrew. I can't—I can't even really talk about why. I—"

"Shh—doesn't matter… doesn't matter at all. I can kiss you… that's okay, right?" Andrew moved back to look into my eyes.

I smiled, his concern and need for reassurance as strong as my need for him. "Yes, you kiss fabulously. I love it when you kiss me. I love it when you hold me… touch me. I just can't… be sexual. Please don't think I don't want you… or that I don't want to. I do, but my body… I start to remember… and I… I can't—" I struggled to explain what I couldn't make myself tell him.

90

"It's okay. I get it. You love me, right?"

"More than I ever imagined I'd be capable of loving someone," I told him honestly, cupping his jaw with my hand, feeling the rough whiskers prickling against it. I didn't know how long Andrew would be able to deal with me and my issues, but as long as he would let me, I'd be here and I'd make him as happy as I possibly could.

"Then that's all I need. Nothing else matters. You're here and you love me. I love you. I'm good with that. I'll take whatever part of you I can have. You just tell me what's okay and what's not. If I can hold you and kiss you, then I'm happy." Andrew smiled, his eyes beginning to light up again as I leaned in and kissed his jaw, nipping at the whiskers there.

"I love you so much." I grinned at the growly sound that came from his stomach and giggled, trying to regain the happiness we had momentarily lost.

"Wait here. Please." His eyes glittered, full of energy and sudden enthusiasm. He bounded out of bed then came back and kissed me. Then he ran to the dresser and began grabbing underwear and socks. He returned, kissed me again, thenwent to the armoire and grabbed jeansand a T-shirt. He came back and kissed me again, then ran for the bathroom, howling as he ran. I laughed as I watched his antics,then waited, listening to water run as he went through his morning routine. I remained perched on the bed where he left me, shaking my head at his clowning around. I didn't move a muscle. He soon emerged from the bathroom dressed, shaved, his hair combed but wet. He scooped me up into his arms, swung me around in a circle, and kissed me.

"Quit it!" I squirmed in his arms. "I'm not a little kid." I flushed red, embarrassed, and rolled my eyes. He ignored my protests, setting me on my feet. Holding my hand, he led me to the kitchen and pulled out the chair closest to the range. He began digging through the cabinets. "We need to talk about all this stuff, Andrew," I said as I looked around in wonder at all the furniture and rugs he'd had the twins deliver.

He stopped only when he saw the dishes. He carefully took down the stoneware I'd designed after his wolf. "What, that stuff?It's just things I've collected over the years. Furniture Dad made, stuff I had when I lived away from the family for a while, working for Stephon. Dad made the cabinets, so really it's just the rugs and some of the other stuff that's new. I'm far from poor, Lance. We live on a farm because we are tied to the land and need a place to allow our wolves to run. It's not our only source of income. We can only be out in professional circles for so long these days before someone starts to question our lack of aging. The twins, not at all. Nobody would take teenagers seriously, even if they didn't act like kids. They do most of their work at a computer. Behind the scenes, we can work quite extensively. I publish occasionally. Mom is a writer in a couple of genres under different pen names. So relax, this is just stuff. Stuff is replaceable. People and experience, love... you can't replace that."

"Okay... I guess." I shook my head as he began to look at each piece individually. "But I'm not your charity case."

"No, you're my lover, and we're sharing this cottage as our home. Sharing is some of me and some of you. So furniture and stuff is me.... These are beautiful. Where did they come from?" he asked, caressing the design.

"I made them, and your brothers were kind enough to take them into town to be fired and glazed. You really like them?" I grinned. Shock crossed his face as he looked at me again. "I made your mom a vase. The twins gave it to her for her birthday."

"They're stunning, and see?This is some of you." He continued to go through the set, pulling each piece out one at a time and admiring the depiction of the wolves on them. He smiled lovingly at me, as if he were seeing me for the first time. He handled each piece as if the simple dishes meant more to him than anything in the world. "They are almost too beautiful to eat off." He grinned and put the pieces back in the cupboard, except for a couple plates and cups. Then he began pulling out pots and pans, utensils, and bowls.

"I'll remember to make them uglier next time." I laughed, watching him move around the kitchen. "Let me help," I said, starting to get to my feet.

He came over and kissed me, then gently pushed me back into the chair. "Nope, I want to cook for you, my love." He laughed joyously at his own words. He mumbled to himself, "He loves me!" Then he went back to pulling ingredients from the cabinets and refrigerator. He was being so silly. I mean, yeah, I loved him. It wasn't a big thing… was it?It was embarrassing to say and admit… wasn't it? I settled back, letting him have his way, watching him cook.

I could watch him all day and never get bored. The man looked blissful. I sat and stared at him, loving every minute. He baked muffins, the smell of raspberries and almonds filling the kitchen. He scrambled eggs, then roasted steaks under the broiler. He fried potatoes with onions and green peppers. Periodically he would look at me, rush over to kiss me, and then go back to his cooking. Of course, in the process of creating the meal, he systematically destroyed the once spotless kitchen. But I laughed and watched him fuss about. He was having fun, and I couldn't help but enjoy seeing him do so, regardless of the mess.

"You love me?"

"Yes. I love you, Andrew."

I couldn't believe how delighted hearing me say I loved him made him feel. It intoxicated me, thinking how what now seemed so simple gave him such jubilance, like it was the greatest gift of all time. I'd given him something he'd resigned himself to never have. I gave him my broken self and he was thrilled. I couldn't have felt more surprised that anyone would want a piece of my heart so badly, and I couldn't help but feel a bit proud of myself that this beautiful man wanted me.

"I love you, Lance. I so do…." He kissed me quickly. I loved to see how his sky-blue eyes danced and sparkled. I loved how he said my name. It was all I could do to keep myself from rolling my eyes and blushing like a schoolgirl under all the intense attention he was giving me.

Andrew could really cook; everything tasted wonderful. I hadn't eaten very well since he had left. I'd had no appetite. But he had me eating like a starving man. When we were both stuffed to capacity, he leaned over and kissed me again, then took my hand and led me to the love seat in the living room. He sat back into the cushion with me on his lap, leaning back against his chest. We were both content.

"You love me," he said again, grinning, but this time with conviction, like he finally believed the feelings were real. His face filled with boyish awe, as if all the years had melted away and he was a child again. I understood completely, because I felt exactly the same. If I died today, I'd be content... loved.

"You look so like the twins right now." I snickered but quickly added, "I love you more than life. You are mine, Andrew, now and forever. Get used to it."

He kissed me softly.

"I'm glad you bonded with my brothers." He shook his head, looking mystified. "I didn't know if you'd ever be able to accept my family."

"They've been very patient with me. Every day your brothers amazed me more with what they were doing. I jumped in where I could, but they did most of the work themselves."

"What did you do while I was gone? I want to hear all about it."Andrew brushed his lips against my hair.

"So much happened while you were gone. I met your mother. She's been here twice. Your father came up with her about a week ago." I struggled to find the right place to begin. "The twins were great. They've been lifesavers. They seemed to know when I needed a laugh and when I just needed to be alone. They worked on the cottage tirelessly, but they were kind of working on me too. They slowly drew me out of my shell, pulled me away from some of my fear. Your mom came to talk to me about a week after you left to deliver your letter and ask me some questions about my past." He nuzzled my neck, kissing me softly as he listened.

"I told her not to…. I hope she didn't push you too much." Andrew looked at me with concern. I could practically feel his intense perusal as he probably checked for signs of anxiety and fear.

I sighed and told him all about the twins going through my records and searching for my birth certificate, and the trip to Dr. Carlson's office. Andrew stopped moving and looked at me as if he'd been electrocuted.

"Oh shit, I'd never have thought…. Oh God…," he stammered, at a loss for any words. Panic warred with the fear in his eyes, and he looked like he wanted to grab me and run.

I put my hand on his face and tried to wait patiently for his warring emotions to settle. "Shh. It's okay." I tried to soothe him. His panic was frightening me. His eyes were flashing, his breath coming in gasps, like he could barely keep the wolf at bay. He held me so tightly against him I could barely breathe. The others had been concerned, but their reactions had been nothing like this—at least, not in front of me. They'd been disturbed and appeared worried, but not terrified. I ran my hands through his hair as I felt his alarm begin to subside.

"Are you okay? What's it all mean?"

"Wow, let me think…." He closed his eyes for a few moments and stroked my hair, holding me against his chest.

"I've so much to tell you. Where to begin…." He paused, fear prominent in his eyes.

"How about you start at the beginning? You can tell me. I'm here and I'm not going anywhere. Remember, you said we could handle anything together." I traced down the side of his face, over his cheekbones and along his jaw. He caught my hand and kissed my palm, then pulled my hand with his between us against both our hearts.

"Okay, the beginning. It's a bit of a Romeo and Juliet story, really. Long ago, before the Great War, we were a free people and a proud warrior race. Along with our ally, we'd fought and won the

Blood War back in the Dark Ages of humanity. We were confident, violent, and very full of ourselves. Some of our leaders thought we were invincible. We were immortal, wild, and free—untamed," he said wistfully.

"The immortals we'd fought alongside, our allies, were the vampires. They'd been our friends for millennia uncounted. The dissension began very simply, I guess, as most of these things probably do. A young vampire, in his early hundreds, barely a youth by their standards, fell in love with a wolf maiden. She was one of our elders' oldest daughters. She belonged to a powerful pack, one of pure blood, a strong family. Her father had promised her to another pack. He wanted to cement an alliance with the royal family. He and the king of our kind had chosen his oldest son to marry the lord's daughter. Unknown to her father, the young vampire had been courting his daughter. Vampire society and ours intersected on a regular basis in those days. The vampires often chose positions as doctors, caretakers, and educators, where we were the warriors and laborers. Our peoples complemented each other nicely." His eyes were far away now as he got into his story.

"When the maiden found out her father had promised her to another pack, she rebelled and ran to the side of her vampire. You have to remember, in those days, she would've been considered of marriageable age after her first shift at puberty, so I'd guess she would've probably been between thirteen to sixteen years old. The vampire petitioned the maiden's father for her hand, putting forth his family as a good match, believing them to be of equal status to the royals. His family was well placed in vampire society and had a lot of influence. He promised he'd love her forever and take care of her for eternity. Her father refused to give up his ambitions and under the pretense of being appalled to have his daughter seek a love match from a different species, he denied the petition." Andrew nuzzled my neck and kissed me, then continued.

"She refused to leave her vampire's side. Her father was furious and demanded his daughter be returned to him untouched and pure. The young vampire lord refused, saying she loved him, and he loved her, and they'd rather die together than be separated. Her family's pack attacked the vampire's stronghold and decimated it. Her vampire had sent away most of his people, not wanting to cause her the pain of seeing her family fighting his, and the ensuing slaughter. Both lovers were believed to have been killed in the fight."

"They died because they refused to be separated. How sad." I frowned as Andrew continued.

"The young vampire's family retaliated against the pack. The violence escalated. One side would appear to gain ground over the other, and then the tide would turn. More and more families were involved on both sides. The war went on for decades and through generations of both vampires and shape-shifters, pulling the entire society of both species to the brink of annihilation. Thousands were killed on both sides. Eventually, though, the vampires won out. Purebloods can have children by birth, same as shifters and humans, but they can also create their children by envenoming them. When a born pureblood vampire bites a human with the intent to turn them into a drone, the venom they secrete will, in a matter of days, turn the person into a vampire drone. The first years of life for a drone child are violent, bloodthirsty, and instinctual; they're the perfect mindless warriors. They're physically fully grown adults, never changing, immortal, very fast, and strong. They must drink human blood to survive. They are nonvenomous, so they can't create more drones. They have pale skin, and their eyes are always black."

"Like Dr. Carlson. He's a drone."

"Yes. He's a very old drone. Long past the mindless stage."

"He seemed all right. I was so nervous being there with your folks, and not really knowing what was going on, I can't say I really noticed a whole lot about him other than he didn't have fangs. I watched for them."

"Believe me. He has fangs." Andrew rubbed my back and continued. "All our children are born and take years to mature before we're able to transform and fight. Even though our people were generally stronger, faster, and even harder still to kill, we were at a distinct disadvantage. Each loss cost us greatly because it took years to replace a lost warrior. In battle after battle, we were always outnumbered. We lost. When our people finally surrendered, there were very few of us left. The vampires named the war 'the Great War' because it was so bloody and decimated families on both sides.Being such an enlightened species, they decided to help to save us from our own folly, a self-inflicted extinction. They split up the remaining packs and families. Each of the born immortals took responsibility for a number of pairs of shape-shifters. We had to be careful with our remaining bloodlines. Inbreeding couldn't be allowed, because there were too few of us left. Family histories and pedigrees became extremely important as we struggled to bring ourselves back from extinction.

"In those days all shape-shifters were purebloods, able to take on the shape of any number of creatures. We could be anything we wanted. The oldest ones couldn't stand the way we had to live, unable to make our own choices. Many of the life-bonded mates were separated in order to save the species—they began to die of broken hearts, unable to live without their mates, forced to breed with others. There were so few of us, the vampires had no choice but to mix our bloodlines with humans.

"The first generation of children of such liaisons had few abilities, if any at all, and could barely control the abilities they did have. Many of these half-breeds didn't have the full long lives of our kind and died after a few decades, more like the lives of regular humans at the time. But their genetic diversity mixed in with the packs.

"Now, we are four and five generations beyond the Great War. Our people are back from extinction, but our abilities are reduced due to the mixture of human and shifter blood. The more diluted the bloodline with human blood, the shorter the lifespan of the individual and the harder it is to shift. Some have trouble holding their animal shape for more than a couple minutes, although some of the stronger bloodlines are relearning to shift into more than one creature. I myself have never tried to be anything other than my wolf. I like him. I've never felt the need to take on another form."

"Do you think you could? I mean, your family seems very strong. You all look so young despite how old you really are."

"I don't know. Maybe if I really tried." Andrew smiled a bit, rubbing his cheek against my hair and inhaling deeply. "When the vampires took over and split apart the packs, we had to rebuild our families. We became bonded to the vampires to whom we owed our lives. They could've destroyed us into extinction, and mythology. In infancy, we're all bonded to our vampire benefactor. My family is also bonded to these hills.It's part of being a wolf. This is our territory. We're the caretakers of the lands belonging to our family. We safeguard it from poachers, maintaining the herds living here. We feel a kinship with nature, as we're so closely knit into the magic of nature."

"Wow, all that devastation because of a pair of star-crossed lovers. How incredibly sad," I said softly. "It's because of them, shape-shifters live as slaves to the vampires."

"We are at the mercy of our vampire benefactor. There are certain parts of my life which I have very little control over, and Stephon has final say. As shifters, we aren't allowed into mainstream education systems, because some of us can't control our shifts. We have to maintain our anonymity, so our education is limited to what we can learn at home. Also, I'm the oldest son of a very strong bloodline. My benefactor wants me to choose a female mate with a good pedigree, so we can grow in strength."

"Oh. He isn't going to like it that we love each other, is he."

"Probably not, but he can't chose who I love. That's what he was trying to do while I was away. He had brought many candidates from across the world, from various families, trying to tempt me with a mate."

I couldn't prevent the growl that escaped my throat. Andrew was mine... but he wasn't, not really. Even if we loved each other, he belonged to the vampire who could make him breed with a female of his choosing. Separate us forever if he so chose. Fear that Andrew was about to be stolen from me sank deep into my stomach. "But...."

Andrew snorted self-consciously, kissing my hair. "When we choose a mate, it's for life. In our society, it doesn't matter if it's a male to female mating, male to male, or female to female. All are accepted and treasured, as ultimately we believe true mates are destined by fate. Male/male life mates happen as often as any of the other combinations. It's not preferable, of course, because there are no children from such a bonding, and although we're gaining strength, our people aren't completely out of danger yet.

"Stephon didn't know, and I hadn't realized, that I'd already chosen my mate." He tightened his arms slightly around me, giving me a possessive squeeze. "It can't be undone. I'd chosen before I left, even though I didn't realize it until the parade of female shifters kept passing by. I compared each to my *leannan*, and none of them could even compare. I told my master I already had a mate." He chuckled softly "He was livid and sputtered in indignation. I haven't pissed him off like that in a very long time. I told him my mate had come to me. I'm not sure he believed me when I told him a free wolf appeared out of nowhere and I'd chosen him to be my mate." He shook his head, smiling down at me. The fear, almost gone from his eyes, had been replaced by overwhelming love. "I think he questioned my sanity for a while."

"He's angry." I sighed heavily, leaning into Andrew, drawing comfort from him as much as I could.

"Well, he can hardly complain if what you told me is true. The lovers in my story, the vampire and the wolf maiden—her name is Sasha Fenrir. I don't know who Fitz is, but Sasha Fenrir was an ancient pureblood. If she's your mother, then she couldn't have been killed in the battle, and she probably went animal when her vampire was killed."

"What does that mean, *went animal*?" I asked in confusion. "Could she be out there somewhere, after having abandoned me?"

Andrew nodded solemnly. "It's a state of grief, really. When our people lose a mate, if one dies before the other, it's common for the mate left behind to go into their animal form and refuse to change back to human. When this happens, the one left behind usually lives the lifespan of their animal and dies, having lost the will to live. They lose the magic of our kind to the mindless instincts of the animal or maybe they just refuse to use it because the pain is too great to bear." Andrew kissed my temple. "I know I couldn't be without you."

"I love you too."

"In your mother's case, maybe because her chosen was a vampire they couldn't really share a complete mating bond. The matings between us and humans had similar problems. The pairs didn't share a true mating bond. She's probably living a life in limbo, unable to truly live because she mourns her vampire love and unable to die because their bond was incomplete. She's trapped in a life of never-ending suffering as the beast." Andrew shook his head sadly and clutched me closer to him.

"Okay—" I paused, stunned. "So I'm the son of a woman who's more animal than woman, with a death wish, over whom a war was started that ended with shifters being enslaved for generations. A war that almost caused her people, and those of the man she loved, to go extinct. Wow, I don't even know what to do with that. There're going to be a lot of angry people when they find out I'm alive. Well, you wanted a pedigree…. Damn." I rubbed my hands over my face.

I knew my life had been a mess, but I'd never guessed things could get worse than they were. It proved the adage "never say never," because things could always get worse. "I'd never imagined knowing my bloodlines would be worse than being an unknown mystery….My family is responsible for a war. There's no way to apologize for a war." My voice drifted. I couldn't even comprehend the magnitude of being responsible for all those deaths.

"No, love, you're the most beautiful creature I've ever set eyes on. My very blood sings your praises." He sounded so sure of himself. "You aren't responsible for what happened over three hundred years before you were born. Don't take that on. We'll just move forward and deal with what comes."

"Okay, then in dealing with what comes… Stephon's coming here, isn't he?" Fear filtered into my voice.

"Probably… eventually. I can't be sure. My family's well-being is very important to him. He isn't evil. He cares very much about us."

"Yeah, right. The slave master cares about his property."

"He really does, Lance. When I was young, like the twins, he called me to him while he attended university. He allowed me to study as well, which is something that doesn't happen often. I thrived there. I learned so much about the world—medicine, society, math, physics, and the stars. Humans have a unique outlook on life because they must live their lives so quickly, in just a few decades, yet their knowledge steadily grows. They stockpile everything they learn for future generations, so nothing is lost. We benefit from their hoarding of knowledge and their striving to pass it on to future generations. We can make their knowledge our own. I have two degrees in medicine and one in physics. I even taught for a while, before we left university because it was becoming apparent that we weren't aging. I came back and taught as much as I could to my brothers and in a few years, when she's ready,to my baby sister." Andrew practically preened, proud of his accomplishments for his family and people.

"But he won't release you. He won't free you from him. You'll always be tied to him," I stated sadly.

"Yes, although his hold on me seems slight in comparison to the bonds I feel tying me to you." He murmured, "I will love you forever," into my ear softly.

I couldn't let him distract me, there was too much left to talk about. "He's going to hurt you, to try and pull you away from me."

"No… I don't know what he'll do. Let's see if we can find out what the test results are, and what Dr. Carlson has to say, before we panic. You've nothing to prove. You're the most beautiful creature on the planet, regardless of your parentage," he reassured me, smoothing the goose bumps forming on my arms and the fear building in my heart. Not fear for myself, I realized, but fear for what could happen to him because of me. It was a new feeling, fearing for the safety of someone else when I'd only worried about myself for so long. I liked having someone to care about.

"If you say I've nothing to worry about, then I'll try not to worry." I didn't want worry to ruin his homecoming. I wanted to go back to this morning and see the happiness in his eyes again.

"I'll need to go see my family soon. They're so glad I'm home. I need to see my father and tell him about my visit, and my mother will want to see me too. She worries when I'm away. Will you come with me? My brothers will be there, and I know they'd love the chance to make fun of me in front of you."He chuckled softly. "I don't want to let go of you, much less let you out of my sight, even for a trip to the ranch."

"I guess. Maybe they'll have heard something from Dr. Carlson. I'd also like to meet your little sister. I haven't met her yet." I smiled up at him. I could do this. It'd make him happy to see his family, and I'd be able to become more comfortable with them. Even his father seemed to be growing on me... slowly. With Andrew there, his love shining from his eyes, I felt like I could do anything, including brave this small piece of the world.

"Seriously, you're okay with this?" Andrew asked, astounded.

"Yes. It's about time I grow a pair, don't ya think? It's not like your family hasn't been completely careful with me. They've given me space and been more than kind and supportive to a squatter in their cottage. They're your family.You love them. I like them, so I need to get over this fear of every little thing. Let's go visit your family." I laughed and snuggled closer to him, "Although I really like the idea of keeping you all to myself." A bit reluctantly, I got up and took his hand, and taking a deep breath, I led him out of the cottage. We walked hand in hand, slowly, to the north, toward the ranch. I would hold my head up high. I could come and go as I pleased. No one owned me. Well, no one but Andrew. I'd be proud. For him, I could be anything, including a warrior. I'd figure out a way to be worthy of him if it killed me.

CHAPTER 6

"I CAN do this," I mumbled, fidgeting nervously. We walked together, side by side,our arms wrapped about each other's waist, around the barn to the large white ranch house. Two sandy-colored wolves wrestled on the lawn—the twins were at it again. I laughed when I saw them rolling around. They heard me, and yipping with excitement, they came running, almost knocking us over in their enthusiasm.

"Hey, guys," Andrew said, patting each wolf lovingly. I bent down and hugged them both, then stood up and took Andrew's hand again. He smiled strangely at my warm greeting of his brothers. Pulling me against him, he wrapped his arm back around my waist, and together we walked toward the house.

Max Reed stepped out of the house and stood on the front porch. He smiled down at us. "So you convinced him to come down and visit the family?" Max chuckled, embracing his son. "How are you, son?"

"I'm good, Dad. Actually, I'm better than that!" he said, smiling at me. I looked at his father, blushing quietly, then stared down at my hands. His dad glanced at the armband Andrew wore and nodded at his son, a grin breaking across his face.

"I'm glad. How did your visit with Stephon go?" he asked seriously.

104

"About as well as could be expected. Of course I had an unforeseen epiphany in the middle of it. But all's well. He may be coming here, I don't know for certain. He may just ask me to bring Lance to him. I don't know what to expect. I also don't really care. There's nothing he can do.My heart has chosen. I can't change it. I don't want to change it. Lance is my mate." He laughed, his eyes sparkling with love as he squeezed me tightly.

"Is that my son I hear laughing?" came a warm voice from inside the house. Laura rushed out, her bright eyes eager. You could tell just by looking at her how much she loved and had worried about her son while he was away.

"Mom," Andrew sighed, his voice full of love. She skipped lightly down the steps and threw herself into her son's open arms.

"I was so worried about you. How are you doing? What... did Stephon forget to feed you?" She looked him over with a skeptical eye, making him turn around before she reassured herself he was okay. Laura noted the armband he proudly wore and kissed him on each cheek.

"I'm fine, Mom, really. You know Stephon wouldn't hurt me." Andrew snorted self-consciously and rolled his eyes. Andrew seemed to have a special soft spot for his mom. He was a consummate momma's boy. I chuckled inside at the thought of my Andrew being a momma's boy. I had a hard time thinking of him as belonging to anyone other than myself.

"Oh my, you're a sight." She pulled me into a hug. "I'm glad you finally feel comfortable enough to come and see us." I blushed, embarrassed, but feeling good, like a prodigal son returning, amazed that she wanted to see me too. She'd been worried about both of us. "I feared we'd never get you to come join us after what happened in Rapid City the other day."

I'd hoped she wouldn't mention the incident with the police. I hadn't told Andrew about almost getting his brothers in trouble. Things were bad enough without adding being wanted by the police for murder to our list of issues. "I'm fine. Your son's been so incredibly generous with me. I owe him far more than I could ever repay. You'll have to come to the cottage and see how beautiful he's made it. It's stunning." I glossed over the police incident and steered things to safer subjects. I needed to get my history out in the open first. "Andrew explained some of the history behind the names on my birth certificate," I told her. "He seems to still want me, even though... things could turn very bad," I told her conspiratorially. I tried to make light of it, but the fear undercut my attempts at joking.

"Don't be silly. You're part of this family. None of that matters." She clasped my hand in hers and wrapped an arm around my shoulders. "Let's go into the kitchen and catch up. Andrew and his father can talk shop, and I'll make you a cup of tea."

"Ahhh... Mom, why don't you let Lance stay with me for now?" Andrew began, but she led me up the steps and into the house. For a moment I thought I saw a flash of pain cross his face, but I must've been mistaken. He smiled apologetically, almost blushing himself while Laura led me away.

"He'll be fine with me. You go on and talk to your dad and brothers. I'll introduce him to Angela."

I gave Andrew a confident smile, telling myself I'd be fine. Laura led me into the foyer. It was a beautiful home; the floors were a dark hardwood, the walls a neutral cream. There was a stairway with a dark wood banister to the right, the entry to a large living room on the left. It was a bright window-filled sitting room with chocolate-colored oversized cushioned furniture and a small grand piano.

"Have you heard from Dr. Carlson?"

"No, he hasn't called yet, but I'm assuming he will soon. Try not to worry so. It really doesn't matter one way or the other to us. You're family now."

"You have a beautiful home."

"Thank you. It's been in my family for generations. When I'm gone, it'll go to my daughter, Angela."

We moved into the sitting room and sat in the overstuffed brown chairs.

"Wow, I would've thought the ranch would go to Andrew," I said in surprise.

"No, dear, we're a matriarchal people. The land belongs to the females of the family. We rule the roost around here." Laura chuckled. "The land passes from mother to daughter. Sons usually go to live with their wives, taking on their territory as their own. Mates will even take the last name of the female they bond with. Children born then have the female's family name. Although children from an unmated pair will take the mother's name as a middle name, and the father's name as their last name."

I chuckled. "That's way cool. A world where the women rule."

"Well, not in every sense, and it wasn't always so, but since the Great War we've taken over the running of the families." Laura straightened her skirt and crossed her legs. "Some things have always been in our power, but now all of it is. I thought you already knew this. You do realize that by giving Andrew a gift of jewelry, the armband, for instance, you've marked him as yours. In our world, it's a promise of love and intent to be mates. By taking that initiative, you've become the 'woman' in the relationship, the one in control." Laura frowned. "Didn't Andrew tell you anything?"

"Umm… well, yes and no," I stuttered, shocked at the implication I'd unintentionally, but quite happily, given. "I gave it to him just before he left to go to Stephon. At the time, neither of us realized how we felt. I wanted him to have a reminder of me with him. I was so afraid he'd forget me. Once he'd left, I realized how desperately in love with him I'd become. He'd declared he loved me, although I think it took him by surprise how much he cared for me as well." I blushed, uncomfortable talking about our feelings to Andrew's mother.

"Well, by giving him the armband, something you made yourself, it's a warning to other females that he's taken, at least in our society. When he refused to take it off, he basically pledged himself to you. Think of it as an engagement ring." Laura chuckled at my shock.

"I didn't know that at the time, but I'm glad." I couldn't prevent the blush coloring my cheeks. This was a subject I wanted to talk to Andrew about, not his mom.

"Come on. I'll show you the rest of the house." Laura and I stood and walked from the sitting room to the hallway.

"Is he here? Did he come?" called a little voice, followed by the thunder of feet on the stairs. Andrew's sister, the youngest of the Reeds, came running from somewhere upstairs. She had her mom's curly blonde hair and her father's gray eyes and dark complexion, giving her a rather exotic appearance. She'd be stunning when she grew up. Full of life and energy, she bounded down the last couple of stairs and spun around the banister, almost colliding with me in her headlong race to join us.

"My name's Angela," she chimed as she spotted me.

"Hi Angela, I'm Lance." I smiled down at her cherubic face.

She grabbed my hand and towed me away from her mother down the hallway toward the back of the house, to the kitchen. It was a warm yellow room, full of light and wonderful smells. Laura Reed had followed after us, smiling indulgently at her daughter. Angela pulled me over to the table and guided me to a chair across from her.

Her mother went to the stove and put on a kettle for tea."Andrew tells me you're fond of tea. Can I make you a cup?"

"That would be nice. Thank you," I said softly.

"So, do you really like my big brother?" Angela asked with the innocence of a child, getting straight to the heart of the matter.

"Oh yes, most definitely. He's the air that I breathe."

"Gross!" she snickered but smiled at me anyway. "What can you turn into?"

"I turn into a wolf. He's chocolate brown with a white belly and white feet. What can you turn into?" I winked at Laura when she turned to look at me, as if Andrew had missed telling me something else. Angela clearly hadn't gone through puberty, and so I knew she couldn't transform.

"Well, I can't decide. I like the wolves and most everyone in my family's a wolf, but I kind of like Cousin Sam's eagle too. I don't want to be a bear, though. They're clumsy." She spoke so earnestly. I envied her growing up in a family like this, knowing that she'd be a shifter, surrounded by those who loved her.

"You'd be too big of a bully if you became a bear. Groooowwwwwlllll!" said Jack from the door of the kitchen, then came at his sister with his arms in the air.

She squealed, got up from her chair, and ran to me, then hid behind me.

"Ha…. What do we do now?" I leaned in conspiratorially over her shoulder."The big Jack Bear is going to get us…."

She squealed again, delighted I'd joined in her game."You can take him. He's just a clumsy bear," she whispered.

I laughed and Jack grabbed her by the waist, flipped her upside down, and carried her from the room like a sack of potatoes on his shoulder. I laughed, watching them leave.

Laura put a cup of tea in front of me and beamed at her oldest son. Andrew stood in the doorway, glowing with happiness. He mussed his sister's hair and kissed her cheek as Jack carried her past him and out the door. He came to stand behind me, leaned down, and kissed me ardently.

"I missed you. I'm not ready for you to be out of my sight yet," he complained softly into my ear. I blushed as his mother watched her son's passion for me flash across his face.

I took his hand, pulled him into the chair beside me, and looked into his eyes. "I missed you too. Love you."

Laura Reed smiled knowingly. She came behind us and gently touched his armband then looked into her son's eyes, kissed him on the head, and then kissed me on the head.

"Welcome to the family, Lance." She quietly left the room.

"Wow, can you clear a room or what?" I said breathlessly, as he moved in for another, much more passionate kiss. "You have to explain this 'I'm the woman' thing to me later."

"I love you, my *leannan*."

"You already said that…it's not getting you off the hook."

He chuckled. "Well, um…." Andrew kissed me with so much need, passion, and tenderness, he took my breath away. I loved Andrew's kisses.

He sighed, placing his forehead against mine. "Want to see my room?" He got a mischievous grin on his face, raising his eyebrows.

"I'd love to see your room." I chuckled, knowing I'd find out about the engagement thing soon enough. I felt a bit like a kid as he grabbed my hand, pulled me to my feet, and led me out the kitchen door to the stairs, then up to a landing that opened onto a long carpeted hallway. He opened the last door on the right and then closed it behind us. It opened into a suite, the first area a lounge or study, dark paneled, with a thick dark-brown carpet. A large dark-stained oak desk sat along one wall with a flat-screen computer monopolizing the space. A stone fireplace filled the outer corner, and a couple of dark leather chairs with a large square ottoman covered in numerous books, sat in front of it. The room seemed to be a combination personal library and living room. I walked along the wall, scanning the shelves. One whole section of shelves was paperbacks by an author whose pen name varied from A. Wolf to L.A. Wolffe and various other spellings. These, I assumed, were his mother's fiction writings. Another shelf held several professional journals, books on medicine, physics, and the stars.

Scattered about among the books were star charts, model planes, trains, and ships. There were shelves and shelves of CDs, and painted canvases of wolves howling. Meticulously carved animals of all types from various woods decorated the room. Clutter of every possible type seemed to fill every nook, cranny, and shelf, depicting years of distractions and hobbies of every kind.

Andrew's bedroom lay through a door at the right side of the room. Decorated in rich blues, the bed had been draped in a blue-jean patchwork quilt. Stars were painted in a mural on the ceiling above the bed. These two rooms abounded with Andrew's life and vitality. Years of hobbies, professional interests, and activities that had served to keep him occupied before we met surrounded me, covering every surface.

"Here we are." Andrew walked over to the desk and looked at some of the papers laying there, giving me a chance to really get a feel for his space. "What do you think?"

"I like it. I can see you spending a lot of time here."

"I did. Now my place is with you." He came up behind me as I read the titles of some of the books on the shelves and drew me back against his chest, kissing my temple. "You're doing much better with my family than I ever hoped. I knew they'd love you. How could they not see what I saw? You're the most beautiful creature in the world."

"I'm fond of your family. I'm kind of jealous of how you grew up. I didn't expect... but I should've known. How could someone as kind and generous as you not be completely loved and accepted by his family?" I closed my eyes and leaned into his touch. "It shocks me every time, but somehow they accept me as I am and they don't judge me for my past. I can't say how much that acceptance means to me. I hope I don't lose it, regardless of how these tests come out."

"The tests are more for Stephon than for acceptance by my family. You just have to get used to it, my love. You're part of this family. My mom will always worry about you, as she worries about me. No matter what the tests say, that won't change." Andrew chuckled.

I bit my lower lip. I couldn't shake the self-preservation instincts I'd honed growing up in foster care, and they all screamed at me that any moment now this dream would end... horribly. I decided to begin with what bothered me the most. The scars on his back had become the personification of vampire evil in my mind, and I needed to know if I was right. I hoped they had nothing to do with his family. "Love, do you mind if I ask you a question?"

"Whatever you want to know, just ask." Andrew swayed from foot to foot as if we were dancing to music only he could hear.

"What happened to you?" I asked solemnly.

Startled, he pulled back a bit in surprise, his arms loosened around me, and I turned around, placed my hand on his shoulders, and looked into his eyes. "What do you mean, what happened to me?"

"Your back, love. You don't grow up the way I did and not know what a beating leaves behind, and those scars aren't just from one beating, but multiple beatings." I tried to keep the pain hidden and my voice even as I slid my hands down his chest and I reached around his waist for the scars on his back, hidden by his T-shirt.

A pained look flashed through his eyes. So he'd noticed the scars I carried that crisscrossed my back as well. He'd never asked for specifics about them, for which I'd been grateful, but I needed to know who'd hurt him. I couldn't imagine his family beating him. I blamed Stephon.

"Oh, don't fret, love. They're from a time long past. Practically a different lifetime." He kissed the worry from my eyes. "Really, they're the result of stupid kid stuff. You aren't the only rebel, you know. I rebelled against everything when I was growing up." Andrew looked into my eyes then sighed when he realized I wouldn't let this go.

"I fought everything. I didn't like the control Stephon had over my life. I behaved like a wild horse, refusing to be tamed. But the only way to live in our world is by acquiescing to the vampires who are our benefactors. My need for freedom, to choose, is the main reason Stephon took me with him to the university. When the pack could no longer discipline me in a way that curbed my self-destructive nature, he took me under his wing personally. He encouraged my education as an outlet for the frustration I felt being tied to the hills and to him. He hoped a wider understanding of the world would help, and it did, truthfully."

"The pack beat you. Your parents beat you," I stated coldly, shocked and astounded.

"No, my parents didn't beat me. But when you become a problem for the pack, which is a much larger group than just my family, you're brought before the pack and they decide guilt and punishment. Some punishments are automatic, based on the crime. Stephon had no choice, once the pack's judgment came down, but to assign the lashes. I don't blame him. My behavior and stupidity resulted in my punishment. I knew the risks, and the penalty. I just didn't care. I felt like a wild animal in a cage too small to comfortably hold it. Stephon tried to show me that I had a great future ahead of me, but I just couldn't see it. All I could see were the bars of the cage. I felt I had no life of my own. Now I'm grateful Stephon stopped me, because otherwise I'd have never met you." Andrew stroked my hair and kissed my temple.

I tried to feel grateful to Stephon, but the more I learned about him, the less I liked him. Everyone justified Stephon's actions, but no matter how you dress up a pig, it was still a pig. I could only loathe him.

"You're such a blessing to me. I don't deserve you." I hid my face in his chest. I didn't want him to see the anger flowing from my eyes. I wanted to kill that vampire and I needed to start figuring out how to do it.

The sun would be going down soon. Andrew's family would want to hunt. I wasn't ready for a group hunt yet.

"Ready to go back to your cottage, my love?" asked Andrew, his mind following along the same paths as my own. He gently pushed my hair back and placed a finger under my chin, then lifted my face so he could look into my eyes.

"Yeah, I'd like to go back to *our* cottage. I'm sure your family will want to hunt soon, and I'm not up for that yet." I laughed tightly, trying to disguise my anger as nerves.

He chuckled softly. "Okay, let's go home." He pulled me up, kissed me once more, then stood, hugging me tightly. We left his rooms and went downstairs. I could almost feel him leaving his youth behind in these rooms. We were going forward—to our home, our cottage. I couldn't describe how loved I felt in that moment, knowing he'd chosen me.

113

His family had assembled on the front lawn. More visitors had arrived while we were upstairs. Seemed I was about to meet some of the extended family members of Andrew's pack. Andrew gripped me tighter, twitching when he saw the visitors. I couldn't be sure, but I thought I saw anger flash from his eyes for a moment.

"Uncle David." Andrew nodded in greeting to a lanky sandy-haired man who stood shaking hands with Max Reed.

"Andrew. Good to see you, my boy." David smiled, peering at me closely.

"Sam! Long time no see." Sam appeared to be a little older than Andrew. He had the same black hair, cut short like Andrew's. His eyes were dark brown and his complexion was the same.

Andrew led me down the stairs of the porch. He pulled me behind him, as if to hide me from the man. At the last minute, he let go and shook hands with David. I hadn't noticed until the minute he let go that the twins had taken up positions on either side of me, almost like guards. Then Andrew grasped my hand again and guided me forward to his side so he could put his arm about my waist. The twins stayed close, flanking him.

"Uncle David, this is my mate, Lance." Andrew's introduction felt very formal, as if he were laying down the ground rules for his uncle's behavior. I smiled at the strange man, a little confused, but I tried to be friendly. I nodded my head shyly in greeting and let my hair fall forward, hiding my face from him. The man glanced at Andrew's armband and grinned widely.

"Wonderful, my boy! Stephon finally found one you liked," the man boomed. Andrew didn't bother to correct him. Andrew's attitude of cool indifference at his uncle's jabs reassured me, but I could tell there wasn't a lot of love between these two.

"Sam, it's so nice to see you. I hope you have a good visit." Andrew's smile for Sam appeared genuine. He actually let go of me long enough to embrace Sam. I heard Andrew whisper, "Ditch our uncle and follow the twins to our cabin. We'll talk."

Sam looked curiously down at the armband on Andrew's arm when he embraced him, touching the braid hanging alongside."It's good to see you too, Andrew. I'm sure it'll be a wonderful visit." Sam winked at us, so we'd know he heard and understood.

"Good night," we said, and I hugged Laura and Angela. The twins punched their brother in the arm.

"Good night, Lance. You're truly good for my son." Max hugged me gently, carefully. If he kept this up, I'd end up liking Max. The man was growing on me, like foot fungus. I wasn't that fond of the man… yet.

With the good-byes done, Andrew and I took off at a comfortable jog to the south and our cottage home.

CHAPTER 7

WE WERE just entering the clearing around the cottage when a beautiful bald eagle flew over the treetops and a pair of sandy wolves bounded into us, almost knocking us to the ground. Andrew and I both laughed as they sprinted ahead to the large log just to the side of the cabin, where the eagle perched.

"Are you ready to go hunting with the twins and Sam?" Andrew asked, smiling at me.

My comfort level was the best with the twins, and my wolf felt okay hunting with them. Sam was an unknown, but there was no getting around the affection Andrew had for his cousin. I had to try, so I nodded and smiled in return. I thought I might actually enjoy running and playing in the woods with the twins in our wolf forms. I could ignore an eagle overhead.

Andrew went into the cabin and brought out three pairs of sweatpants. Before my eyes, the wolves became Jack and Joe, and the eagle appeared to unfold from itself into Sam. There was much arm punching and rough housing as male bonding abounded between the cousins. I could see from the look in Andrew's eyes how deeply he cared about his cousin. But, of course, he'd never actually come out and say it openly. Punching Sam in the shoulder and being punched back was so much easier. "Hi, Sam. Welcome." I extended my hand. I wanted this person my Andrew cared about to like me.

"So you're the one who stole my cousin's heart." He scowled at me, but it was obvious he was teasing as a grin lit his face. He took my hand and shook it firmly, then punched me ritualistically in the shoulder as well. "Good for you. I've never seen him so happy. Thank you." He laughed boisterously as Andrew blushed red. Sam had just become one of my favorite people, his kind gesture endearing him to me.

"Thank you so much, but he makes me just as happy," I boldly announced. I ended up blushing at my own words, as Andrew pulled me back into his arms. When had I become this blushing bride? Why did my nerve always fail me when it came to talking about emotions? I wanted to growl at my own idiotic reaction.

Just then, Jack and Joe froze, their attention focused at the tree line. "What the—" the twins said simultaneously.

Andrew spun and dropped into a defensive crouch, pushing me to the ground partially beneath him. His body rippled with his transformation as his face elongated and claws sprouted from his fingers. I saw the intruders asthey stepped out of the trees, coming slowly toward the cottage, into *my* meadow. There were two of them; one dressed all in black leather with swords strapped across his back. The other wore jeans and a black T-shirt but carried machetes instead of swords. Neither one covered their faces. They were pale chalky white with black eyes. They hissed, their open mouths revealing vicious fangs. Blue-black veins radiated out from around their black eyes, standing out against their white skin.

They both crouched defensively and drew their weapons. Their fingers, tipped in claws shaped like talons, appeared as deadly as the weapons they carried. They were clearly vampires, possibly drones, in some sort of hunting form. Their appearance only vaguely reminded me of Dr. Carlson. I suddenly realized I needed to transform. My wolf would be much better equipped to handle these warriors than me. The wolf was more aware than me. He pushed his way to the fore, rending my clothes in the process—a minor inconvenience as far as the wolf was concerned. The others were already in their animal forms as I belatedly joined them.

The two vampires approached slowly, swinging their weapons. They walked in a semicrouch, hissing, moving around to take opposite sides. They appeared to glide across the ground, looking for a way around Andrew, who had taken point. They hissed and snarled as they searched for openings. Clearly, they were trying to get to me.

The twins stayed on either side of me, taking up my defense. Sam hovered above, intently watching each move the advancing vampires made. Andrew growled viciously.

His snarls sent chills down my spine. Fear rolled from me in waves, but my wolf was mightily pissed. How dare they come here and invade my meadow, threaten my pack and my Andrew? My wolf forced me past my fear and filled me with his rage.

I was changing again, but I didn't know I could modify my wolf form; my fangs grew longer and my mouth filled with saliva. It dripped from my teeth as if I were venomous.My claws were thicker, longer, and sharper. My fur stood on end, a ridge going down my neck, over my shoulders all the way down along my tail. I felt larger, heavier than I'd been before. My wolf wouldn't let anything happen to Andrew or our little brothers. To him, the twins were barely more than cubs, regardless of the fact that they were older than me. Their wolves were smaller, their bodies clearly as adolescent as their fifteen-year-old-appearing human forms. I tried to push past Jack, who stood between me and one of the advancing vampires, but he wouldn't let me past him. I growled at him, but waited. Jack thought he needed to protect me, but my wolf was far stronger and more powerful. I'd never felt such aggression in all my life. My wolf wanted the invaders dead.They were no match for us. He said we didn't need the help of the others to destroy them.

The drones attacked incredibly fast. Andrew and Joe charged the vampire on the right.

I could hear the drones hissing and snapping their teeth, and the whistle of steel through the air as their blades slashed at someone I loved. I didn't have time to look. Sam dove for the vampire in front of me, talons extended like knife blades, his wings flapping, battering at its face, while Jack attacked from the right. The beast appeared satisfied with his odds, but I was confident that would soon change.

I saw Jack go for the vampire's legs. I attacked just as the monster swung his swords down toward Jack, catching him on the shoulder. I heard the bone and muscles crunch and snap. I heard Jack's yelp of pain. The creature never had the chance to get his swords back up, to defend himself. I had it by the throat, my wolf snarling as we bit down hard. My teeth met more resistance than I'd experienced with any prey we'd ever hunted before. My teeth rent through flesh with more force than I was aware I was capable of, shredding its throat with my fangs. I swung my head, violently snapping the neck of the vampire and ripping his head clear off his body. Jack stared at me in shock for a moment before he crumpled to the ground, his wounded shoulder refusing to hold his weight. I glimpsed the blood running down his leg and onto the ground.

I didn't have time to think. Sam screamed, and I turned to find Andrew and Joe circling the other vampire.

They'd held him at bay but were trying to get an opening to cut him down—I wasn't waiting. I lunged straight at him, snarling. When they saw me coming, both Andrew and Jack attacked from either side, each catching an arm above the blades he held. I leaped for the throat, flying through the air like an arrow. I closed my jaws around his neck with a sickening crunch. I knew to expect the resistance this time. I let my weight spin around, carrying me over Andrew and wrenching the vampire's head and neck along with me, decapitating him.

Sam transformed to his human shape and began gathering wood, I assumed for a large bonfire. I couldn't stop snarling, and I watched as Andrew and Joe viciously dismembered the body. I turned around to check on the other vampire. Jack had risen and begun ripping the other vampire viciously apart. I went to help him.

He seemed better initially. At least he was no longer in shock and standing, despite the trail of blood continuing to run down his leg. I went to Jack's side. I was beginning to calm down now that the danger lay in pieces at our feet. Jack ignored me, trying to hide his discomfort, but he could barely put his injured leg to the ground. I whined and he froze, trembling, but he let me look at the wound, rolling his eyes wildly with distress.

The deep gaping laceration seemed to be festering with strange yellow viscous ooze. I could only assume the swords had been treated with poison, or the metal itself was dangerous to shape-shifters. Before I realized what I was going to do, my wolf licked along the bloody gash. Jack groaned and my wolf began seriously laving the wound, cleaning it of the yellow ooze. To my astonishment, my saliva cleaned and sealed Jack's injury. I watched as it began to heal right before my eyes. Andrew and Joe had transformed. They stood beside me, staring as the raw edges knit themselves together, the bone and sinew reforming until even his fur coat had grown back together, almost like he'd never been struck. In seconds, the only proof of his injury was a faint white line of fur marring his perfect sandy blond coat.

Sam gathered the body parts of the vampires and threw them into the raging fire, weapons and all. Having seen the poison in Jack's shoulder, they handled the weapons with great care. Everything went up in flames. The vile scent of burning vampire flesh—it smelled like burning sugar, tar, and diesel fuel combined—made my eyes burn and water. Sam had ringed the pyre with large rocks to prevent the fire from getting out of hand and becoming a threat to the surrounding forest. We all moved upwind, to the front of the cottage, to get away from the stench drifting to the west.

I went into the cottage and transformed. Andrew came in behind me, just in time to catch me before I crumpled to the floor. With an arm around my waist, he steadied me on my feet.

"I'm good," I assured him, but he didn't look convinced. Fatigue and shock were starting to set in as the adrenaline wore off. We went to the bedroom. I grabbed a pair of sweatpants and a T-shirt for myself and got dressed, while Andrew did the same. He grabbed three extra pairs of sweats and went out to his brothers and Sam, who donned them. Shifting was hard on clothes.

I stood by the door, my legs unsteady, leaning against the frame for support, afraid to let go. I shook like a leaf in a hurricane; with the grip I had on the door, I was surprised the cottage remained standing. Andrew came back in, looking for me. He'd thought I was right behind him. He saw me gasping for air. I hadn't realized I couldn't breathe, or how cold I suddenly felt. My mind told me it was shock.

Andrewgently gathered me into his arms. "Shh... it's over. You're safe. We're all safe. Come, see for yourself."

He drew me through the door, holding me upright as I leaned heavily against him. Sam, Joe, and Jack were smiling as he pulled me outside. I couldn't fathom how they could be happy after what had just happened. They were all looking at Jack's scar, a thin white line across his beautiful tan skin, running from the back of his shoulder blade to the top of his shoulder. He sat there grinning as if it was the best present in the world.

"Oh, Jack, I'm so sorry. I didn't realize... I was too slow to stop him." I reached out toward Jack's shoulder, hesitantly reaching for the scar but afraid to touch it. Instead I threw my arms around him and hugged him fiercely. I didn't want to think about what could've happened; if anyone had gotten killed, I'd never be able to forgive myself.

"No worries, Lance, I'm fine. Look what you did, though. That wound should've taken at least twenty-four hours to heal, if it would've healed at all, because of the poison on the sword. But when you cleaned the wound, something in your saliva must've sped up the process, clearing out the poison. I've never heard of one of us having the gift of healing." Jack hugged me back a bit self-consciously and patted me on the back. I let him go and looked questioningly at Andrew, who pulled me back into his arms fiercely. For a moment it looked like he was about to attack his brother, but that couldn't be right. Andrew loved his brothers.

"I don't know. The legends say pureblood shifters were known to heal almost instantly, but maybe it wasn't an ability but something in their saliva that caused the healing. Instant healing is a gift none of us have shown." Andrew scanned the tree line as we talked, watching for any sign of more intruders.

"Well, I guess we can be pretty sure someone somewhere knows about you, Lance. I'm guessing they think you're a threat or know who you are and want revenge." Joe stood very near his twin, as if he couldn't get close enough. They were two parts of a whole, and Joe seemed more upset than Jack, who'd almost been killed.

"We'd better get back to the ranch and tell Mom and Dad what happened." Jack sighed. Fatigue started to show as the adrenaline began to recede. I could see the first telltale signs of shock as he began to pale.

"We'll do a perimeter sweep first and make sure those two were alone, but I'm betting they were. Joe, you go around to the left and I'll go to the right. Jack, you head to the ranch and tell your folks to expect us." Sam watched Jack closely. I could tell he wanted to get Jack moving so they could get him home before he fell asleep on his feet. I felt myself sagging too, my will to stand having fled while they were talking. I swayed slightly and Andrew was there with a steadying hand.

"I can run," Jack complained.

"I know you can, but there are three of us and three jobs. Your parents need to be warned so they can search the ranch to make sure no one's hiding there," Sam said with conviction. We all nodded, but it was obvious that Jack felt railroaded; he growled softly. "I'll be back in the morning, Andrew." They all stripped, transformed, and were gone before I could thank them for risking their lives for my sake.

Andrew kept an arm firmly around my waist as he led me toward the door, but we didn't go in until Sam screamed an "all clear" and had headed down the road toward the ranch, flying just above Joe. Once inside, Andrew brought me straight to our bathroom. I vaguely remember him scrubbing me from head to toe, removing all trace of blood and gore that covered us both, before drying us and leading me into our bedroom. We lay down on the soft cool comforter. He pulled me up halfway across his chest, so my head rested on his shoulder, and he gently smoothed my hair back out of my face.

"I love you," I sighed in a whisper, as my eyes closed. I couldn't fight it any longer. He kissed the top of my head. Every once in a while I would feel him kiss my nose or my head, or run his fingertips along the side of my face, like he was afraid someone might snatch me away from him or I'd shatter into a million pieces.

The nightmares came back with a vengeance. This time Andrew and I stood back to back, surrounded by black-clad vampires with black dead eyes. Still the evil laughter rang. When would my subconscious be done with that damn vile laughter? The vampires attacked us with whips and swords. I tried to defend Andrew, but I was too slow, as if I were moving in molasses. They cut sliced Andrew's throat from ear to ear. I screamed.

I awoke to find Andrew clutching me to his chest in the darkness of our bedroom. He rocked me gently, crooning softly. I relaxed immediately and began to feel better. Fearfully he looked into my eyes, but when my clear gaze met his, he relaxed and love replaced the fear.

"I'm okay. Really." I stroked his face. He didn't seem convinced, but we managed to go back to sleep. I slept peacefully the rest of the night, safe in Andrew's arms.

CHAPTER 8

MORNING arrived clear and blue. Lying on my stomach, with my head resting on my forearms, I could see the sky through the window over the bed. The morning blue had nothing on Andrew's eyes. I slowly realized I lay alone, in an empty bed—I could hear the sound of the shower running. Getting up, I went to the kitchen. The mess from the previous day had disappeared. Andrew had also begun a load of laundry. I felt sure sweatpants were in great demand. I hoped Andrew's family owned stock in both the sweatpants and T-shirt industries.

He'd thought of everything; hot water awaited me in the teapot on the stove. I stretched and decided I wasn't quite ready for tea yet. I debated joining Andrew in the shower. Smiling to myself, I decided against it, but maybe I could just tease him a bit. I crept into the bathroom, but the glass shower was empty. He jumped out from behind me. I squealed and spun around into his arms. *Did I just squeak?* I thought to myself.*Damn, how embarrassing.*

Laughing, he picked me up off my feet and tried to kiss me good morning. I gently pulled away, putting a hand against my mouth and making a face. He laughed. I needed to brush my teeth, and badly, before I'd be ready for kisses. With a loving smile, he pushed me toward the shower and left me to my morning ablutions.

While I washed my hair and body, I thought about the attempt on my life. I could only come up with one person who could want me dead, and who knew I was here—*Stephon*. But I might still have a chance. If the genetic tests and his dead assassins could prove I was from a strong bloodline, maybe he'd reconsider and decide I was good enough for Andrew. I mean, it wasn't as if we were a breeding pair. Stephon just needed to be shown that I wasn't a misfit.

The stronger the shifter, the better the bloodline. Strong shifters could take more than one shape, so if I could take on a second shape that would prove I was a strong shifter and came from respectable pedigree.

If I could choose to become something besides the wolf, what form would be most useful? I mean, the wolf was great. I liked him a lot, but he chose me, not the other way around. I liked the idea of having wings. If Andrew were forced to leave, I'd easily be able to follow him on the wind. But on the other hand, the idea of being a large feline also had merit. I'd be very impressive and imposing as a lion, or a tiger, maybe. I vaguely wondered if I could somehow do both. Andrew had said some could do two forms, but he hadn't mentioned three. The wolf seemed to think we could do both, but I'd settle for achieving one more... today. I got out of the shower, dried off, andwrapped the towel around my waist. I brushed my teeth and combed out my hair as I debated with myself which form to try. When I turned around to head for the bedroom and some clean clothes, there stood Andrew in the doorway, watching me with a hungry look in his eyes, my clothes forgotten in his hands.

I strutted slowly over to him, took my clothes, stretched up on my toes, and brushed my lips against his lips for a proper, lingering, passionate good-morning kiss. I could feel the shivers it sent along Andrew's body. I chuckled softly. "What are we doing today, my love?" I sighed into Andrew's open mouthas he groaned.

"You, my love, are dangerous." Hestroked my bare arms as he struggled to control himself, even as he continued to touch my body. I chortled, enjoying the reaction his body had to mine. I turned him around and pushed him from the room so I could get dressed, although part of me ached to be touched. *Seriously, you lean into him... he squeezes your ass... you go screaming into the sunset. Not exactly romantic.* My sarcastic internal voice was unfortunately right.

There was no way I could have sex with Andrew, no matter how much I wanted to. I could see no way around my past—as if the nightmares weren't proof enough of my messed-up and broken state.

I quickly dressed then went back out to the kitchen, pulling my thick hair back. I couldn't believe how long it was getting. It had grown well past my shoulders. I drew it into three sections and braided it into a thick plait that hung between my shoulder blades, then secured it with a rubber band at the base. The stereo played a background of soft eighties rock while Andrew cooked breakfast. I grabbed a leftover muffin and some tea while he fried eggs and flipped pancakes. He had a large stack on the table already and bacon waiting on a plate, covered with a paper towel to keep it warm.

"We need to see Dr. Carlson for those test results today. Sam should be here shortly. I don't know what he has in mind, especially after last night," Andrew said as he continued to cook.

"Why don't you spend the morning with Sam and find out what he wants to do? I'll stay here at the cottage. There's plenty to keep me busy. I have laundry to do and I can relax a bit before facing people again." I gave him my most relaxed smiled. He looked at me warily, concern coloring his eyes.

"All the people—my family has been a big stress factor for you, and now the attack last night. I suppose you could use a little alone time," he agreed ruefully, but he seemed to be drawing away as if he feared I intended to kick him out. I stood and draped myself around him, hugging him tightly.

"I don't need time away from you. But I do need some time to try and adjust to everything that's happened." I reached up on tiptoe and kissed him again, then sat back down in my chair at the table. "You and Sam can come back for lunch, and then we can go see Dr. Carlson and get the test results. We can even check in on the twins and make sure Jack's doing okay. I know you want to spend time with Sam. You haven't seen him in a while."

Andrew still seemed unconvinced. He appeared divided. He didn't want to leave me alone, but wanted to spend time with Sam. I knew he wanted to talk strategy and theories about who might be behind this. He wouldn't want to hear my opinion, because I believed it had to be Stephon.

"I don't want to leave you alone," he admitted, leaning across the table to kiss me. "I'll worry about you the entire time we're apart."

"I'll howl if I need you and you can come running. I know you need quality time with Sam, and I'm trying to be okay with that. I like Sam and you love him. Which, I admit, my wolf hates."

"We grew up together. He's like another brother."

"If my wolf had his way, you'd never leave this house. Ever." I voiced my possessive feelings. Andrew snickered, obviously enjoying my possessiveness. "But I'm an adult and I know you love me. I promise I won't leave. I'll be here when you come back. Or, if I get bored or my wolf thinks you and Sam have bonded enough, I'll come and find you. My nose works too, you know," I teased.

"You're sure?"

"Yes. Look, it's nothing against you, Sam, or your family. I just really could use a little time to myself, especially if you want me to be surrounded by your family and the doctor this afternoon."

"If you're sure you'll be okay," he conceded reluctantly.

"I'll be fine."

A knock at the door interrupted our conversation.

Andrew rose and answered it. He clapped Sam on the shoulder and invited him in.

"Hi, Sam." I rose and gave him a friendly one-armed hug, then went into the bedroom to start gathering clothes and towels for laundry. I hummed happily to myself as I gathered things together.

Sam and Andrew visited quietly out in the kitchen. I could practically feel how uncomfortable Andrew was talking about the attack where I could hear him, but he didn't want to leave either. He stood where he could see me as I moved around the bedroom making the bed and tidying up. They chatted while Sam dug into a plate of pancakes and eggs. I went into the bathroom and started cleaning the shower. I wiped the glass walls down, removing the spots and streaks. Maybe it seemed a little OCD to be cleaning a brand-new shower, but I liked bathrooms to be clean. I could still hear their conversation—God bless wolf hearing—but Andrew could no longer see me as I worked.

As their conversation began to get more in-depth and speculative, I heard Andrew shifting restlessly from foot to foot. Finally, satisfied that I intended to fuss about with chores, Andrew came into the bathroom,pulled me out of the shower, and into his arms so he could kiss me soundly.

"Okay, Sam and I are going on a run around the hills. We're going to do some tracking to see if we can find any clues about where our visitors came from. We'll probably be a couple of hours. If you need me, howl, and I'll come at a dead run. Or you come looking for us. I don't like leaving you, even for a little while." His eyes were full of concern.

"You worry too much. I can take care of myself, which I think I proved quite nicely last night." I ran my hand down the side of his beautiful face and cupped his jaw gently. "Go, enjoy being with your cousin. Do your tracking. Have some fun, while you're at it. You remember fun, it's where you laugh and play around instead of frowning and worrying all the time." I all but kicked him out the door after Sam.

He growled softly, but pulled himself away, then shed his clothes in the kitchen. I heard the eagle scream and Andrew's wolf bark as they took off on their adventure. I quickly finished the shower and started the laundry. After that, I cleaned up the kitchen and removed the ashes from the fireplace. Then I went outside and removed my own clothes.

Okay, I thought to my wolf. *You choose—feline or bird*. The wolf chose feathers, and the pain began in my stomach. I kept the idea of feathers in my mind, focusing on wings. The wolf told me they should be black feathers. I trusted him and pictured the black feathers in my mind's eye. I felt myself folding in on myself, getting smaller, as I'd seen Sam do. The feathers were prickly as they sprouted along my arms. But nothing prepared me for the eerie sensation of my bones going hollow. I closed my eyes because I didn't like how my vision seemed to mutate. My hands disappeared and my shoulders folded back on themselves. When the pain finally stopped, I stood still, wobbly, on two feet. I'd succeeded. My bird trembled and panted through an open beak, the stress of transformation hard for the bird's system. I didn't know what kind of bird I was, but guessing from the talons and hooked beak, I was probably a raptor of some kind. I was a rather large bird. I examined my wings and tail, running my beak through my feathers, giving my wings a couple of test flaps. I realized I'd forgotten to ask Sam if he knew how to fly or had to learn how, but the wolf—or rather bird, knew we could fly. He screamed, the call echoing across the treetops. We opened our wings and took two hopping leaps and then, with a downward flap of enormous black wings, I rose into the air.

Flight came to the bird as easily as running did to the wolf. I felt free and exhilarated. I could fly! I'd completed the shift into another animal! Andrew would be floored, but I hoped in a good way. I rose above the trees, looking for the bald eagle. I knew Andrew would be with Sam and I had to share this with him. I spotted Sam soaring on the updrafts. He circled lazily above a beautiful white-gray wolf. Even though they were miles away, I could see the wolf's blue eyes. Gotta love birds' eyes. I called and flew straight for them.

I flew as fast as I could, until I soared above the bald eagle. I called down to him, and he, curious about me, rose on the air currents to meet me. I found I could fly circles around him. I was smaller than Sam, but not by much. My wings were shaped a bit differently, making me faster. I flipped over to look at him and then back around under him. He clucked, laughing at my playfulness. I screamed, calling down to the wolf below. I tucked my wings and dove toward the wolf. I buzzed over his head, laughing, a jeering sound coming from my bird. The bald eagle followed after me. I landed smoothly, touching down with grace, before I realized I had no idea how to land. My bird laughed at me; I could fly, so of course I could land. I hopped slowly forward to the wolf with my wings folded against my body, bobbing my head a bit nervously. Looking up at the wolf, I considered for the first time the possibility that I could get myself eaten. The wolf cocked his head at me curiously, growling a warning to keep my distance. The bald eagle transformed into Sam.

"It's a black falcon. They're very rare, if not extinct. I've never actually seen one. I have no idea what he's doing here. Where could he have come from?" asked Sam.

Andrew transformed. "I've no idea, but he's beautiful."

"Look at those vivid markings, solid black except for the white on his chest, and check out those flight feathers—they look tipped in blood." I hopped closer to Andrew, getting right next to him. I cocked my head up to look into his sky-blue eyes and clucked, practically willing him to recognize me. *How do I tell him who I am?* I couldn't transform back yet.

"He must be from a sanctuary or a zoo," Sam said, looking at the falcon. "Unless… you don't think…."

"What…?" Andrew asked, confused. He reached out to me carefully. I put my head in his hand and clucked softly.

"Could he—? Could he—he have done it? No, he couldn't have…." Sam looked closely at Andrew, shock in his voice. His eyes had gotten huge as he looked from Andrew to me. Andrew had the bird's head snuggled into his hand. "Lance…."

I screeched and bobbed my head when he said my name.

"Oh! Lance!" Andrew exclaimed, shocked. "What did you do!"

My bird… a falcon, evidently… laughed and dipped my head to the side. I pranced around in a circle so he could see all of me. I wanted him to be happy and proud. I was thrilled with my achievement.

Andrew held out his arm to me. I knew I'd need to be very careful with my talons. I hopped up onto his arm with my wings partially outstretched to help me balance. He winced slightly at first, as if he expected the claws to pierce his arm, but I held on carefully with the pads of my talons, not the claws. He lifted me carefully, working with my balance. He watched as I adjusted my grip, keeping the sharp claws away from the flesh of his bare arm. My balance wasn't as sure as I would've liked, but keeping my wings partially open seemed to help. To grip his arm any tighter would've drawn blood.

"Yep, definitely Lance. Any other bird, even one raised in captivity, would've shredded the flesh from your arm by now with their talons," Sam commented. My falcon agreed with Sam, and a strange jeering clucking noise came from my throat.

"Sam, have you ever heard of one of us being able to pull off two shapes within the first six months of our first transformation?" Andrew asked, a fearful note in his voice.

"Never. Something like that would've been way before my time," Sam replied thoughtfully. "I'd say you're right. He's very special indeed."

I rubbed my face on Andrew's chest again. He turned to me then. "Go back to the cottage, please, love. I don't have wings. I can't find you if you get lost." My falcon found his fear of us getting lost amusing and a jeering clucking sound erupted from my throat.

"He's laughing at you, you know," Sam said, a huge smile on his face. "You have no idea how hard it would be to get lost as a falcon. He can see for miles and miles."

"I'll be home soon. Please, for me?" Andrew sighed tiredly. I rubbed my face against his chest, cooing softly. Then pushing against his arm, I launched myself into the air. I thought he'd be happy I could transform into a second shape. But he almost seemed more troubled than before. Sam flew right behind me. But he was a larger bird and he couldn't keep up with me, although he could float endlessly on the thermals and I had to work at it. I watched the progress of the wolf below. The bald eagle twisted and spun in the air.

I spiraled and dove. I wanted to be closer to Andrew. I folded my wings and dove down below the treetops to fly directly over him. He ran full speed and I easily kept up with him, dodging the trees and branches as easily as he dodged the hedges and jumped logs. I raced above him, screaming my joy at our race. When we poured out of the trees into the clearing around the cottage, Sam had already landed, changed, and put on clothes. I landed easily on the dead tree by the fire pit. I felt exhilarated. Flying was truly an expression of freedom. Running as the wolf felt wonderful, but flying felt like freedom.

Andrew transformed in front of the house and put on his clothes. He grabbed a couple towels, wrapped them around his arm so I wouldn't have to be quite so careful, and extended his arm for me. I hopped on, still being careful, knowing my talons could rip the towels with ease. I didn't want to hurt him.

"He won't be able to transform back yet, Andrew. He needs to spend some time in this skin. You know how it works.Maybe in a couple more hours he'll be able to change back."

The falcon in me agreed with Sam. I bobbed my head at Sam's words.

"I know you're right. He just has me freaked out. He shouldn't be able to do this, Sam."

"Let's take him down to your parents' place. Your dad's been around a lot longer than I have. Let's see what he thinks."

"Is Uncle David still here? He can't see this, not yet."

"No, he left shortly after you and Lance did yesterday. I think he was sent to check up on you. Stephon probably wanted to know if you really had found your mate."

"Okay, then let's go see Dad."

Andrew raised his arm and I launched myself back into the air and circled above the cottage. Andrew briefly went inside, then returned with some clothes for me. After nodding to Sam, they ran toward the ranch. I floated in easy circles above their heads until they entered the woods, then I flew in close, just above their heads, like I had with the wolf. I liked being close. I tried to fly as close to Andrew as I could without getting into his way. "He's going to crash!" Andrew exclaimed, alarmed by my progress through the branches as I zoomed along above their heads.

"Not likely." Sam laughed. "He's playing. This is for him like dodging trees is for you in your wolf form." I screamed my joy.

"He's really enjoying himself. I'd say he's rather proud of himself too."

"He's magnificent." Andrew sighed with longing. I cocked an eye at him and flew so my flight feathers gently brushed against his arm as I glided through the trees at his side. He looked lovingly at me as my wing grazed his arm.

We emerged from the forest and entered the yard at the ranch. Andrew hollered for his father at the top of his lungs. I screamed my falcon's call. The family came running from all corners of the ranch. Sam and Andrew stopped running, and I glided in to land lightly on Andrew's wrapped arm. My balance seemed to be getting much better with practice. His mom and dad stood stunned, staring at the falcon. They had probably expected to see Sam in eagle form after hearing the scream. When they saw the black falcon perched on their son's arm, everyone looked decidedly confused. The twins looked at each other with knowing grins; they were the first to realize the black falcon was me.

"We have news to share with everyone. Lance has discovered he's more than a wolf. You're looking at his second form. According to Sam, he's a black falcon." Andrew's smile faltered as he looked to his dad for reassurance. "Dad, have you ever in your life come across someone who could take two shapes after only a couple months?"

"Son, the only ones able pull that off were the purebloods, and some of them would have struggled to pull off multiple shifts before six months. I don't know what to tell you. This is unprecedented. There are cases of the royal family being able to do it almost immediately from the time of their first shift. I wonder if Dr. Carlson knows any more about Lance's parents? If he has royal blood in his family, it could explain this talent."

I screeched in surprise, my talons tightening reflexively in shock on Andrew's arm, but I loosened them just as quickly when I felt him wince slightly. I just wanted to prove I was good enough for Andrew, not scare him or turn out to be a part of the royal bloodline.

"I think I'll go call Dr. Carlson and see if he has the results of the test yet." Max chuckled, going into the house.

Andrew and Sam sat on the front porch, talking to the rest of the family, as I felt my muscles beginning to relax. I could feel the ability to transform back into myself creeping closer. The falcon felt confident and pleased with himself, telling me we could be anything we wanted to be. I believed him. I felt a confidence I had never known before. I could feel the urge to shift to the cat, but I knew I'd be able to make the shift whenever I chose. I wanted to get good at being the falcon first, and then I'd try the cat. Andrew was my first priority; I needed to reassure him that I was all right. He seemed very upset, which further amused my falcon. He told me Andrew held himself back unnecessarily. Andrew was ours and he could be anything he wanted to be too, if he would just talk to his wolf. According to my falcon, Andrew and his wolf limited themselves unnecessarily.

I rubbed against Andrew's chest and clucked my tongue, looking at my clothes in his other arm and then at the house. I rubbed my head against his chest again.

"I'm guessing he's ready to change back. His grip on my arm's relaxing. I'm going to take him in," Andrew walked into the house and up the stairs to his bedroom. I gingerly let go of his arm and hopped onto the bed. He piled my clothes beside me and then went out to the office while I transformed and dressed.

I felt like I exploded out of my falcon as my joints righted themselves and the feathers receded, everything expanding internally. My legs lengthened and bones solidified. I slowly resumed my human shape. I remembered to close my eyes, because the visual changes were truly nauseating. My shift only took a couple minutes, although it felt like much longer. The pain I felt was hard to explain—it hurt like muscles and joints being worked in ways they hadn't been in years. Dull, sometimes stabbing pain, but not like the first change I'd made into a wolf. Once again human, I took a deep breath, filling my lungs with air,and stretched my arms and legs. I felt like I had been crammed into a box or wearing clothing that was way too small. Yes, the falcon would take some getting used to, but the freedom to fly was well worth it.

I quickly dressed and went to Andrew. When he saw me come out of the bedroom, he immediately rushed over and clutched me to him. He was terrified, literally trembling, as the waves of his fear washed over me.

"What's wrong, my love? Why're you so scared?" I asked him, holding him just as tightly to me as I could, trying to reassure him.

"You don't understand how rare what you're doing is. Love— it's so dangerous. Some of us change and are never able to return to human. They lose themselves in the animal. One shape is one thing, but a second? What if you couldn't find your way back?" He shuddered involuntarily. "You'd be stuck as a falcon and I couldn't fly with you. We would be forever separated."

"Shh… I'm fine. I'm here. I'm not going anywhere."

"But you might have gotten lost in the bird. Why…why did you do this?"

"I needed to find a way… I had to be able to prove that I could be worthy to be with you."

"You're my *leannan*. You have nothing to prove. Please don't do this again. You have no idea how terrified I was that you would just fly away… that you'd be gone."

"Love, you should know, you've been what we are much longer than I have. You do know your wolf, don't you? You listen to him? Talk to him?" I asked Andrew softly. I led him to a large leather chair. He sat down and pulled me onto his lap. "My wolf is very sure of himself. He tells me I can run like a wolf and I believe him. He says I can fly and I believe him. He's part of me, yet separate. I trust him."

"I used to hear my wolf, when I was young. He hasn't spoken to me in a very long time, since I became resigned to my servitude. I guess I feel his excitement during the hunt. His joy when he sees you. Most of the time he sleeps." Andrew had a faraway look in his eyes.

135

"Well, my love, I think it's time to wake him up. My wolf—my falcon, they're one and the same. He's always here. Even when I'm human, his voice is there in my head, telling me my limits. He won't let me get lost." My words were filled with the conviction of my animal spirit.

"Just be careful, my love. I couldn't bear to lose you." He crushed me against his chest.

"Can't… breathe… Andrew!" I gasped. He loosened his hold slightly but didn't let go of me.

"My *leannan*, I'll die without you. Please, don't take chances like that with your life. If you feel the need to try another animal, please, at least talk to me first," Andrew begged.

"Okay, Andrew. Before I try another shape, we'll discuss it. I think, in the meantime, you need to wake your wolf and have a couple heart-to-heart conversations with him. My wolf seems to think you underestimate yourself greatly. He's sure you could fly if you wanted to." I smiled into his eyes and ran my fingers through his hair.

"Yeah?"

"Yes. I think you would like flying. There's nothing like it. The closest comparison I can make is that it's like pure freedom."

"I'd like that."

"Do you think this will do it? Do you think I'll be able to prove myself good enough to stay? I'm so afraid Stephon or someone will try to take you away from me, and I'd do anything to be able to stay with you."

He suddenly looked very tired. "You did this, risked your life, because you're afraid you won't be seen as worthy of me?" I saw his incredulity in his eyes. "Lance, you're so far beyond worthy of me I'm sure they'll try to take you away, because I can't keep up with you. None of us will be your equal. There will be a line for miles just to get the chance to pass by, in case you might find something even remotely interesting and catch your attention."

"No! I don't want anyone else!"

"As soon as the word gets out—I don't even want to think…."

I couldn't prevent my shock. How could he even think I'd be interested in anyone but him? "Andrew, I don't care who or what parades past. I see only you. You're my life. You are my love."

"It won't matter, they will still come."

"Don't you knowyou are my angel?" I shook my head. "You are the only one who ever saw me and tried to help...t-to even attempt to heal me. No one else matters but you." I clutched him to me. I shook my head in disbelief. How could I, a runaway with a bloody past, even begin to measure up to Andrew? I sighed, running my fingers over the armband. "This tells everyone that you're mine. Nothing and no one will make me change my mind. I've just wanted to be good enough for you."

"You are, and so much more."

"Let's go see what your dad's found out from Dr. Carlson. Then I want to get you home, my love. You look exhausted," I said, concerned, as I stroked his face gently.

"I'm sorry. I didn't rest much last night. I watched you sleep instead. I was so worried about you and the attack. Then you had such awful nightmares. Now I guess I worried about all the wrong things."

"I'm fine, Andrew, really. Let's go, okay? I love you." I held him close to me.

I stoodand pulled him to his feet, then led him downstairs and out to the front porch. The whole family was pelting Sam with questions about my falcon as we arrived.

"Like I said, black falcons were considered messengers of the Egyptian god Horus, who had the head of a falcon and the body of a man," Sam explained.

"Hi, everyone," I said, my cheeks flushed with embarrassment as everyone stared at me.

"How are you feeling, Lance?" asked Laura, her voice full of concern, coming over to put a hand on my shoulder and give me a little hug.

"I'm fine, just a little stiff."

"I bet," Sam said, shaking his head.

"What's the news from Dr. Carlson?" Andrew asked, looking at Max.

"He said the results from the tests are in, and he wants to talk to all of us. He said he would come up to your cottage tomorrow with the rest of us, in the morning. He said there's a lot to talk about." Max smiled at me.

"Okay, then we'll see you all tomorrow morning." We said our good-byes and were passed around for hugs.

When Jack pulled me in for a hug, he slipped something small into my left hand with a wink. "See you tomorrow morning, brother," he said, snickering.

Andrew looked almost angry with his brother. Jack just cuffed him on the arm and grinned at him. We took off at a wolf trot back toward the cottage. We ran easily together, but we didn't speak, the silence comfortable between us. Andrew seemed lost in thought, so very far away. I feared interrupting him before he was ready to talk.

I gingerly fingered what Jack had put in my hand. A small ring. My platinum ring! I could finish Andrew's necklace now. I smiled to myself, thrilled I could complete his present. I slipped the ring into my jeans pocket.

When we got to the cottage, afternoon had turned to evening. I pushed Andrew into a chair and began taking food from the refrigerator. He watched me, attempting to help.

"This time, love, you sit. I'll cook." I made him a cup of coffee and then went back to making dinner. I found some chicken breasts, cut them into pieces, and made chicken fried rice and egg drop soup. I hummed and worked carefully, cleaning up behind myself as I went. His gaze never left me as I buzzed about the kitchen. When I came into range, he'd grab me and pull me to him for a kiss, then let me go. I filled a plate for him, put the extra soy sauce on the table, and ladled the soup into bowls.

I went to sit in my usual chair across from him, but he pulled me onto his lap and proceeded to try to feed me. I laughed so hard after the second forkful of scattered rice that he gave up and handed me the fork. It's an odd thing to want to feed your lover. For

Andrew, it was his Alpha nature screaming at him to provide for me. His wolf needed to prove he could still take care of me. That I hadn't left him behind. I kissed him, put the fork down, and picked up a pair of chopsticks I had made myself, and sat next to my plate. I positioned the sticks and gingerly scooped up the fried rice and fed it to him.

"How do you do that?" he said, astonished.

"Do what?"

"Continue to surprise me at every turn."

"Just lucky, I guess." I grinned and licked a piece of rice from the corner of his mouth. I fed him and myself, snickering when he took the chopsticks from me and attempted to use them, with disastrous results as he sent rice flipping across the tabletop. We both enjoyed the soup. He'd finally begun to relax, but occasionally he stared off into the distance, focused on troubles he kept to himself. I wouldn't be satisfied until I could keep his focus firmly on me instead of problems neither of us could solve. We both needed rest. Too much had happened lately, and we were both struggling to cope.

I didn't want a mess left for later, so I cleaned up the kitchen, then went into the bathroom and turned the water on in the tub. I hid the ring in the armoire, with the rest of the necklace that had been awaiting that one piece to make it whole. When I returned to the kitchen, he still sat where I'd left him. He stared in my direction but didn't appear to see me.

Andrew looked so tired. So much had happened since his return—it felt like weeks, but had been only days. Exhausted from his trip back from Stephon's and not having slept the night before because of the attack, my love was in danger of making himself ill.

His gaze followed me as I turned the stereo on. I had no idea what CD was in the player, but I just let it play, turning up the volume. I took him by the hand and led him into the bathroom. Andrew's preference in music was jazz or rhythm and blues; either would go well with a steamy bath. He stood in the bathroom, looking around like he'd gotten here by mistake somehow. I smiled mischievously up at him and took off his shirt. I recognized the

139

second song, by the funky divas of soul, En Vogue, and began singing along as I divested him of his clothing, swaying with him slowly back and forth to "Giving Him Something He Can Feel." I helped him out of his pants. He wore no underwear, and I could see I definitely had his complete attention now. I pushed him toward the tub as I danced around the bathroom while the divas crooned. Andrew groaned slightly as he eased into the hot water. I danced over to the cabinet, took out bath salts, flipped the switch on the wall that turned on the whirlpool jets, then returned to the tub and poured in the salts.

I never realized I could be such an exhibitionist, but I enjoyed having him watch me. I held a sponge on a handle and lip-synched with the divas, pretending the sponge was my microphone. He chuckled, a leering grin on his face, his gaze riveted on me as I sang and twirled, suggestively stroking my hands across my chest. I sashayed my hips slowly in time to the music, making a fool of myself, but enjoying myself nonetheless because of the hungry look that filled Andrew's eyes. I bent over and pretended to draw the sponge up my leg, tossed my hair, and glanced over my shoulder at him. I slowly two-stepped back across the bathroom, sponge in hand, and rubbed it slowly down his chest while standing beside the tub. He made a grab for me. I turned quickly out of his reach, wagging a finger, and shook my head.

I began slowly pulling my shirt loose from my jeans, starting to take it off but mostly dancing and singing. The music changed as Queen Latifah crooned "I Put a Spell on You" while I continued to move. I rolled my hips, shifting back and forth, just out of his reach, teasing him with my entire body. He watched me, his mouth half open, sweeping his tongue across his bottom lip as he moved to stretch out along the back bench of the half sunken tub. He groaned and began to stroke himself below the surface of the water. The shirt came off over my head, and I played with it, rubbing the soft cotton over my stomach before tossing it into the corner with his clothes. I began to play with the button fly on my jeans, popping each button in time to the beat of the music and then easing them down around my hips and to the floor, my ass in the air, continuing to sway from side to side with the music.

I got down on the floor on all fours before him and slowly inched closer to the tub. My briefs—now the only thing between me and the last dregs of coy modesty I'd decided to give up before coming into the bathroom—displayed my enjoyment for him to see, as my erection pressed against the cotton barrier. Teasing him seemed to be an aphrodisiac for me, making me feel like a god, as I strutted my stuff just out of his reach. Once I got just a touch too close, he lunged for me a second time. I dodged, not missing a beat in the dance. I shook my finger at him again, smiling wickedly. I totally enjoyed playing the tormenter, and I couldn't get enough of the hungry looks Andrew sent me. He slowly moved to sit at the back of the tub again.

Another jazzy number, and I weaved and gyrated slowly toward the tub. I slid onto the tiled ledge and perched there. I arched my body and watched his eyes bug out of his head. I laughed and kicked the water at him with my toes in little splashes. That was it— he couldn't take anymore. With a growl, he grabbed me and pulled me into the tub, creating his own mini tsunami across the bathroom floor. Water went everywhere. He held me and kissed me until my skin burned. I had his undivided attention. I panted under the onslaught of his intense kisses.

"You are so dangerous, my love—God, Lance," he groaned, holding me pressed between him and the edge of the tub. I could feel his hard cock rubbing against mine through the wet cotton of my underwear.

"You think so?" I laughed a heady laugh. I still hadn't caught my breath, and with his erection grinding against my own, my senses began to overload as I struggled to hold on to his wet arms.

"Oh, most definitely. You drive me to distraction. When you're around, you push all other thoughts from my head." Andrew panted as his heated gaze penetrated the haze that was beginning to wrap around my senses.

"That was kind of the point, my love. You needed distraction."

141

"Well, you succeeded, because all I see is you." His kissed me, sending a line of fire from my ear down my neck to my collarbone. Desperately pulling at my underwear, we worked them off, allowing them to sink to the bottom of the tub. Holding our cocks pressed together, Andrew began stroking us both. I moaned and leaned forward, resting my head in the crook of his neck; he nibbled on my earlobe, sending shivers down my spine. I put my hands on his chest, finding his nipples; I pulled on them gently, eliciting a deep groan from Andrew. He thrust his hips up into his tight grip.My hand joined his,moving in synch as we stroked our erections. Panting, unable to control myself, I thrust my hips wildly. I encircled his girth with my hand, sliding along the slick length in time with the rhythm he set, then fisting the head and wrapping around to caress the glans beneath his mushroom cap.

"God, Lance," Andrew gasped as I slipped a finger in the crease of the head of his cock. A tingling sensation built at the base of my spine as my balls drew tight against my body, reaching for a blinding climax.

"Andrew—coming!" I gasped, throwing my head back as I screamed. He followed me; I heard him cry out my name as he continued to stroke us, milking our shafts until the last of the tremors shook our bodies. He groaned and dropped his head back against the edge of the tub, his body completely relaxed.

I kissed him gently, then moved around behind him in the tub. He knelt on the bottom, while I sat on the bench behind him. I started to massage his shoulders. His muscles were one huge mass of tension. He began to rock with my ministrations, so I eased him forward until his arms lay on the ledge, his head pillowed on his arms. I worked the muscles across his shoulders and down his back. He moaned and groaned as my hands released the pent-up tension. The bubbling hot water swirling around us helped to erase the stress. I felt each muscle relax beneath my fingertips all the way down his back. When his breathing started to become steady and deep, I coaxed him up out of the tub, then dried him with one of the oversized, fluffy white towels from the vanity. I grabbed one for myself, dried off quickly, then left the damp towels strewn on the floor. I'd clean up the bathroom later. After grabbing some lotion, I led him back to our bed and pushed him down onto his stomach. I positioned his arms overhead and began again, kneading the tension from his exhausted, beautiful body. I worked every muscle group, enjoying the texture of his skin and the hardness of his muscles beneath my hands, until I heard him snoring, soundly asleep.

I pulled on a pair of underwear and shorts then went into the bathroom, let the water out of the tub, and wrung out my soggy underwear before throwing damp towels and laundry into the hamper. Then I went out to the living room, turned the stereo off, and returned to our bedroom.

He'd begun to fuss; even in his sleep, he seemed to know when I left the room. I went to the armoire, grabbed the necklace and the platinum ring I'd hidden there, then climbed onto the bed and stretched out against him. I softly hummed a lullaby that had been with me for years, although I couldn't have said who'd sung it to me.

I worked on my gift, weaving the platinum ring into the center, smiling as I looked at the now completed present. A single strand of bone beads in gold and black, woven into the heavy braided cord of my hair, made up the necklace. The platinum ring hung at the center. The ring symbolized the never-ending circle of life, and, of course, the moon. The carved bone wolves' heads on either side of the ring appeared to hold the moon in their teeth. I quietly slipped from the bed, put it away, and returned to my spot alongside my Andrew.

He slept so peacefully. I continued to hum the song until I lulled myself to sleep, laying my head on his back. I could hear his heart beat under my arms. I figured even if it was just a nap, the sleep would do both of us good. I realized I'd never in my life been so happy, and I prayed it'd never end.

CHAPTER 9

WE MUST'VE needed the sleep, because we didn't awaken until the early morning light of the next day. I really needed to get those damn curtains. When I awoke, Andrew had stretched out on his back and I lay across his stomach. He was awake, stroking my hair.

I didn't want to move. I enjoyed listening to his heartbeat, feeling safe and peaceful in his arms. I opened my eyes and turned my head to look up into his. They were thoughtful, but no longer as tortured as they'd been the previous day. Sleep had given him perspective, at least. I just looked at him—my Andrew, my love. I didn't say anything. I just watched him watching me. Eventually, smiling and sighing contentedly, he rolled his eyes and shook his head, pulling me up so I could lie alongside him and he could kiss me.

"You're a fox, not a wolf. I swear, man. I'll never get the image of your dancing out of my mind. It's going to make my skin boil my entire life. Every time I see you, I'll think of you singing and dancing for me." He growled softly, and I kissed his hot needy lips.

"I know you enjoyed yourself. I really enjoyed watching your eyes bug out."

"Dangerous. You are *so* dangerous. If you didn't already own my heart, there'd be no holding it back now." He stroked my hair.

"If I wasn't sure of your heart, I wouldn't have been able to dance." I laughed, showing him my own insecurity and self-consciousness.

"What am I going to do with you, my love?"

"Feed me? I'm famished." I sat up as my stomach growled.

"Okay. I want to try something, though. You told me I need to listen to my wolf. He's been whispering to me all morning as I watched you sleep. I've asked him if he thinks we could fly. He's unsure, and I'm afraid to try," Andrew said.

"My love, you're my mate. My heart beats in your chest. If I didn't love you, I wouldn't have had the courage to try, no matter what my wolf said," I whispered. I kissed him softly as I started to get out of bed.

Shock and fire lit his eyes at the same time. I felt his heart skip a beat and then speed up to double time. He suddenly grabbed me and held me in place, not letting me get up.

"Really? Am I really? Do you accept me, love?" His voice cracked with an emotion thick with agony, bordering on pain.

"Yes, of course. You know I love you." How could he even question how I felt about him? I told him I loved him all the time.

"No, love. Oh, I forget, you're so new to our world, you don't understand." He sighed with impatience, trying to calm his nerves and control his emotions. I'd obviously said something he wanted very much, but he already had my love.

"Andrew, you have my love. What else do I have to give? Everything I have you've given me, but if there's something else…" I was at a complete loss, but I held onto him as tightly as I could, trying to tell him without words what was in my heart, since he wasn't understanding or I was clearly misunderstanding something critical.

"I can call you my mate all I want. I can tell the world that you're my mate. Announce it to the stars, the moon and to anyone who'll listen, as I shout it at the top of my lungs. You gave me your blessing to court you when you gave me the armband. You claimed me as a suitor, but that is *all* it means." Andrew paused,pushing me back a bit, holding my eyes with his gaze alone. "By making the first move with a gift, you took the female role. It's the most powerful position in a mating relationship." Andrew drew me against his chest and he rubbed his cheek against my hair. "You gave me a chance to become your mate. Only you can decide if I'm your mate, if I'm worthy to be your mate. I can confess my feelings and tell everyone, but until you confirm and accept me, it means nothing. If you accept me as your mate, my love, nothing can ever separate us, no matter the consequence."

"Nobody could separate us?" I asked, and Andrew shook his head.

"We'd become one in spirit, and it'd be forever. Only you can decide. I started the process by telling you I loved you and by calling you my mate. I'm purely declaring my intentions to everyone around me, staking my claim to your heart and hoping you'll choose mine in return. Only you can accept me." He tried to smile; his voice trembled with emotion as fear crossed his eyes. He realized he'd just given me the power to reject him.

I put my fingers to his lips. My angel should never have doubts like this. "Shh, there's only you in my heart… now and always. My lover, my Andrew, my mate, you're my one and only. I'd bind you to me in any and all ways possible. I'll never allow you to go anywhere again without me. If I could put my blood into your veins to seal you to me permanently, to make you part of my physical being, I'd do so gladly, no matter what the cost to me." I quieted his fears and his trembling ceased.

His eyes filled with love and joy. I stroked my fingers down the side of his beautiful face. I got out of the bed, holding up one finger when he protested. I was so glad to have finished the necklace while he slept; now I could give him his gift. I grabbed it from the armoire and brought it to the bed, climbed back in, and handed the necklace to him. "I don't know how else to show you my love."

"Lance, a necklace like this is like a wedding ring in our world. This tells everyone we're mates and is a physical representation of our bond," he said, holding onto the necklace. "A gift like this would be given when you agree to be mates, to declare our relationship as mated... to everyone who sees us."He stroked my face gently from temple to jaw. "I could never leave you. There's no place that one of us could go that the other couldn't follow. If you were to leave, regardless of my benefactor, I'd have to follow." He held the necklace in trembling hands and looked down at the two wolves holding the moon.

"It's how I feel about you, my love." I stared at the necklace in his hands. I pointed out the ring first. "We're the circle, you and I— never ending and never beginning. We're the white bone inside the ring, the moon; always one and solid, yet always changing from phase to phase. The wolves hold us in the sky, our ever-changing moon. Our love is always constant, always changing, always one." I looked up into his eyes. "I don't have anything to give you but—me."

"Will you secure it for me?" He trembled as he handed me the necklace, leaning toward me. I knelt and tied it securely around his neck. Finally, he belonged to me and I loved him more than my own life. Damn the consequences, any time we were together would be worth it. Beware anyone who dared to try and hurt him—they'd face me, and then they'd learn we were a force to be reckoned with.

"So, my love, you were saying you wanted to try something?" I asked curiously, tilting my head.

"Wings. My wolf didn't think we could, but now my soul soars so high, he seems to think wings aren't such a stretch anymore. He says with you as my mate, anything is possible." A wild freedom sent flames into his eyes like I'd never seen before, and I liked it. Andrew's soul was born to soar.

"Then, by all means, I think you should go for it." I chuckled.

"My love, I feel like a pup, a baby in this world with you. The possibilities seem endless at this moment. I've got to try."

"Don't just try, my love. Join me—soar on the wind. We can hunt. Oh, and I recommend when you start to change, close your eyes. The visual shifts from human to bird are really nauseating." I laughed when he rolled his eyes. I kissed him once more, then got out of bed and headed for the bathroom. "But before I do anything, I've got to brush my teeth."

He laughed and rose with me, following me into the bathroom to do the same; he finished first. He waited, standing behind me, beautiful and naked, looking in the mirror; he fingered his new necklace as I ran a comb through my hair and brushed my teeth. He pulled me back against his chest and I felt his excitement harden between our bodies. I leaned heavily into him as he started kissing my neck. Every time he held me, it never failed to amaze me how safe and cherished he made me feel. Part of me never wanted to leave the warmth of his embrace.

"Ready?" he asked as I put down the comb.

"Yes." I slipped out of the shorts and underwear andthrew them into the hamper. I'd slowly begun to be more comfortable with my own nudity, at least around Andrew. Modesty in a shape-shifter really wasn't conducive to the lifestyle; getting over mine was a work in progress.

We headed for the front door. When we stood in the morning sun, the warmth sank into my skin. I smiled at my mate, my Andrew, and released the falcon, first calling for wings and feathers. I shifted quickly, becoming my falcon before Andrew had sprouted the first of his black plumage.

He'd moved away from me; I watched him clutch his stomach. His usually smooth transformation was marred as I watched the pain cross his face. Black fluffs were sprouting across his arms and body, poking out of his hair; he began shrinking in on himself. He cried out in pain, but it turned into a screech partway through. His body began to change quickly. His legs didn't look like they could support him, but his joints were not in the right direction to let him fall to his knees. His chest dropped and his tail feathers lengthened. His shoulders expanded and reversed direction. Feathers covered his head and the sharp angular beak emerged.

Finally, before my panic could truly set in, he stood there whole. Andrew as a black falcon. He panted as he struggled to steady himself, touching his wingtips to the ground for balance. I watched him carefully. I called softly, clucking my tongue. He'd taken much longer than I had, and I couldn't keep the fear from showing as I remembered he'd told me some who tried to change never returned to human, the animal taking over. He looked at me then and clucked his tongue back, answering my nervous call, reassuring me he'd be okay.

Around the falcon's neck, a silver moon hung at his throat, secured by feathers; the rest of the necklace appeared to have been absorbed by his feathers, along with the armband. The natural materials transformed with him, but the ring and white bone piece secured in the center remained, held in place by feathers.

He appeared to be all right. I hopped closer and rubbed my face against his chest. He draped a wing around me and cooed softly, still panting slightly from the exertion of transformation. I tried to kiss him, clicking my beak with his. He chuckled, a jeering sound coming from the bird. We weren't identical.His bird was larger than my own, his markings slightly different. But we were clearly two of a kind. I hopped away and opened my wings. I looked back at him, cried out, and launched myself upward. He followed immediately behind me, chasing me into the open blue endless sky. His scream of joy and exhilaration filled the air. I shrieked with him. We wheeled and dove. We locked talons and spiraled toward the earth, then let go and opened our wings to come out of the dive at the very end, playing in the thermals. Flight was… freedom completely unlike anything else in the world. The whole sky became our playground. The only ones who had more freedom than the birds of the sky were the gods themselves.

We hovered on the updrafts high above the meadows. Looking down, we could see everything for miles as clearly as if it were two feet in front of us. I watched deer moving through the trees. I watched the mice scurrying about, gathering seeds for their winter stores. The squirrels leaped from the trees and played games, and the rabbits…. Oh the rabbits, they were down there too! A large warren of rabbits moved about, gathering food and nibbling at the vegetation. My falcon watched them intently. I could see Andrew had spotted the warren as well. My falcon chose a rabbit, and I saw Andrew had done the same. We folded our wings tight against our bodies and plummeted like bullets toward the ground. At the last minute, I opened my wings, landing talons extended like knives into a rabbit, severing its spine, killing it instantly. When I glanced over, Andrew had also killed a large hare, just a little ways from me. We both screamed and ripped into the rabbits, enjoying our meal.

When we finished enjoying our spoils, Andrew hopped over to me and rubbed against my chest. I clucked and rubbed back. He looked in the direction of the ranch, then looked back at me. I understood and bobbed my head. He wanted to go see his family. Wouldn't they be surprised? I laughed and a jeering, clucking sound erupted from me.

We both took to the air and lazily flew to the ranch. We had some time yet before Andrew would feel relaxed enough to be able to transform back. He needed to become familiar with this shape. He needed to spend time as his falcon. Flight speed, even at a leisurely pace, seemed quick. In no time, we were above the ranch in the air currents, playing, catching each other's talons, flying upside down.

We began to spiral in a great circle, slowly losing altitude. I began to wonder if Sam would be staying with the family for a while yet or if he'd gone home. What would they think of Andrew being a falcon too?

Andrew began screaming, again and again, trying to get the attention of everyone at the ranch. I joined him in screaming as we floated gently downward. Family members poured from the barn and the house. They gathered in front of the large house to stare at the two black falcons circling overhead. We landed on the clothesline pole, side by side on the crossbar. Sam and the twins were the last ones out of the house.

"Oh, man!" exclaimed the twins together, gawking at the falcons.

"Lance?" Sam asked. I clucked and bobbed my head up and down. He paused, looking at the other falcon. "Andrew?" he said in

150

a whisper, mystified. Andrew clicked and bobbed his head, then screamed at the top of his lungs elatedly.

"Wow!" Max sighed loudly in his shock. He dragged his hand across his face, stunned. "I don't know what to say or think. Son, are you okay?" His voice trembled with concern and fear. Andrew whistled, swaying from side to side, then rubbed his head against me.

"You two crazy lovebirds." Joe laughed. Andrew cackled too, the sound coming from his chest, fluffing his feathers and waggling his tail feathers, trying to let the others know he was all right.

"You kids are a daily surprise." Laura sighed, too worried to see the humor.

I cooed at her concern and ruffled my feathers. I understood her fear; I had felt it before Andrew had completed his shift. Andrew hopped on the pole until he stood at the end, as close to his dad and Sam as he could get without getting down. He stared pointedly at Max and Sam, then looked toward the cottage, clucking again, and then looked back at Sam.

Sam understood, "He's wondering when we'll be heading to the cottage."

"I have a couple chores left to do, and then we can head up there. Dr. Carlson should be here in about an hour. So I figure about an hour and a half." Max sighed. Again.

Andrew dipped his head in understanding. He looked at me and then launched himself into the air, and I quickly followed. This time, though, I power-winged myself forward as fast as I could, calling to Andrew, who'd begun to climb to altitudes above. He dove down as he saw me dart into the woods. I held back 'til he caught up with me. Then I sped up, racing him through the trees as I had when he'd run as the wolf. I wanted to show him how I'd felt flying through the forest at top speed. We raced through the trees, dodging the branches, as fast as our wings would take us. He screamed, losing himself in the race, and brushed his wing tips against mine. I spiraled around him, flipping upside down with precision.

Almost as quickly as we entered the forest, we emerged into our meadow around the cabin. We burst from the trees, flying highstraight up into the clear blue sky, then flipping upside down at the height of the climb to turn over, tuck, and plummet back to earth. We opened our wings at the last moment, completely synchronized as we landed on the log by the fire pit. I hopped to the ground and let the person expand out from the bird's body, becoming human again. I stretched stiff joints, and the muscles in my arms, shoulders, and legs. I ducked into the cottage, grabbed a pair of sweatpants, dressed, and returned to the log to wait for Andrew to relax enough to return to being human. He hopped closer to me and I stroked his head and shoulders. I rubbed his flight muscles. He cooed and leaned into my hand. He clucked and picked gently at my fingers with his beak.

"You make a beautiful falcon, my mate," I told him.

He screamed at my words, which seemed to fill him with delight. I laughed at his antics as he nodded his head and hopped from one foot to the other. I could tell how much he'd loved flying. I sat in the sun, patiently stroking his back. Eventually Andrew clucked and leaped into the air, gliding toward the front door of the cottage. I got up and followed him. As I approached, he began to expand, and Andrew began to unfold from the body of the bird. He appeared to explode out in all directions and then reform into Andrew.

He screamed in pain when his legs reformed at the right angles, and he dropped to his knees, his shoulders folding back around forward, his tail disappearing as his chest expanded back to normal. His head expanded and the beak withdrew. I noticed with a little smile that he had his eyes closed tight against his changing vision. He took less time shifting back into his human form than he'd taken to become the falcon, but it appeared to be just as painful. When he finished, he knelt by the door, his muscles trembling from the stress, panting with the effort it took to transform. I put a hand on his shoulder, and he slowly stood and stretched his muscles. I noticed his armband and necklace had also returned to just as they were before he'd changed.

"God, I hope that gets better. That's the strangest feeling, exploding from that small body." Andrew's voice cracked as he gripped the doorframe, trying to maintain his balance. I put my arm around his waist to help steady him. Taking a couple of deep breaths, he stood up straighter, sighing. I watched him, very concerned. He really had to struggle to regain his equilibrium. His recovery time had been much longer than mine.

"Are you okay?" I asked. He'd really scared me with the amount of time his shifts had taken, and how painful they seemed to be. I didn't want him to have to struggle so hard.

"Yeah, I'm fine. The first is always the worst. Next time will be better." He sighed as we walked into the house, headed for the bedroom and clean clothes.

"So, did you like it?" I glanced over at Andrew, who was pulling on a pair of jeans.

"Did I like it—are you crazy? I loved it! There's nothing like it in the world. When you flew upside down and then I flipped upside down—that was so cool. And when you locked talons with me and we were way up high then plummeted toward the ground—God, what a rush," Andrew raved.

"So you did like it," I teased as I changed out of sweats into a pair of jeans.

"Of course I liked it! I never felt so free in my entire life. I still like being human best of all, because then I can hold you in my arms." Andrew pulled a blue T-shirt over his head, as I pulled a red T-shirt over mine. He walked over to the bed, sat down, and pulled me between his thighs. He rubbed up and down my back, pulling me down for a hot kiss that melted every bone in my body. I groaned and leaned into his kiss.

I felt his hands cup my ass and although my body froze, the tingle of fear that usually accompanied the sensation wasn't there. I pushed back against him and his arms immediately loosened, although he whimpered.

"Andrew, I explained this. I can't—I can't do anal intercourse. I love you and I can do a bit of yanking off, but that's really pushing my limits. Actually, I was really surprised when that didn't freak me out. You're the only person who I've been able to even be that intimate with." I closed my eyes and rested my forehead against his.

"It's okay, love. Whatever you can give me is enough. I love you." Andrew's body trembled and shook. My body shook right along with his as we held each other through the tremors of our desire until we both had a grip on ourselves once more.

"Your family should be here any moment."

"Really, Lance. Nothing compares to this. Being with you makes this the best time of my life." His deep voice rumbled huskily with the love he felt for me. I could listen to his voice all day long. It sent such longing through me I began to wish I could let Andrew physically love me.

We went back to the kitchen. I put on a pot of water for tea, while Andrew fished around in the refrigerator and came out with an apple. We relaxed together at the table, Andrew sitting in the chair and me sitting so close to him our thighs touched under the table. I reached over and snatched the apple from him and took a bite. He rolled his eyes and took my tea, taking a sip and curling his nose.

"How can you stand this stuff?" he grumbled.

"I like it. It's soothing."

"Yuck." He pushed the tea cup back toward me and took back his apple. I rested my head against his shoulder, just enjoying being with him. I didn't think about anything. I didn't want to. I just wanted to be with him and drink in the fact that he loved me.

The stress Andrew felt the day before seemed to have lessened, which I didn't understand. Maybe the sleep had helped or the freedom of flying, but I hadn't expected this much of a change.

"You seem so much more at ease today than before. Why?"

"Because you accepted me. It changes everything for me." He saw the confusion and total lack of understanding in my eyes. "You still don't get it, do you?"

I shook my head. "Not really, I guess. I must be missing something. It doesn't change anything. You're my mate and I never want to be parted from you. If I can bind us together by accepting you as my mate, I'm more than willing to do that, because I love you."

"I love you too, *leannan*, but this goes beyond that. Our pairings are for life and absolutely binding. Once a mating is accepted it can't be undone. So now, although Stephon can throw his fits and be angry, he can punish me and do anything he likes, but we're mates forever, as long as we live." He kissed my hair. "We bond so completely, our forms tend to be linked. Since you were a falcon, I became a falcon. Since Sam is a Bald Eagle, his mate would need to be another Bald Eagle, or at the very least another bird of prey."

"So what will Stephon do now that I've accepted you, my mate?" I enjoyed watching him, as my words seemed to make him tremble with happiness.

"I'll never get used to you saying I'm your mate. It touches me right to my soul. Thank you so much. You have very little idea how honored you make me feel to be your mate. I need to think of a gift for you." He sighed, fingering his necklace thoughtfully and snuggling his face into my hair, nibbling on my ear.

"I feel the same about you, my love. You make me feel so proud. I only hope somehow, some way, I'll be worthy to be your mate and Stephon won't have cause to hurt you. You all seem to like him so much, I'd hate to have to kill him," I said seriously, feeling the wolf inside growl at the thought of Stephon. I still believed he sent the assassins, and I'd end his miserable vampiric eternal life if I could prove he was behind it.

"Let's hope it doesn't come to that." I could feel Andrew's indulgent smile. "If we had more time before—"

Andrew's thoughts were interrupted by the sound of four-wheelers ripping up the road toward the cottage. "That'd be Sam, Dad, and the twins." He smiled down at me, his eyes full of love, and sighed, leaning in and kissing me gently.

SUI LYNN

"You know I really like your family, but I'm feeling very greedy right now and I regret having to share you with anyone. I like having you to myself."

"I understand, love. I don't like the idea of sharing you either. I almost ripped my brothers apart when you gave their wolves a hug the other day out in the meadow." I giggled at his discomfiture.

"Jealous?" I asked innocently, cocking my head to one side to look him in the eye as I raised one eyebrow quizzically.

"Very! And if I ever catch you dancing where someone else can see you, I'll go insane." He kissed my head and neck before we heard the knock at the door. He groaned and growled softly in annoyance.

I attempted to get up, but he held me in place and hollered, "Come on in, already."

"Oh, that's rude!" I smacked him on the arm, forced my way out of his embrace, and went to greet our guests as he laughed at me.

"Ignore him," I said, opening the door and letting the guys in. They took places around the table with Andrew amid much laughing and teasing. "Can I get anybody anything? Tea... coffee...," I offered. I carefully watched my proximity to Andrew. He looked like he'd grab me the moment I came within range of his long arms.

There were mumbles of "no, thank you" from the guys, so I made my way back to Andrew and let him pull me back onto his lap.

"I'm guessing he's accepted you as his mate?" Max smiled at me and looked closely at Andrew's necklace.

"Yes. He's mine now." I grinned at Andrew, which sent a volley of shivers through Andrew's body and elicited knowing chuckles from the men around the table.

"So, what do we know?" asked Andrew, blushing slightly, hinting at the pile of papers the twins had brought with them.

Jack pulled out a copy of my birth certificate and laid it on the table. "Dr. Carlson should be here soon. I'm sure he'll have something to say too."

"A pureblood," whispered Sam, shaking his head as he saw the name on the birth certificate. I didn't realize he hadn't been told. "That explains so much. Lance is free because his mother wouldn't have been bonded to a vampire family. He could have vampire vassals. I don't know what the condition of the vampire's family was after the war."

"But where's his mother now?" asked Andrew in frustration.

"If his mother is Sasha, then she must've gone animal when her chosen vampire died." The awe was plain in Max's voice.

"It explains what Lance can do and what he's drawn out of Andrew." Jack rubbed his shoulder, reminding them all of the instant healing.

"Yes, and it would make his bloodline the rarest, purest of us all, a veritable prince among our kind even if his bloodline isn't actually royal." Max tried unsuccessfully to keep the concern from his voice.

"It could also put a price on his head. His mother's part of the reason we were enslaved in the first place."

Sam shook his head. "There'll be some who'll be against him for that reason alone."

"But he had nothing to do with what happened before he was born!" Andrew growled defensively. He clutched me so tightly and protectively I began to get scared.

"Be calm, son. This is all speculation at this point," Max tried to soothe Andrew.

"Could the assassins the other night have been from Stephon? Who else knows there's even a possibility that I might be something other than a throwback?"

Andrew's gaze flew to me, shocked, a loud dangerous growl coming from his lips. I put my hand to his face and drew his eyes to mine. "It's okay, love. Shh, it's all right," I said very softly, holding his gaze until his breathing calmed down, even if his heart still pounded against my shoulder.

He took a deep breath. "Sorry," he said, looking at his dad and the others. "Sorry, love," he said, looking back into my eyes. "My emotions are a bit raw."

"It's possible, but not really Stephon's style. The only other person who knows is Dr. Carlson, and I trust him. He's been good to this family for centuries." Max shook his head, scowling.

"Lance, it could've been someone who tagged your birth records, knowing you were born but not where you were. They might've been waiting for someone to come looking for you, and when we found the records, they followed them back to us, and you." Joe frowned.

"Unfortunately, we hadn't considered someone might be looking for you when we found your birth record online. It could easily be someone we don't even know." Jack sighed. I could see the idea they had been traced disturbed the twins.

"Okay, let's say the twins are right. I thought the vampires prized pure blood above all else. Wouldn't they want to preserve my bloodline, regardless of which family I belong to, as long as the bloodline is pureblood?" I asked, not at all sure I wanted to hear the answer to that question.

Sam shook his head. "Maybe, but many vampires are no fonder of that particular family than many of our people. Sasha's family was thought to be extinct from the beginning of the war. Some may want to save it because it was a very strong bloodline, close to the royals, but others will hunt you down. They view the overall cost of the war negatively and have long lives and memories."

"It's the name Fitz I find curious." Andrew's deep voice practically sent tremors through my body.

"Obviously Lance's mother had to have gotten pregnant by another shape-shifter or his blood would be diluted. Probably by another shape-shifter who had gone animal? It's a common enough thing to do when a mate's killed out of turn. It's the only way to stand the pain.They live out the remainder of their lives in their

158

animal shape, mindlessly.Do we know anything about the family name Fitz?"

"No, I don't remember ever hearing that name before the day we took Lance to see Dr. Carlson. He recognized both names, saying Sasha Fenrir's protector's name was Henry Fitz and he was a shape-shifter," said Max. "We may need to go into the clan histories to find which family he came from."

"You know, being he's the son of a pureblood, and if his father is a pureblood as well, Lance could claim 'Right to Rule'. He could essentially free us all. You said it yourself.If he's of pureblood, it'd make him a prince among us," said Joe softly. We all stared at him, dumbfounded. "It was the only stipulation our people were able to add to the surrender agreement. If one of royal pureblood was to ever be born, our people would be freed, and allowed to rule ourselves. Of course, at the time, there were no purebloods left other than the wild ones, and they were too far gone to help us. Sasha must've finally been touched, because her star-crossed love had been directly responsible for the war and our enslavement. She just couldn't face life as a human without her mate, so she did the next best thing. She gave us her pureblood son."

They all stared, first at Joe, then at me, with a strange expression of mixed horror and admiration. My mind began to whirl with incomprehension, panic, and fear. They couldn't be serious. No way could I possibly be what they were thinking. I was a runaway orphan with a price on my head for murder. I couldn't be a prince to these people. When we all heard a vehicle race up the road and slam on its brakes, spewing gravel, my brain screamed with panic, and everything went black.

When I started to come around, I could hear the voices around me, as well as a combination of growling, snarling, and exasperated talking.

"Andrew, really, you're not helping. Lance is fine. He just fainted. He should be coming around in a minute or two. You all frightened him so badly his mind protected itself the only way it could." The voice sounded familiar, but it wasn't one of the family.

My sluggish brain registered it as the voice of the good doctor. The snarling continued, getting louder and more aggressive. It must've been Dr. Carlson's vehicle I'd heard pulling up in front of the cottage.

Slowly, I realized I'd been laid on the love seat, my feet up on a pillow. They must've put me here. I opened my eyes. Andrew hovered over me in a defensive stance, growling at everyone who came near me. I smiled slightly; seeing him so protective of me made me feel warm and cherished.

"Andrew… he's waking up. Look at him. He'll be fine. Calm down." The doctor continued to calm my worried mate, trying to get close enough to me to check on me. The rest of the guys sat motionless in their chairs around the table. They were trying, through their silence and stillness, to calm Andrew. He refused to look at me.He wouldn't take his eyes off the doctor. I put a shaky hand on his arm and almost sent him to the rafters.

"Shh, love," I whispered. I couldn't get any more out.

"Lance—" His voice cracked.

"Easy. I'm—"

"Don't say good… just don't…," he cried hoarsely.

He buried his face in my chest, and I placed a shaky hand in his hair.

Dr. Carlson hovered at my side. Looking into my eyes, he placed a hand on my forehead, quickly checking my temperature. "Lance, can you sit up? Slowly now, not too quickly."

Andrew helped me into a sitting position. I put my head between my knees when the room wouldn't stop spinning, threatening to go black again.

"Take deep breaths," Dr. Carlson coached from the stove. He poured me a cup of lukewarm tea and returned with lightning speed. He'd added milk and a hefty amount of sugar, which I usually used sparingly. He handed me the cup. "Drink," he commanded gently.

After taking a sip, I mumbled, "Too much sugar."

He chuckled. "Good. You need the sugar to fight the shock. Be a good boy and drink the tea, so you can keep your mate from ripping my arms off," he teased, but he watched Andrew like a hawk.

I looked up and saw Andrew again in a protective stance, hovering over me and snarling at the doctor, who had squatted down in front of me, trying to be small and submissive. He sat very still. I put up a hand,grasped a fistful of Andrew's hair, and coaxed him down out of his crouch, to sit beside me. I took one of his hands in mine, pulled it to my chestand trapped it there. He whined at me. I glanced up at him, giving him a hard look.

"Get a grip," I told him sternly, but my voice cracked. The men at the table began to relax and talk softly again among themselves. They knew I had Andrew in hand; in his desire to protect me and help me, he'd do as I asked.

"See, Lance is going to be fine," Dr. Carlson said, standing slowly and then moving over to the men at the table, so they could bring him up to speed.

Andrew whined in my ear. He began to stroke my hair with his free hand, but could do nothing with the other because of my grip. The room had finally stopped its death spiral; I began to relax my shoulders and slowly stretched the muscles in my neck. My head ached. I needed to find some Tylenol. I chugged the last of the super sweet tea, then looked at Andrew and released his hand. He immediately, slowly, and carefully lifted me to his lap and cradled me against his chest. I melted into him, right where I wanted to be. I felt him relax, knowing he must feel more confident with me safe in his arms.

"Are you really all right, my love? You scared me so badly. I couldn't get you to wake up. Poor Dr. Carlson walked in just as your head fell back. I damn near attacked him, because he saw you unconscious and swept you off my lap and onto the love seat so quickly. I freaked out. He tried to tell me you needed to have your feet elevated above your heart so you'd recover, but I couldn't get my mind to understand. Everything in me said he had attacked my mate," he whispered into my ear. I felt the hot tears running down his face as he gently rocked me back and forth, trying to comfort himself as much as me.

I had to remember to do whatever it took to never faint again. Andrew couldn't handle me being unconscious. I'd need to become strongerto protect him, even from myself. "I'm sorry, love. I didn't mean to pass out. I guess I felt overwhelmed by what everyone was saying and I forgot to breathe. You were getting so upset, I felt completely lost and confused, and everyone kept staring at me. Then everything went black," I said, shaking my head in confusion.

I looked at his face and wiped the tears away. I took his worried face into my hands and drew him to me. I kissed the furrows on his forehead. I kissed each eye and his nose and then softly kissed his mouth before letting go. He shuddered and relaxed. He finally seemed to realize I'd be all right.

"I'll remember to breathe in the future." I snickered softly into his lips.

"When you put it that way, it sounds so silly. Only it didn't feel silly," he complained quietly.

"Don't dwell on it, love. We're okay. Now, you owe Dr. Carlson an apology. He only wanted to help, and you threatened to take his arms off. I need to get some Tylenol.My head is killing me." I slowly stood. When the earth didn't move under my feet, I sighed and let go of Andrew. I watched as he ducked out of the room, returning from the bathroom with a couple of little white pills in one hand and a glass of water in the other. I took them gratefully, and we made our way back to the table and the others.

"I'm really sorry, Dr. Carlson. I didn't mean to get so hostile," Andrew said, offering the doctor his hand to shake.

"I've told you, Andrew, please call me Tim. You too, Lance. And really, I understand. I pushed you hard, a bit too quickly. I'm sorry." The doctor shook Andrew's hand.

"No, never apologize for pushing me when you need to help Lance. Sometimes I get too thick to realize I'm more of a hindrancethan a help." Andrew smiled slightly as he took his chair and pulled me back into his lap, where I'd been before I passed out.

"The test results came back as expected. You have royal pureblood running through your veins. Your father,Prince Henry Fitz, was Sasha's protector and the oldest bastard son of His Highness, King Henry. During the time before the Great War, it was customary for families to have fosterlings from other families living with them. Usually a family you were trying to establish an alliance with would send their second sons or their bastards to be raised away from their own families. Often these sons would become friends with the girls in their foster family, and when they became old enough, they would declare them as mates and cement the families together. Fitz was the surname of the bastard children of the royal family. In this case, I happen to know his full name was Henry Joshua Fitz. He was the oldest son, but because his mother was the mistress and not the king's mate, he was ineligible to rule, but as a son of the king, he retained the title 'Prince'."

"My father was a p-prince?" I know they suspected me being part of the royal family, but he was a prince! I just couldn't get my mind around it.

"I remember seeing him flying in his preferred form, a black falcon, weeks before the war began. It was rumored at the time that his father hoped he'd mate with Sasha and tie the families together. Sasha's father wanted a connection to the royal household, and so did Prince Henry, who'd been totally smitten with Sasha and a close friend of My Lord Nathaniel. Many thought she had fallen for Prince Henry as they were often seen together and seemed to have a great affection for one another. She shocked many when she declared herself mated with her vampire instead, but Prince Henry stayed with her. Lord Nathaniel couldn't hunt with her or protect her when she went into any of her animal forms, so Prince Henry pledged to be her protector for as long as she lived, even though she'd refused him as a mate. When her vampire sent her away, knowing he'd be killed in the fight, he believed she would get away in her animal form, so Henry left with her. He refused to leave her side even then.

Your father is the first son of King Henry, prince of the royal family," Tim said softly. "Breathe, Lance," he reminded me, as my vision began to tunnel and darkness crept in around the edges.

"But how?" I struggled to understand, shaking my head in complete confusion and disbelief. "She was alive more than three hundred years ago. You can't tell me I'm three hundred years old and didn't know it."

"No, son. You're really eighteen. I suspect both she and Henry are still alive, spending their lives as their animals. But since Sasha and Lord Nathaniel couldn't complete theirbond as a mated pair, her life continues instead of fading at the end of the animal's natural lifespan. Henry likely remains faithfully with her." Max frowned, looking to Tim for confirmation.

"I'm not sure of the lifecycles of the purebloods, to be honest, Max. I know they were as immortal as we vampires. I know they had mating cycles, because some of the attacks during the war were specifically timed to coincide when the older wolves would be most distracted, but to be honest, my knowledge is limited." Tim shook his head.

"So… my mom, a wolf, and my dad, a falcon, mated. Nine months later I'm born and abandoned with paperwork filled out for my birth records, and left for adoption at some hospital." My voice rose in agitation, my frustration and confusion evolving into anger. I tried to stand, but Andrew held me tight.

"I'm sorry, Lance. We really don't know what happened." Andrew's deep voice calmed me though I didn't want it to. I wanted to be angry with her for abandoning me, leaving me with people who hurt me."All we know for sure is that the ancients gave birth as humans. Your mom would've had to become human when you were born."

"My best guess is Henry took her to the hospital when the time came.You were born in a hospital among humans. I can't imagine why she didn't give you to a shifter family to raise." Tim looked to Max and then Andrew.

"Unless maybe she was afraid you'd be killed because of her. So she tried to hide you among humans to keep you safe." Andrew rubbed his cheek against my shoulder, trying to soothe me. "It's all speculation, really. We may never know her reasons."

"We'd need to find a drone older than myself who worked among the pureblood shifters, or we could ask one of the born vampires. They might know. Otherwise, we're going on your folklore and the few things I am able to recall from a time in my life I barely remember." Tim seemed deep in thought.

I took a couple of deep shaky breaths. "Oh dear God, could this get any more complicated." I leaned forward, putting my head in my hands. Andrew's arms were steel bands about my body. I could feel the silent rumbling of Andrew's growls in his chest, even though they weren't loud enough to be heard by others.

"Wow." Max shook his head. "I have no idea what to do now. Where do we go with this, Tim? This is so much more complicated than I even vaguely thought possible."

"I believe Lance is exactly who the records say he is." Tim sat back in his chair, crossing his arms over his chest. "I find it rather ironic that here before me sits a combination of both my people's greatest hopes, to find a royal pureblood shifter whose parentage is untainted by human blood, and our worst fears, that a child of the Fenrir blood line which is responsible for the death of thousands and caused the Great War, coexist in one person. It'll make them crazy trying to decide what to do with you, Lance. The question becomes, what will they do?" Tim dropped his arms to the table and shrugged.

"What do *we* do?" asked Andrew, so forlorn and fearful his voice trembled.

"Well, we'll start here. I'm your vassal, Lance." Tim leaned forward in his chair. "I pledged myself to your mother's honor when she accepted my Lord Nathaniel as her mate. Their mating didn't have quite the same binding nature for the two of them as it does for shape-shifters, because they were of two different species. Even though they truly loved each other and were bound together, it didn't carry the same ramifications as those with which the two of you

165

have bound yourselves. There are a few of us vampires still around who'll be loyal to you because of her love for our lord. Most of us were killed in the war, trying to avenge him. I've been trying to contact as many as I can find since the first test results started coming back positive a couple days ago. Max, I'd suggest you contact the packs and any families with Fitz blood, or any of the royal house. Try to reach the most pureblooded of that family that you can. I'm sure there have to be a few members of the royal family somewhere, even if they don't hold court or power. We'll need to contact Stephon and bring him here, if possible. We don't want to ignite another war, but we'll have to convince him to release you, Andrew. If Lance is to be a savior to your people, you'll need to be free to help him, and to protect him as much as possible. The future isn't going to be easy, kids. It's about to get ugly, very quickly. But I get ahead of myself. Let's take it one step at a time."

"Okay," I said. "Step one—get the vassals together. Step two—convince Stephon to free Andrew. Step three—get the royals to acknowledge me as a prince or whatever. Step four—save the world. All without getting anyone killed. Sure… piece of cake," I said sarcastically, sagging back into Andrew's chest and shaking my head.

The entire table burst into laughter at my sarcasm, all except me.

"That's the spirit, brother!" Joe laughed, nudging Jack with his elbow, and both of them grinned like I'd given them the greatest birthday present ever.

I shook my head in disbelief. Even Andrew had begun to chuckle. The whole concept was so far beyond reality, I couldn't even fathom where to begin. The men around the table grinned and looked more hopeful than I felt.

"Okay, then, that's settled." Max laughed. "I'll start making phone calls in the morning."

"You might be having a lot of guests in town soon." Tim stood and stretched his arms over his head. "I'd start considering a third shape. You'll need to be able to produce at least three to prove you

166

are of the royal pureblood lineage. None but a royal pureblood could do three, and Andrew will probably be forced by your mating into a third shape as well. You might be able to put it off for a while, Andrew, but eventually your blood will ring with the need to keep up with Lance." Tim frowned, looking at us carefully. "His power will help you, but I'm sure it won't be a comfortable experience for you." Tim contemplatedus for a minute, deep in thought. We rose from the table and began to file toward the door, still discussing details.

"I also want to talk to you about the healing properties of your saliva. That was a very interesting phenomenon. Sometime when you are in town, I'd like you to stop in to the clinic so I can get a sample and run some tests. I would be very interested to see if I can determine the chemicals involved. The applications of such a boon to society in general would be fabulous. The immense healing gift you could give to the world would be beyond measure."

The twinsleft the copy of my birth certificate on the table, giving Andrew a strange look I didn't understand. He followed them out the door. Max stopped me before I could follow Andrew and the twins out. He started telling me about the different members of the royal family he would contact. Tim joined him, adding tidbits of information here and there about different members of the royal family.

Eventually Andrew returned, looking ashen, as he looked at me then stared at the ground in what I could only assume was humiliation. In that instant, my greatest fear, that the twins would tell Andrew about the murder I'd committed, seemed to be coming to life before my eyes. Andrew kept looking at the ground. Was my mate ashamed of me?Maybe he didn't want me anymore, knowing what I'd done. I felt tears come to my eyes, but I tried to listen to Max and Tim. I focused on them, trying to get them out the door… and yet the longer they stayed, the longer I didn't have to face Andrew and find out what he was thinking. Yes, that was the coward inside me screaming it was better to pretend and not know.

"Thank you for everything. I'll be making those calls tomorrow morning. As soon as I hear when they'll be here, I'll let you know." Max smiled and patted me on the shoulder. "It's not all that bad, Lance. Everything will work out. I'm sure of it."

"I'm glad you think so." I tried to smile but I couldn't. A glance over my shoulder at Andrew filled me with dread. He'd sat back down at the table with his head in his hands. Tim frowned. He stared at Andrew, then looked at me. The sound of the four-wheelers heading off toward the ranch filled the silence in the house. I was torn between going to Andrew and running into the bedroom and crying.

Tim took care of the issue for me. "Okay, children, what's going on? Why aren't you mated? You've both declared it often. I've heard you both, and I can see how much you adore each other. You must realize it'll only get more painful each time you declare your intentions and don't consummate your relationship," Tim stated as if he were explaining the birds and bees to an adolescent.

I felt confused, because the way I understood it, Andrew and Iwerealready mated. Andrew stood and began pacing about the kitchen, then with a loud growl headed out the front door. I hurried after him, with Tim right behind me.

"Tim, what are you talking about? I don't understand," I said, looking from Tim to Andrew, who stood with his hands clenched into fists beside the log in the front yard.

"You didn't explain this to him? Why not?" Tim looked accusingly at Andrew, almost angrily. "It's not fair for him to be declaring this and not know what's involved, or the changes it begins in both of you."

"Tim, I'm strong enough. I can do this." Andrew growled.

"Andrew, you aren't human, either of you. You're old enough to realize there's no such thing as being 'strong enough'. Your species doesn't give you that option. If you intend to be mates, then the compulsion will steadily get stronger. I can smell you both, you're practically polluting the air with your pheromones. Both of you are clearly in heat. If you don't consummate this relationship soon, while you can still control yourselves, it'll eventually happen violently, without the consent from either of you. You don't have a choice."

Tim shook his head and put a hand to his forehead, as if he had a headache. Could vampires get headaches? "What is the holdup here? Andrew, you're one of the gentlest, most considerate of your people I've ever met. I've always admired you. Surely he hasn't rejected you?" Tim now looked at me.

Confusion filled my mind, but as Tim spoke, I began to realize reluctantly what he'd been driving at. When it came to sex, my brain was concrete. I didn't want anything to do with any part of it, and the turn this conversation had taken terrified me. My brain froze solid, and I went into complete denial.

"*No!*" I shouted, shaking my head vehemently from side to side. I couldn't deal with this. I moved to the log and sat down, wrapped my arms about myself, put my head in my hands, and trembled uncontrollably.

"I don't understand," said Tim, watching my outburst with concern.

"Tim, I-I don't know what to do." Andrew's voice faltered. "The twins just told me. He was brutalized, raped, beaten, and then forced to watch the rape of others by his foster father before he came here." Andrew shook his head."We were involved before I realized what had happened. I didn't know about his past. He didn't tell me, and there're so many things I take for granted, but he doesn't understand. Lance declared me as his mate, before I realized he didn't understand what it meant. I didn't know why he refused me. I thought he just wasn't ready, not that he couldn't stand to have anyone touch him sexually. I can't hurt him, so I'll just have to make myself strong enough to keep my distance from him but still love him as if he really was my mate." Andrew practically sobbed, standing behind me but not touching me.

"No, no, no, no," I mumbled incessantly, but Andrew just kept talking.

"It's getting harder all the time. I tremble constantly when he's out of my arms, and I can't stand to have any others even look at him.It makes me want to rip them apart." The sob became a menacing growl, filled with pain."He's feeling the pull too," Andrew pleaded."I know he is, but his pain and fear are greater. I can see that now. Maybe if I can hold out long enough…. But if this goes on too long, his fears could become reality. I don't want to hurt him. God, Tim—I'd rather die first."

I could hear every word of his pain, and I could feel the longing in myself to make his pain go away, but my brain screamed *no*. I just couldn't go through with it, and because I couldn't, I'd end up making Andrew force me. I just wanted to scream. I began to rock violently on the log.

"I'm so sorry." Tim shook his head and squatted down in front of me. He put a finger under my chin and made me meet his gaze; I flinched slightly at his cold touch. "I'm so sorry you were hurt. There's something, though, you don't realize, and I think I can make it clear for you in a way Andrew can't. It's ultimately the reason your mother, despite her love for my lord and his love for her, was able to leave and go animal, to live on. Her grief was insurmountable because of her love for him. So much so, she chose to live the rest of her days as an animal rather than face the pain of her grief as a person. The problem here is a truly mated pair wouldn't have been able to separate in the face of such a threat. They would have died together."

I tried to pull away from him.

"Look at me now. This is very important. It's horrible, what happened to you, and doubly so because the aggressor was a human. You, dear boy, are a shape-shifter, *not* a human. You've been raised among them and have believed yourself to be human so long that I'm sure it's hard to see yourself as a shape-shifter and not a human being."

Tim paused, and I tried not to close my eyes in resignation.

"Even as a child, I'm sure you realized you were different from the other kids—that you didn't fit in. Subconsciously, humans know we—people like you and me—are dangerous to them. We're natural predators. They fear us and loathe us without knowing why. There were probably children who were kind to everyone else, but went out of their way to be hurtful to you." Tim sighed and shook his head in dismay as confusion continued to cloud my mind. "At one time in history, your people preyed on humans as much as mine. It's how all the vampire and werewolf legends began, as warnings to others to beware.

"Both of our peoples have alternatives for our natural impulses these days. Your people have taken to hunting animals to curb both your aggressive nature and appetite. My people have taken to harvesting blood from volunteers to sate our thirst, using donated blood from blood banks owned by vampires. Don't you see, child, when that human brutalized you, it wasn't just the physical and mental harm because of the act. He went against the natural order. It would be like an adult rabbit attacking a wolf pup before the cub was eating solids." Tim seemed to get a bit frustrated with me, as I shook my head and closed my eyes, trying to understand what he was telling me.

"The brutality and violation you felt with the human became exacerbatedbecause he's your natural prey. That won't occur with Andrew. Even if the worst happens, and you make him wait until he attacks you, because of the overwhelming sex drive of your species, there will be no shame, no anger, and no revulsion. Even then, the feeling of violation won't be there, nor would the feeling of brutality. If that happens, the sex drive will take hold of you as much as it has a hold of him, and neither of you will be able to deny it. It would be better if you could release your fears and accept him willingly, and the sooner the better. Do you understand what I'm telling you?" asked Tim softly.

"You're saying because the man who attacked me was human, and I'm not, that's why I feel so violated, beyond the attack itself. You're trying to tell me sex won't be like that between Andrew and myself because we're both the same species." My voice was flat, without feeling. "But why doesn't it feel different in my head, then,

Tim? I love Andrew. I want to be able to be with him. But I only see what that man did to me, and the violence and pain."

"It's because you weren't raised among your own people and haven't really accepted that you aren't human." Tim sighed. "Haven't you noticed yet? Your people don't treat you the way humans did. Not just Andrew, but his whole family. They all love you. They all welcomed you into the fold. That's the way of shape-shifters. Their whole society is matriarchal and pack-oriented. Everyone has a place and is welcome in the pack. Without the support of the pack and the ones they love, they go insane. That's why Andrew is in such agony, and why you're hurting so much right now. Your very nature is trying to drive you to each other, to be in constant contact with each other. The drive for connection, touching and holding, is the most important instinct of your species. Most packs are so tightly tied together they live together every day of their lives in constant contact with each other. Some have no compulsion to wear clothing at all, because they feel clothing impedes their true nature. They spend their entire lives immersed in touching and holding each other with nothing between their skins, because they need to feel connected to feel whole." Tim rubbed my arm, and I shivered at his cool touch.

"I know you're hurting and fearful, but look at Andrew." He stood behind me, not touching me. Andrew's whole body shook; he'd wrapped his arms around his body, practically mirroring my own position. He seemed about to fall apart. I wanted to hug him tight and hold him together. "What do you see?" asked Tim.

"He looks like he's about to fall apart," I whispered.

"You look just as bad as he does. You're trembling so hard, you're causing the log to fall apart." Tim tried to steady me, but his touch only made me shake all the harder.

In truth, the log did seem to be shedding large amounts of wood as I rocked where I sat.

"Andrew, kneel down behind Lance and wrap your arms around him." I went a little stiff, but relaxed immediately as Andrew's arms circled me. My trembling slowed, and then stopped, as did his. We both breathed a sigh of relief. "Do you see? Apart, you'll shake yourselves to death. Together you're one, whole and strong. It's who you are. Don't fear it, child. It's the greatest, most wonderful form of love there is. For your kind, once you find your mate, that person is the love of your entire life. You become one, a true expression of your love for centuries. You do love him, don't you?" asked Tim critically.

"More than my own life," I whispered without hesitation, resting my head against Andrew's shoulder.

"Then this is just an expression of that love. Do you understand what I'm telling you?" said Tim sternly. "You need to allow your wolf to finally tell Andrew how much he loves him. It'll make so many things easier for him as well. Right now, he's halfway in the magic. He can barely control himself or his emotions. You'll need to take a third shape. If you haven't consummated your relationship first, it'll probably kill him. I know you don't want that."

"God, no!" I cried in dismay, trying to grasp everything Tim was saying.

"Okay, then. I'll take my leave of you, unless you have questions for me?" Always the good doctor, Tim wouldn't leave before he felt I completely understood what was happening to me.

"No, I understand," I mumbled softly.

"This isn't some horror, child. You'll see. Don't overthink the physical act. Just let Andrew show you how much he loves you, and let yourself show him as well," Tim said softly, then he leaned in and hugged me.

It was a cold hug and it sent goose bumps up and down my skin, but it was enough to demonstrate what he'd been saying all along. It was unnatural for him to be that close to me, just like when the human man had held me. But Andrew's arms never repulsed me. From the very first time I had leaned back against his chest, I'd always felt right in his arms. I relaxed as Tim stood and walked to his car, giving us a wave as he left.

"I'm so sorry, my love. I didn't realize you didn't understand, and then after what I found out from the twins—well, I was lost, I had no idea what to do. But I finally understood your rejection, even while your body kept telling me something else." Andrew just held me tightly, sounding hopeless. As he let me come to terms with everything I'd been told, he slowly caressed my hair and rubbed his face against my temple.

I took a deep breath, and the wolf in me said I was being stupid. He wanted Andrew. I trusted him on everything else, why not this? "I'll really try, Andrew. I will. We'll have to go slow. I want us to be mates. I don't want someone to be able to take you away from me. I won't stand for it. I won't give someone the opportunity to separate us. You'll have to be very patient with me. I don't know how to do this, how to overcome this."

"Okay, my love. Somehow we'll make this work." Andrew sighed, holding me tightly. "Are you ready to go into the cottage? I just want to talk to you some more. We don't have to do anything today."

I sighed deeply. "Okay. But Tim's right. We have to complete this before you contact Stephon and all the others."

"Yes, he's already calling to me, and I've been ignoring him. Our connection helps. We need to talk about that connection some more too, because Tim, for all that he's a great doctor, he's still a vampire drone, and there are things about being a shape-shifter he doesn't know. The mental connection between a mated pair can get intense and it's something about ourselves we don't share with other species. I want you to understand everything before it happens." Andrew kissed my temple. "When Tim was telling you, it dawned on me just how much you don't know. I'm so sorry, love. There's so much I take for granted." Andrew sighed helplessly.

"It's okay, Andrew. I know, I'm learning. I don't blame you for not telling me about things you take as second nature." I stood up and tried to smile. Andrew stood with me. He kept his arms wound around me, and we walked back to the cottage together.

I felt cold. The air outside had been a bit frosty. Andrew felt the goose bumps on my arms and rubbed them briskly, then went into the kitchen and laid a fire in the fireplace. I went into the living room and sat down on the love seat, pulling a blanket down over me. I kept my eyes on him, watching every move he made. My mind kept going a thousand miles an hour. The wolf in me was arguing the case for making love to Andrew, vehemently. He hungered for Andrew. It was the little human voice in the back of my mind that screamed in fear. The wolf told it to shut up; we weren't human. I felt the lust begin to fill my eyes—maybe I could do this after all. The wolf was right.

The cottage began to warm up almost immediately once Andrew had the fire going. He went to the stereo and put on some soft music. I vaguely noted the classical, soft, and soothing tones. He came back to me and sat down, easing behind me on the love seat. He then pulled me up and turned me so I sat across his lap with my back resting against the back of the love seat and my shoulder against his chest, with my head pillowed on his shoulder. He held my hands up to his lips, kissed them, and took a deep breath.

Andrew began solemnly, "What Tim couldn't tell you, because it isn't something we share outside of our race, is that when we choose a mate, it's a blending of spirits. We become tied together, not just emotionally, but mentally as well. For a time at least, we'll be joined in thought. You'll know my every thought and I'll know yours. There'll be no secrets. Everything you know and have experienced will become part of me and everything I've ever done or known will become part of you. The more pure the bloodline, the longer it seems to last. Dad told me when he and Mom became mates they were joined mentally for two months solid. Even now when they are together, their minds join for a short time, although not as intensely as it once was. He believes that the more pure the bloodline, the more intense and long lasting the sharing will be. Purebloods, when they mated, could be joined in thought permanently. It didn't seem to matter how far apart they were, the pair was always in contact with each other." Andrew paused and nuzzled my neck gently. "Our family's bloodline is more pure with every generation, even for our people. Stephon's been very careful to build up our pedigree, never allowing our bloodlines to be torn down or weakened. But your bloodline is pureblood on both sides. I don't know how permanent our mental bindings will be. It could be that we would be forever bound in every thought and emotion, our lives spent forever as one." He watched me carefully. "Our stories say the purebloods are forever bound to their mates, that they're two beings with one mind, one soul."

"So, we would be forever in each other's thoughts, knowing each other's feelings as if they were our own. No secrets." A bit of awe crept into my voice as I considered the ramifications of sharing every thought, dream, and deed with Andrew. "Well, that's a little disturbing, but you already know the worst experience of my life. I've nothing else to hide from you. We'd be bound together forever, not just emotionally, but in thought too. We would be inseparable, and there could be no misunderstandings." The wolf was winning this battle and my fear was fading. "I like the thought of being tied to you in every way. I want to share everything I am with you, Andrew, never doubt that, my love. I do want you—and I desire you." I pulled one of his hands to my heart, and I put my hand on his heart. "Two hearts and one being. I *really* like that, my Andrew, my love. I want you—I choose you—you are my mate." I said the words very deliberately, stressing each word individually, leaving no doubt as to my intentions.

When the trembling began, I moved in to kiss him with all the need my wolf possessed. The trembling moved like an electric current from him through me. The need I felt for him flowed from me into him, and then back again. I knew this time we wouldn't be able to stop, and I didn't want to. I could feel Andrew struggling desperately, trying to get control of himself, but the wolf in me wanted him wild and free, the need in us so strong that neither could control our desire.

Too much clothing, my wolf growled. I clawed at Andrew's shirt, then slipped beneath his T-shirt and caressed the planes of his chest. When I reached his nipples and rolled the nubs between fingers and thumbs, I felt them harden.

He groaned; the need in his voice set my body on fire. His kisses were full of tenderness, yet they burned with a fire that threatened to consume us, until where there once were two, only one whole being arose from the ashes, reborn. He whimpered softly against my mouth, struggling for control. I darted my tongue out, tasting his lower lip. My teeth were on his jaw, nipping, and then I kissed him hard. He moaned with pleasure as I raked his chest with my fingernails.

As his handsmoved beneath my T-shirt, his fingers left burning trails across my chest. They moved around my body to stroke across the muscles of my back. I arched into his caress, pulling away from his mouth for a moment, my head falling back. I moaned with the pleasure of his hands on my body. He kissed and nipped down my neck and across my collarbone, then down my chest. He licked an erect nipple, rolling it between teeth and tongue. I gasped and panted, struggling to catch my breath in the onslaught of pleasure.

Beyond thought—beyond fear—I surrendered to instinct and pleasure. I'd give myself to him and hold nothing back. He undid my jeans and slipped his hand inside to grasp my cock. He began to fondle the head, rubbing the sensitive tip while he slipped his other hand behind and separated the soft mounds to press against my hole. He massaged the muscles around the tight opening, coaxing it open for him. I groaned and rubbed myself against him, seeking much needed friction.

He growled and scooped me up in his arms and ran into our bedroom. He laid me on the bed and with swift movements removed my clothes and tossed them to the floor. Leaning over me, he whimpered softly, biting my neck and my ear as I clawed at his back, tugging at his clothing. He sent his shirt flying to the floor, followed quickly by his jeans.

He knelt on the bed, and I shifted to my knees facing him, running my hands up his body from his abdomen to his chest, my eyes locked with his. I sank my teeth into the soft flesh of his neck and sucked and kissed him. I moved down along his body, sucking and kissing every inch as I made my way back down, tasting and nipping, leaving red marks spread across the surface of his golden-brown skin. With a slight press of his hands on my hair, he guided my kisses down to his erect shaft.

"So beautiful," I mumbled, licking the long thick rod standing hard with his passion for me. I took him into my mouth and began to kiss and lick him. He tasted so good as I raked my teeth against the sides of his erection. He moaned and trembled at my touch.

"G—ah—so good." Andrew buried his hand in my hair as he pressed my head tighter against his prick, forcing more of himself down my throat. I opened my throat to him, taking as much of him as I could, gagging a little as I struggled to swallow more of him. I worked at breathing through my nose. He grew bigger under my active tongue, with my lips locked around him. I sucked hungrily, hollowing my cheeks as my throat massaged his length as I swallowed around him. "Ah—God!" He pulled me off him with a popping sound when he glanced down and saw the tears streaming from my eyes. "I'm so sorry!" he said in panic, pulling me up and kissing the tears from my cheeks.

"I'm fine. I'm not hurt," I reassured him, trying to kiss him back, answering his tender kisses with passion-filled ones of my own. He laid me down on my side and stretched out alongside with my leg draped over his hip, kissing me while one hand went to work on my painfully erect cock. He stroked the cleft between my asscheeks, followed the crease to my quivering hole and teased the muscles, tracing the edge as I relaxed. He slid a finger inside, and I pushed my hips back to meet the thrust of his finger. He stroked my cock at the same time, working both in a rhythm that had me gasping his name. "And—da—drew," I groaned and clutched at the sheets of the bed.

"You are so hungry for me, but I have to be careful. I don't want to hurt you. I want this to be good for us," Andrew said huskily. "You're ready to come, aren't you?"

"Gah—God—Andrew," I panted.

"You're so beautiful—I want you," Andrew whispered, but I felt him move away. I watched him lean over and open the drawer on the nightstand, then return.

I gasped when I heard the crinkle of the safety seal being ripped off and the snap of a cap. Andrew had grabbed the bottle of lube from the nightstand. He'd obviously been planning this for a while as the lube must have come in with the rest of the supplies. I felt the cool drizzle as the slick slipped down my ass, coating his digits as he slippedtwo into me. He scissored his fingers, rubbing, opening me up, then caressed a spot inside as electricity flashed through my balls. Moans of pure pleasure, sounds I had never made before, flowed from me. I felt like I could fly on wings of pure bliss as I ground against him. Gasping for air, I clawed at his shoulders, whimpering.

"Andrew... I need... need you inside me. Don't make me wait anymore. Andrew, please...," I begged.

He snarled and rolled me over onto my stomach. Reaching under me, he grasped my hard cock, spread my legs, and slipped three fingers into me, rubbing vigorously but holding my cock still and tight, preventing me from coming. I cried out in pain, but pushed myself against his hand, matching his rhythm with the movement of my hips.

"I can't hold back anymore, Lance." Andrew gasped and pulled his fingers out of my body, causing me to cry out in loss. He rubbed the engorged head of his cock along the spread crack of my ass, pressing against my opening then backing off, teasing us both for a moment before sinking slowly, gently into me. He moved his hands to my hips, guiding his steady thrust until his balls brushed against me. "So hot... tight...."

We both panted, trying to catch our breath. I gripped the sheets, pushing back against him as he inched inside. His cock felt huge, like he'd split me open with the aching burn of each inch of him. I wanted more of him—all of him—to be sunk so deep inside.

"More," I panted, pressing my hips against him.

179

"You want more?" Andrew drew himself back, leaving only the head of his cock within,then thrust his hips forward, forcing himself deeper into me.

I screamed, lit from the inside with a burning pleasure. I rocked back, meeting him, taking him still deeper until I felt his balls slap against mine. He tightened his grip on my hips with both hands and began a feral rhythm, pounding into me.

"You feel so good—so fucking tight. Ah—hot—Lance!" Andrew panted each word, thrusting harder.

I cried for more and he slammed into me faster, sliding along my prostate with each pass, sending waves of pleasure crashing through my body. I felt the wave rippling through his body. A never-ending cycle of pleasure rocked from my curled toes through my body into his and through him back to me. He laid his chest along my back and continued to thrust into me, and he closed his teeth over the nape of my neck, biting me hard as his wolf demanded my submission. My head dropped down and to the side, giving my everything to Andrew.He was mine—I was his.

"I'm gonna come. I can't—" I screamed.

"Yes—Lance—love—now—" Andrew roared as he thrust into me.

I arched my back and forced myself onto him. I turned my face and his mouth crushed mine in a fierce kiss as we came together, every muscle in our bodies tense with our release. Our ecstasy spewed from our bodies, as he filled mine with his seed and I came all over my abdomen and chest.

Our minds burst into one another. Another release, like another transformation, only there was no pain. For one brief moment, there were two people and two wolves, then everything flowed together. One mind—one wolf—one life—one soul—shared by both of us. The wolf howled his joy. We felt nothing but pleasure; our bodies moved as one. Our minds joined. I knew how he felt—how much pleasure he took in my body. He saw I had no more fear, only joy in being with him and the complete wonder of feeling whole with him locked inside my body, of having his arms around me, holding me, keeping me safe.

We melted into each other, becoming part of the whole. Exhausted and spent, we lay spooned together, heady in the afterglow as the visions began. We were each a raft on the ocean of the other's life, helpless but to watch as it passed before our eyes. Through my mind spiraled every warm moment with his family, every conversation with Stephon. The years he spent learning everything his mother had to teach him, his time at the university—studying everything that took his interest, detailing each distraction until the subject waned. The endless blurring parade of uninteresting, faceless women Stephon sent past him, hoping he'd find one of interest to pass on his genetic line. The rebellious behavior against his slavery and the lashes it had earned him, which his uncle had dished out for his behavior at the council's behest, his punishment for trying to run from his benefactor. I saw his wolf's denial and hatred of the restrictions of his freedom, year after year, as he tried to live within the restrictions of his people for the sake of his family.

His mother's tears finally brought about the change in his behavior—he couldn't stand to see her cry when she watched him being punished and then nursed him back to health afterward. Seeing his mother cry had been worse than all the punishments they could have dealt him.

I saw the years since his capitulation to being a good responsible son, even though he felt sure he'd die soon if he couldn't be free, and the seething hatred he still felt for his uncle who'd taken pleasure in his beatings—Andrew's very soul all there, laid out like an open book, nothing held back.

At the same time, Andrew got the complete story of my years in the foster-care system, including the people who were in it for the money and didn't care about the children they'd taken in. He saw the abusive and malicious behavior of children and adults alike, which I now understood, thanks to Tim. He saw the years I struggled to fit in, none of which mattered anymore. He saw it all—that life was gone,

181

never to return, and good riddance to it. He also saw my shame at the murder of the man who'd hurt me the most, and still he loved me.

"You're so beautiful," he said both out loud and in thought. I could feel he really meant it, and I could see what he saw in me that he found beautiful. Somehow it was everything, my entire being he found beautiful.

"You're my hope—my light. My angel," I said to him, showing him how he comprised everything good in the world and had given it to me. His eyes blazed with love.

We had no concept of time. We made love, we slept, we gloried in each other's minds, and we slept again. It could have been hours, days, months, I had no idea. For us time stood still.

CHAPTER 10

THEY say it's always brighter in the morning. Well, morning came through crystal clear. Suddenly I saw my fear multiplied through Andrew's eyes and mind. Almost everything I'd been worried about, I could see reflected in his thoughts which flowed seamlessly into my mind. My fear of us being forced apart was the only fear he didn't carry.

Somehow I'd gone from a runaway punk thief to a pureblood prince who could save the shifter world in one fell swoop. Not to mention if anyone wanted to get rid of me all they had to do was call the authorities and turn me over to the police—the murder rap would have me behind bars in no time. I wondered if they'd put me in regular jail or I'd end up in a zoo or a gilded bird cage somewhere. Andrew scowled, knowing my self-recriminating thoughts.

"Quit already. I won't let that happen. You defended yourself—it doesn't matter anyway, that life is over." Andrew growled and pulled me into his arms. He kissed me then sat me back down at the table. He poured me another cup of tea while he foraged through the refrigerator, grabbing cheese and eggs, bacon and potatoes. I couldn't concentrate on what he was making. My mind had become stuck on autopilot, circling the same issues over and over.

He went to the stereo at one point and turned on some soft music.

The smell of frying bacon and eggs filled the kitchen; with my overactive emotions, I began to feel nauseous. I vaguely remembered hearing the toaster pop. Andrew put the toast into my hands, trying to distract me. I held it but couldn't eat; my stomach refused to cooperate. My tea sat untouched in front of me. I couldn't move. I'd begun to let my fear overtake me. The panic must've been plain on my face, despite the reassurance and love I felt coming from Andrew; I was all but hyperventilating.

The sound of a four-wheeler kicking gravel up out front brought me out of my circular thoughts, and if it hadn't been for Jack's familiar scent, I'd have transformed because of my own fear.

"Shh… stop, love." Andrew ran his hand along my jaw and gently kissed me. I inhaled deeply of his reassuring scent. It calmed me more than anything else on earth could. "I'll go see what he wants."

"Okay." I watched Andrew go out the door. My thoughts once again started to spin of their own accord.

"Nothing's going to hurt you. I won't let it. We'll be okay." I didn't hear him come back in or his brother leave. I just found myself wrapped in his arms. He sounded so sure of himself. I wondered where he got his strength. "I get my strength from you, my love," he whispered.

"How did it happen? How did I go from being a guy in love with you to the world's savior? I'm nobody's savior," I raged. "I couldn't even save myself." Flashbacks of my childhood flowing just under the surface, like they always did when I felt insecure, threatened to send me racing into the dark.

"Shh… love." Andrew held me as if I were the finest crystal on the verge of shattering into a million pieces. If he moved just an inch in the wrong direction, I'd be gone.

"I'm okay… I'll be okay." I reined in my frenzied emotions, and although I had no idea what to do, maybe I could focus. I closed my eyes and clutched at Andrew, my anchor in my new world. I needed a distraction, "What did Jack need?"

"He had some information for me. It's good news, I just don't—"

"Just tell me." I shook my head. One more thing to deal with. Maybe it was something I could get my mind around and fix or explain.

"They found the police report. They told me," he said softly, carefully.

"But you already know what happened. You saw it all, you've heard my nightmares, you know." I frowned as he led me to the sofa and pulled me into his lap.

"I know what you think happened." Andrew's smile was sad as he rubbed my back.

"I killed him. End of story." My shoulders slumped in defeat, and I hung my head. I'd been found out. "I'm not proud of it. I don't remember much from that night. I remember the bloodeverywhere, hot and sticky. The scent of it—"

"Lance, you'll always be my *àlui*—"

I interrupted him before he could continue. "I'm not beautiful. I'm scarred and a killer. The bloodcovered my hands. I held the switchblade that slit his throat." Why didn't he understand if he saw the police report? How could he continue to hold me if he really knew?

"Shh," he soothed, trying to calm me. "Do you really remember taking the knife and slitting his throat? He was a very large man, much taller, stronger, and heavier than you. How did you hold him and slit his throat at the same time? How?"

"I don't know—I can't remember. Why does it matter? I killed him, isn't that bad enough? I know I did it, why do I have to remember it too?" My voice faded to a whisper as the horrors of that night washed over me."I remember what he did. I remember him going after one of the little girls because I couldn't scream anymore, and he didn't find it as much fun when you stopped screaming." I shook involuntarily, anger mixed with shame. "I remember sitting beside the body, my hands covered in his blood, trying to hold his

185

throat together. I was talking to some woman on the phone and then the ambulance arrived. I remember screaming at the rescue people because they couldn't save him, because he was dead when they arrived. And I remember washing and washing because I couldn't get the blood off my hands.Isn't that enough to remember?"

"Lance, he raped and beat you. Then he raped and beat a young girl, and made you watch. You don't remember slitting his throat because *you* didn't. Although if you had, I'd still say the man got off easy." Andrew rocked slowly with me as the stress of the memories refused to let me remain still."No, what you can't seem to recall is there were two other teenage boys in the house at the time. They jumped him while he was beating the second girl. One of them held him while the other slit his throat from ear to ear. They ran. You, my love, called 911 and tried to stop the bleeding. You tried to save the life of the vile monster who had attacked you. But you had no chance; the other boys did a good job of it and he bled out before the ambulance arrived." I stared at my hands as if I could still see the blood.

"But—"

"You were so traumatized and hysterical the EMTs had to sedate you just to get you to the hospital. When you woke up at the hospital, you screamed and ranted that you'd killed him, that you were a murderer. They sedated you again. The police picked up the two boys when they came to the hospital to check on the girls. They gave statements admitting to the murder of the man and the circumstances you had all lived under. When you woke up the third time, you just ran." Andrew clutched me against him and kissed my temple as he told me my own story. "Over a year and a half later, you appeared in my barn. *Leannan*, you didn't kill him. The boys who did admitted to doing it long ago. They couldn't stand hearing him attack every night, or the stress of wondering who would be next. One of the girls was the sister of one of the boys that committed the murder. When you saw the girls the other day and the police chased you in Rapid City, they were trying to tell you that you'd been cleared, and the boys had been acquitted due to special circumstances and their age." I leaned heavily against his chest. I couldn't believe what he was telling me. It didn't seem right—my mind couldn't accept that it had happened that way.

"No. They must have gotten something mixed up. I killed him. I—"

"No. You didn't. You couldn't have, my love. It took two of them to kill him. You couldn't have done it alone either." Andrew soothed me as I saw the reality of what had happened in his eyes. Andrew kissed my temple and stood up from behind me, then went over to the table and picked up the police report Jack had brought with him, in its entirety.It was impossible to refute the words. It was all there in black and white. Theo Larson and William Davidson had committed the murder. It wasn't me.

"It wasn't me. But the vampires…. I—I still killed."

"With the drones, you were attacked and you defended those you love. We're warriors, love. Our people are born predators. We hunt—we kill. We're part of nature, and nature isn't always fuzzy bunnies and ducklings. Killingis*part* of who we are, but not *all* of who we are. Before we changed our nature to hunting animals, we were blood hunters, like the vampires, killing humans to feed. Now we teach our children when they are young how to control and focus their needs. We hunt to alleviate the desire, releasing the animal. It's why you're so angry. It's not in your nature to accept being weaker than a human, even without knowing why. You were too young for the wolf to rescue you. Part of you, the wolf inside, raged against your weakness, but he couldn't help you. Do you understand?" Andrew trembled.

"If that man wasn't dead, I'd be blood hunting right now." Andrew's voice grew cold with his own confession."So who's the monster here, the seventeen-year-old boy who tried to save the life of the human who attacked him?Or the seventy-seven-year-old man who wanted to rip the skin from that creature's body because he dared to hurt my mate? You tell me which is worse." He spoke so softly, I almost missed the way his voice cracked at the end. I could still feel his rage, tightly contained but threatening to bubble through.

Andrew in no way joked about killing that man. I could feel his conviction, and it made me feel loved, cherished, and treasured above everything else in this world.

I wrapped my arms around his chest and my legs around his waist. I had to be able to hear his heartbeat, to look into his eyes. I needed to see as well as feel his emotions. His eyes were hard and angry, but not at me.

"I didn't want you to know any of this." My throat was so tight with emotion, it hurt to get the words past my lips."I know you saw…everything… and that you were okay, you loved me regardless. I was so afraid you'd see me as less—I don't want you to think of me as weak, beaten, and broken. Even though part of me is… or was—" I stuttered as I looked up at him.

"Shh…," he cooed, holding me cuddled against him. I listened to his steady heartbeat and let him rock me slowly to the rhythm, which matched my own. The soft thump-thump, thump-thump of his heart eased the last of my fear and worry away. He calmed me. When the trembling stoppedand I'd relaxed, he kissed the top of my head, placed a finger under my chin, and brought my gaze up to meet his. "I could never think of you as anything other than perfect. You are my*leannan*. Now and forever, nothing can ever change that. Better now?"

"Yes," I sighed. "He hurt me so badly, Andrew."

"Yes, he did, my love. I'm so sorry." Violent memories flashed lightning fast through my mind like a slideshow on fast-forward. I could still hear the vile laughter that had haunted my every nightmare. I could feel his two-inch-wide belt cracking and snapping against bare skin—feel the skin welting up, burning, splitting open with the next strike, and the memory of his violation of my body, being ripped open by his assault, and how I'd struggled to breathe as he choked and shook me, because I'd started to pass out from the pain. The human had been disgustingly repulsive and evil, and I was glad he was dead. Now that I knew I hadn't murdered him, the part of my soul that had felt ripped to shreds could start to mend.

"I'm so sorry. I know it's illogical, but I wish I could've been there to help you. I love you so much, and I'm not as good a person as you are, because I'd have gladly ripped out his throat. I wouldn't have tried to put him back together." Andrew rubbed his face into my hair as he cuddled me close, as if trying to absorb me into himself so he could be my armor and protect me from the rest of the world.

"I'm glad you weren't there. I'd never want you to have to kill someone, no matter how horrible they are. I wouldn't want that on your beautiful soul." I finally understood his anger.

"He wasn't a person. He was a human monster, and he hurt you. I'm glad he's dead and I'll praise those two boys, whomever they are, for all eternity. I owe them a very large debt."

"Love, I've been angry for so long." I sighed and slumped against his chest. "Angry with myself, because I thought I'd killed him. Angry that I was glad he was dead. Angry that no one had helped us. Then, to find out that the other boys had helped, when I thought we'd been abandoned. I hated everyone, and most of all I hated myself." I looked up into his eyes, which smoldered with rage. "Now I'm just tired. I don't have any more emotions to give," I whispered as I struggled to keep my eyes open; he continued to growl angrily.

"Are you okay?" I asked him, looking into his eyes for any sign of repulsion or disgust. I didn't feel any coming from him but I wanted... *needed* reassurance. I could feel his love through our bond, but I wanted to hear it from him.

"No, I'm not okay. For some unfathomable reason, you seem to continue to think I'm better than you. I'm not perfect. I've hurt people—my family, and friends. I've lived a long time and made a lot of mistakes. You, on the other hand, have lived such a short time, and had so many horrors forced upon you, yet you still find courage to go on." He frowned. "I'm so worried about you. I want to protect you. You're so important to me. I can't bear to lose you."

"You've put me back together, Andrew. Your family has taught me that not everyone, in this or any world, wants to hurt me.

189

You've shared your love and your life with me. You've been generous to a fault, giving me a sanctuary to hide and heal to regain some portion of my humanity, while I discovered just how inhuman I really am." A strained chuckle escaped me. "You're the reason I'm still alive, my love. You give me hope. The future, no matter how scary or complicated it becomes, will be okay, because you'll be with me. I can do anything, be anyone, as long as you're at my side. You've accepted me as your mate, even though I'm broken. You've managed to mend my broken self, something I believed beyond repair."

"I'm amazed, not disgusted. I love you so much. Nothing will ever take you away from me. You're my solid ground and my blue sky. You're the freedom of my soul." He held me tenderly now, the anger finally gone from both of us.

He rubbed my back. I nestled up close to him, closed my eyes, and let him take care of me. The tension gone from our bodies, we relaxed together. The future would take care of itself. I had Andrew and he had me. Nothing could separate us. He'd made me whole and I'd given him wings to fly. All beneath a changing moon.

THE BEGINNING

SUI LYNN is a born and raised Midwestern gal. She loves rock 'n' roll but can get a little bit country too. She has been writing for as long as she can remember and is always found with a book or pencil and paper in hand. She has two Cocker Spaniels who are the comic relief in her life. She loves orange soda, *Doctor Who*, and her computer, all of which she could not function without.

Sui received two M/M Goodreads Romance Group nominations: one for Best Paranormal Story of 2012 and the other for Best Word Created for 2012. She has also been nominated for the Preditors & Editors Reader's Poll in the category of "all other" Novels.

Website: http://suilynn.com/
Blog: http://suidlynn.blogspot.com/
Facebook: https://www.facebook.com/sui.lynn.9
Twitter: http://twitter.com/#!/suidlynn
E-mail: sui.d.lynn@gmail.com

Also by SUI LYNN

http://www.dreamspinnerpress.com

www.ingramcontent.com/pod-product-compliance
Lightning Source LLC
Chambersburg PA
CBHW060102260626
47160CB00005B/1772